ABOUT THE AUTHOR

Alex Bell has published novels and short stories for both adults and young people, including *Frozen Charlotte*, *The Lighthouse* and the Explorers' Clubs series. She always wanted to be a writer but had several different back-up plans. After completing a law degree, she now works part-time at the Citizens Advice Bureau. She lives in Hampshire with her husband and sons.

ABOUT THE ILLUSTRATOR

Tomislav Tomić was born in 1977. He graduated from the Academy of Fine Arts in Zagreb. He started to publish his illustrations during his college days. He has illustrated a great number of books, picture books, schoolbooks and lots of covers for children's books. He lives and works in the town of Zaprešić, Croatia.

THE EXPLORERS' CLUBS SERIES

ALEX
BELL

EXPL✦RERS AT
STARDUST
CITY

Illustrated by
Tomislav
Tomić

faber

First published in 2022
by Faber & Faber Limited
Bloomsbury House,
74–77 Great Russell Street,
London WC1B 3DA
faberchildrens.co.uk

Typeset by MRules
Printed by CPI Group (UK) Ltd, Croydon CR0 4YY

A CIP record for this book
is available from the British Library

ISBN 978–0–571–35975–2

FSC
www.fsc.org
MIX
Paper from
responsible sources
FSC® C171272

2 4 6 8 10 9 7 5 3 1

For my son, Toby Dayus.
I look forward to reading this book to you one day.

Contents

CHAPTER ONE

Ursula swam a short distance from the *Blowfish* with the snow globe clutched tightly in her hand. Her friends had urged her to be quick since there was a storm coming. Fortunately, Ursula was a very fast swimmer because she was half mermaid and changed from her human form as soon as her legs touched saltwater.

The waves churned restlessly and the sky above had already turned purple and black with clouds. Ursula could smell the storm in the air and imagined that somewhere nearby a storm maiden was already preparing to hurl lightning bolts and hurricane cats. This wasn't a good time for the *Blowfish* to be above the ocean, but the submarine's water reserves were almost empty and they had had to stop to collect fresh supplies.

Since their eventful visit to Pirate Island, the explorers had been travelling hard for a week. They were still fired up after their encounter with the villainous Collector Scarlett Sauvage. Although they had rescued some children she'd taken prisoner, the explorers hadn't been able to prevent Scarlett escaping from them, and taking Stella Starflake Pearl with her. The Collector had ensnared the ice princess in a pair of magical golden handcuffs that would compel Stella to do whatever Scarlett told her. And the explorers all knew it was a very dangerous thing for Scarlett to have ice magic at her disposal.

Scarlett was part of the Phantom Atlas Society, a secret organisation that had been stealing places from the world for years and locking them up inside magical snow globes. The Collector had finally run out of snow globes, so her stealing had stopped ... for a while. But now she held Stella captive, she could force the ice princess to use her magic to make new ones, and even more places would be stolen. Scarlett had to be stopped, and quickly.

So Ursula and her friends had set off in the *Blowfish* on a new mission. Apart from a brief stop to drop off their Polar Bear explorer friends, who had helped them on Pirate Island, and another to release a sea gremlin they'd taken prisoner, they'd hardly slowed down since.

But submarines needed water and now they'd stopped to fill up their reserves, Ursula took the opportunity to swim out with one of the snow globes they had rescued that contained a water horse. On their recent visit to Mercadia, the mermaid city, the explorers had met Princess Coral. The mermaid had been caring for a water foal whose mother had been stolen by the Collector. Now Ursula was eager to help reunite them.

Thunder rumbled ominously overhead as she unscrewed the glass dome from the base of the globe. Immediately, a fully grown water horse burst forth, snorting, stamping and prancing over the waves in its delight at being free. Ursula felt a huge smile spread over her face. She didn't think she'd ever get tired of being up close to these majestic beasts. Water horses were magical creatures made from the sea itself, and this one had frothing white foam for her mane and tail, sparkling blue water for her body and pearly shell hooves that glinted in the last beams of light slanting through the storm clouds. After a short while, the horse stopped frolicking and turned back to Ursula, leaning down to nuzzle her hair.

'I don't know whether you can understand me,' Ursula said, looking up into the horse's blue eyes, 'but I hope you can because I need to tell you that your foal is waiting for you in Mercadia. She's safe – Princess Coral is looking after her. I'm afraid we're a long way from the mermaid city, but hopefully that won't matter too much to you.'

Water horses were the fastest sea creatures in existence, able to fly over the waves with astonishing speed. The beautiful horse whinnied and pressed its soft nose against Ursula's head for a moment before she turned and galloped off across the ocean.

'Goodbye,' Ursula whispered. 'And good luck.'

She began swimming back towards the *Blowfish*. The wind had really picked up now, whipping her hair around her face, and enormous waves were already crashing over her head. Ursula ducked beneath the surface and swam underwater. It was calmer below, although she could still sense the ocean's restlessness and was keen to get back to the shelter of the submarine as quickly as possible. She was almost there when she saw a water horse dive beneath the surface. At first, she thought it was the one she'd just released from the snow globe, but she soon realised that this was a different horse altogether. In fact, it wasn't a normal water horse at all, but something even rarer – a storm stallion.

The stallion was massive, its entire body rippling with speed and strength. Its coat was dappled black and grey rather than blue, its hooves were the colour of lightning and its green eyes flashed with wildness.

It looked so untame that Ursula was a little afraid to get too close, but the horse spotted her at once and galloped over, leaving a churning tunnel of bubbles in its wake.

Ursula couldn't help shrinking back as it skidded to a halt and reared up on to its hind legs, but then she saw that it had a golden shell in its mouth, which it dropped in front of her. Ursula recognised the shell as one of the ones used to send messages on the bubble tide – the mermaid postal service. These messages were usually delivered by the tide itself, or sometimes by dolphins if the message was particularly important. She'd never heard of a water horse messenger before though, let alone a storm stallion, and she knew this message must be incredibly important. The horse was watching her expectantly, so she reached out and grabbed the shell before it could float away.

'Thank you,' she said.

The stallion snorted into the water, then turned and galloped off, quickly disappearing into the darkness of the sea. Clutching the shell tightly, Ursula hurried back down to the submarine and entered through the swim-out hatch. As soon as the water drained away she used the intercom to tell her friends on the bridge that she was safely on board. The engines immediately came to life and she felt the vibrations through the floor as the *Blowfish* dived deeper below the surface.

Ursula was so curious about the message that she didn't even wait to dry off her tail, but raised the shell to her ear straight away. The cool tones of Princess Coral came through to her at once:

'Ursula, I've sent this storm stallion from my own stable to instruct you to make your way to the Seashells Mermaid Academy in the Jelly Blue Sea with all due haste. It's too complicated to explain everything now, but it's to do with the fire magician who provided Scarlett with the magical handcuffs. The coordinates are engraved into this shell. Yours truly, Princess Coral.'

Ursula removed the shell from her ear and saw that there was indeed a set of coordinates engraved into it. She lost no time in drying off her tail and changing back into her engineering coveralls. Dressed like this, it was hard to tell that Ursula was half mermaid. The only things giving it away were the streaks of blue and purple in her otherwise black chin-length hair.

Taking the shell with her, she exited the swim-out hatch and ran along the submarine's gleaming wood-and-brass corridors. Through the portholes she could see they were already under way, streams of bubbles racing past, along with the occasional blurry glimpse of a passing fish or eel. Like most Ocean Squid Explorers' Club submarines, the *Blowfish* was sleek, speedy and gigantic, almost like a floating hotel with its onboard library, skating rink, cinema, ice-cream parlour and other facilities.

Although the *Blowfish* was designed to carry an entire team of explorers, Ursula and three other children had been the only ones on board when Scarlett Sauvage had stolen the Ocean Squid Explorers' Club all those weeks ago and so escaped the Collector's clutches. They had been travelling together ever since. Along with snow globes containing the water horse and several places, they had managed to rescue the one with the club from the Collector's stronghold on Pirate Island, and the explorer Zachary Vincent Rook had recently set off to return it to its rightful place in the Jelly Blue Sea.

Of course, technically speaking, Ursula and her friends should have returned the *Blowfish* to the Ocean Squid headquarters now the club was safe again. But the children knew that if they returned there, or made radio communication with anyone, then the president – or their various parents and guardians – would be sure to force them to come home, and none of them wanted that. Not when there was still an ice princess to be rescued and a villain to be foiled.

It took Ursula a few minutes to reach the bridge and she was out of breath by the time she finally arrived. Jai was at the controls, making some adjustments to their course. He was the acting captain of their team and spent a lot of his time on the bridge. Max was over in the corner tinkering with his new robot shark. Although he was renowned in the club for misbehaviour, he was also an extremely talented robot inventor and his various creations had come in handy more than once during their adventures. Finally, Genie stood at one of the windows waving at her shadow kraken Bess, who had attached herself to the side of the submarine and was peering in at them, her gigantic eye taking up the entire window.

'Genie, could you ask her to move?' Jai said, glancing up. 'She's blocking our view.'

But Bess had already faded away. As a shadow animal, she had no physical substance and could appear and disappear at will. She was never far from Genie though, as Genie was one of those rare breeds of people known as a whisperer, meaning that she could communicate with a particular type of animal – in this case, kraken. No one knew for sure why whisperers had shadow animals that accompanied them wherever they went, but many believed they were a little piece of the whisperer's soul given physical form.

'Hi, Ursula,' Genie said now, turning from the window. She and Jai were brother and sister and both had the same brown skin and black hair, although Genie's hair was partially covered by an extraordinary hat. She was very skilled at making hats and seemed to have a never-ending supply of imaginative creations. Today she wore one in the form of a coral garden. Several bits of coral were the same shade of sparkly pink as the cowgirl boots she always wore. 'Did it go OK with the water horse?' she added.

Realising that their friend had appeared on the bridge, the others turned towards her too.

'Yes, I set her free,' Ursula replied, finally catching her breath. 'But as I was returning to the submarine, a storm stallion appeared and delivered a message.'

Max frowned. 'Storm stallion?' he asked.

'They're a type of water horse,' Ursula said. 'Very rare. Princess Coral has some in her private stables. In fact, this message is from her. It says ... well, you'd better listen to it yourselves.'

She held up the shell and the message from the mermaid princess replayed. Once it had finished, everyone was silent for a moment. Then Jai came over to look at the shell and exclaimed in dismay. 'But these coordinates will take us back the way we've just come,' he said, 'in the opposite direction from where we need to go.'

Before parting from the Polar Bear explorers, the Ocean Squid team had been given the *Phantom Atlas*, a book that Stella and her friends had discovered, containing a record of all the places that had been stolen by the Collector and where they had come from. Now the Ocean Squid explorers were trying to reach the Nebula Sea, the original location of the captured Stardust City, home of the galaxy fairies.

Ursula and her friends planned to release the city from its snow globe and then ask the fairies who lived there for help locating Stella and Scarlett. The galaxy fairies had wings made of moon dust, which meant they could fly all the way into space, and were even said to have invented rockets. With their help, the explorers would be able to find the Collector much more quickly.

The Nebula Sea was a week's journey away, which was precious time to them. They had discussed setting the city free in some other part of the ocean, but they couldn't know for sure how large it was and how much space it would need. Max had suggested it wasn't likely to be huge, being a fairy city, but the explorers had made a bad mistake the last time they'd released a stolen place from a snow globe, and the Sunken City of Pacifica had been destroyed as a result. No one had been hurt, but all Pacifica's beautiful buildings and books had gone. And Jai had pointed out that a new city suddenly appearing somewhere it wasn't meant to be could upset the sea's delicate ecosystem too.

'We have a responsibility to the galaxy fairies and the rest of the creatures in the ocean,' Jai had said. 'So we need to put Stardust City back where it came from.'

'I know it will cause a delay,' Ursula said now. 'But I don't think Princess Coral would have asked us to go to the mermaid academy if it wasn't important. And any information they can give us about the fire magician could be helpful in rescuing Stella.'

Jai sighed. 'I suppose so. I hate to lose the time, though. Scarlett could already be stealing more places, and who knows how much longer we'll be able to remain hidden from her spies.'

They all peered at the pickled parrot charm on the bridge. After their city had been destroyed, the Pacificans were angry with the explorers and had started to work with Scarlett. They possessed psychic abilities and had used these to discover where the children were, forcing them to go to a sea witch for a charm to disguise themselves. This charm took the form of a pickled parrot in a jar, and the sea witch had told them that when all its silver feathers turned green, the charm would run out. The parrot still had a decent number of silver feathers, but they weren't sure how long this would last.

'What do you two think?' Jai asked, looking at Genie and Max.

Jai could be a little pompous and was a bit of a stickler for the rules sometimes, but Ursula loved that his style of leadership involved consulting the opinions of his entire team and always listening carefully to their views. Rather than handing out orders, he preferred the four of them to discuss matters and reach a decision together, or else take a vote if there was any disagreement.

'I don't see why she couldn't have sent a longer message giving us all the information,' Max grumbled. 'But I guess we'd better do as she's asked, just in case.'

'I agree,' Genie said. 'The mermaids have been useful allies until now, haven't they? Especially with the magic ice cream they gave us, and the trident.'

Although mermaids and explorers had historically been enemies, Ursula and her friends had managed to form a tentative alliance with them in order to help stop the Collector. As a result, they'd been given some special mermaid ice cream that allowed humans to breathe underwater for twenty-four hours, and Princess Coral had loaned the royal trident to Ursula too. She was still learning how to use it, but it was potentially a very powerful weapon that could shoot out lightning bolts from its prongs.

'All right,' Jai said with a sigh. 'We'll turn the *Blowfish* around. I only hope it's worth it.'

Ursula stared down at the shell in her hand and hoped so too. They were all very aware of the need to stop Scarlett and rescue Stella. It felt wrong to all of them to turn the submarine around, but at least they weren't too far from the mermaid academy.

'We should get there tomorrow,' Jai said, looking down at the controls.

'It's a very famous academy,' Ursula said, in an attempt to encourage the others. 'My mum told me that only the smartest, most gifted mermaids go there.'

Ursula had often secretly dreamed of visiting the school. She'd never had much opportunity to experience mermaid life because many mermaids had disapproved when her mermaid mother had fallen in love with her human father. The three of them had only lived together as a family for a short while before living on land had started to make Ursula's mother ill and she had to return to the sea. Ursula had gone to live at the Ocean Squid Explorers' Club with her father, but she always looked forward to the times when her mother visited her, bringing mermaid gifts and tales of underwater life.

'I'm sure if anyone can help us, the mermaids at the academy can,' she added.

The others nodded but none of them said what they were all thinking – that for this expedition, they would need all the help they could get.

CHAPTER TWO

The storm raged all night but the water was calm beneath the surface and the explorers arrived at the mermaid academy in the afternoon of the next day. It was deep under the sea and would have been as black as space, but the area was lit up with an abundance of glow jellyfish. The golden light they gave out was very similar to sunshine, turning the ocean an attractive turquoise blue and clearly illuminating the school itself.

It was housed in a grand building made of white coral that sprawled upon a golden seabed scattered with shells and starfish. In fact, with its four turrets, the school looked more like a castle, especially as it also had balconies and statues of dolphins holding up the rails. The main thing giving it away as a school was the merstudents swimming around. Some were attending to a sea garden, while others rode water horses and giant seahorses in the sea nearby.

As usual, Ursula felt a little twist of envy at seeing

this slice of mermaid life – one that might have been hers if she'd been entirely mermaid rather than half one thing and half the other. The explorers left the submarine docked a short distance away and Genie asked Bess to stay with it so as not to startle the mermaids. Then they all went to the swim-out hatch.

Max, Genie and Jai wore their swimsuits and had all eaten some Ocean Discovery mermaid ice cream. Since the others weren't as fast in the water as Ursula, they had the help of small robot dolphins that Max had made, which allowed them to move more quickly. Jai only had one arm, but Max had adapted his dolphin so that it could either be used one-handed or with one of the prosthetic arms Jai sometimes wore. He had one of these on today and used his robotic hand to enter a command into the control panel of the submarine.

The next moment, the cold ocean began bubbling up through the floor and Ursula's legs immediately transformed into a green mermaid's tail. As soon as the hatch was fully submerged, the explorers released the door and swam out into the water. Their submarine had clearly been spotted because there was a small welcome party of mermaids waiting to greet them at the school's entrance. They were all adults and Ursula guessed they were teachers.

'Hello, explorers.' One of the mermaids came forwards. 'Welcome to Seashells Academy. I'm Mrs Parnacle, the headmistress here.'

She had a pale blue tail, grey hair tied back in an elegant bun and a delicate pair of pince-nez glasses perched on her nose. She peered at the explorers over the top of these now and went on, 'Thank you for coming. I know any detour must be frustrating but this is important.'

'It's a pleasure to meet you,' Jai replied before introducing each of them in turn.

When it came to Ursula, she felt the eyes of the other mermaids linger on her curiously. As far as anyone knew, she was the only half-human, half-mermaid being in the world, and both groups were always curious about her. Ursula didn't think she'd ever get used to people staring with such open curiosity, though. They stared at Genie a bit too, but that was probably because she'd made herself a waterproof swim hat in the shape of a rainbow fish with rather startling bulbous eyes.

'In her message, Princess Coral said something about the fire magician who made the magical handcuffs?' Ursula prompted.

'That's right,' Mrs Parnacle replied. 'He's waiting for you in my office.'

The explorers were surprised. 'He's here?' Max asked.

'Not for much longer,' Mrs Parnacle said with a grim expression on her face. 'He's due to be taken to a mermaid prison, but first he needs to speak to you about these handcuffs.'

'How did you manage to capture him?' Jai asked.

'We didn't,' Mrs Parnacle replied. 'He turned himself in. He said he only helped Scarlett to save his granddaughter, and now that she's safely back he's willing to take the consequences.'

'But why did he turn himself in to you?' Genie asked, puzzled. 'It's an explorer he helped imprison, so why didn't he go to one of the explorers' clubs?'

'They were all too far away,' Mrs Parnacle replied. 'And anyway, he may have helped imprison an explorer but he stole something from one of our merboys in the process. Come with me and I'll explain.'

She swam through the school's front door and the explorers followed. The other adult mermaids all looked desperately curious, but they drifted back to their various pursuits. The explorers found themselves in a grand lobby carved from ivory sea rock. A double staircase curved around to an upper floor, adorned with noble-looking dolphin statues. The walls were studded with tiny galaxy starfish, all giving out a soft blue light.

Mrs Parnacle led them down a corridor with elaborate chandeliers made from golden coral hanging from the ceiling, and ornate shell tiles on the floor. They passed the open doorways of various classrooms where a range of different lessons was being held, from magical singing to sea science. It seemed that pets were allowed at this school because Ursula glimpsed several students with a terrapin perched on their shoulder, or a turtle nestled under the desk. She felt another pang of regret that she had never been able to attend a mermaid school like this, but instead had grown up at the Ocean Squid Explorers' Club with only grumpy old Mrs Soames for company. Her engineering mentor Old Joe had always been very kind to her but it would have been wonderful to study with a whole class of merpeople her own age.

Before long, they arrived at Mrs Parnacle's office. It was very large – more like a drawing room – with tall bookcases, portraits on the walls and sofas and armchairs arranged around a fireplace in which a strange blue flame flickered. It seemed to be made from water rather than fire, and didn't give out heat but instead a scent of sea flowers and starfish perfume.

Sitting in one of the armchairs before the fire was a merboy about Ursula's age, with grey eyes, a blue tail fin and blue and black hair. He got up at their arrival and Mrs Parnacle introduced him.

'This is one of our students, Kiran.'

The merboy raised his hand in a wave but didn't speak.

'His voice was stolen,' Mrs Parnacle went on. 'By the fire magician.'

The explorers were all shocked.

'I thought only sea witches could steal a mermaid's voice?' Ursula asked.

Mrs Parnacle shook her head. 'There are plenty of ways to steal a mermaid's voice,' she said. 'The persuasive magic in it can be used as a very powerful weapon so there are many nefarious people who want to use them for their own means. It's a long story as to how this fire magician stole Kiran's voice and you don't really need to know the details. All you need to know is that he trapped the voice inside the handcuffs and that's how Scarlett is able to control the ice princess.' Mrs Parnacle gestured to the sofas. 'Why don't you sit down and let me explain?'

Everyone took their seats – which was a little tricky to do underwater – and then there was a knock at the door. A maid entered with a tea trolley and set out a plate of cream buns with dolphin sprinkles on top, as well as a pot of mermaid tea. Mrs Parnacle told the explorers to help themselves, but as soon as they bit into the buns they realised they were seaweed-flavoured, and the tea was thick and jelly-like and so salty it burned their throats. Luckily, Mrs Parnacle didn't seem to notice they weren't tucking in because she was too busy talking.

'If you can break the cuffs, then Kiran's voice will be freed and the magic will no longer work,' she told them.

Genie smiled. 'Well, that doesn't sound too difficult,' she said brightly. 'When we saw the handcuffs before, it looked like they were made of glass.'

'Hold on.' Mrs Parnacle held up her hand. 'It's not as simple as that.'

'Of course it's not.' Max sighed.

'There are two things that might complicate the matter,' Mrs Parnacle went on.

'Only two?' Max asked sarcastically.

Jai shushed him.

'The first is that you need to be careful that Kiran's voice isn't lost forever in the process,' Mrs Parnacle said. 'It requires a special receptacle to go into.' She swam over to her desk and came back with a spiral shell strung on a golden chain. 'This is enchanted to contain a mermaid's voice safely. You must have it with you when you break the cuffs. As long as it's nearby, Kiran's voice will go inside and you'll be able to return it here to us.'

Ursula took the necklace and hung the shell around her neck along with the clam necklace she always wore.

'And what's the second problem?' she asked.

'I think it's best if the fire magician explains that himself.'

She swam over to the doorway and spoke to someone outside. A moment later, the magician swam into the room. Or rather, he bounced and rolled his way in as he was ensconced inside a giant bubble. Ursula guessed it was some kind of magical creation that allowed him to breathe underwater, but it looked rather unwieldy in the small room and she winced as he bumped up against a bookcase, causing a whole load of books to fall out.

Mrs Parnacle sighed and swam to his side to help him navigate the room and park his bubble in front of the explorers.

'Thank you,' the wizard said. 'Much obliged.'

Ursula would have known at once that he was a fire magician because both his robes and pointy hat were bright orange, with glittering flames stitched on them. He had a long white beard and piercing blue eyes that suddenly became filled with tears as he looked at the explorers.

'You must be the young people from the Ocean Squid Explorers' Club,' he said. 'My name is Rudolpho and, first of all, please allow me to say that I am so terribly sorry. Sorry for everything. For stealing this young man's voice, of course.' His eyes flicked to Kiran. 'But also for helping the Collector to imprison the ice princess. My behaviour was inexcusable, I know that, but try to understand that Scarlett took my granddaughter Klara and I would have done anything to get her back.'

'You're right,' Mrs Parnacle said sternly. 'It was quite inexcusable.'

'But understandable,' Max said, looking at the wizard. 'I was in your position, sir – my sister was also taken by Scarlett. So I understand what an impossible choice it was and how it can force you to do things you're not proud of.'

Ursula was a little surprised to hear Max speak this way as she knew he was ashamed of the short period of time during which he'd been in secret communication with Scarlett. Yet the wizard seemed so sad that she was glad someone had spoken out in support of him.

He gave Max a pitifully grateful look. 'Thank you, my boy. That is kind of you to say.'

'What's done is done,' Mrs Parnacle said briskly. 'Perhaps you might oblige us by telling the explorers about the difficulty with the cuffs? And the solution you've suggested?'

'Of course, of course,' the wizard said. 'The problem, you see, is that the cuffs are made from a type of enchanted glass and there's only one thing in the world that will break them.'

'And what's that?' Genie asked eagerly.

'The bite from a dizard.'

The explorers looked at one another in confusion.

'What's a dizard?' Ursula asked.

'Oh, it's a charming creature,' Rudolpho said, smiling. 'A cross between a lizard and a dragon. Here, let me show you.'

He rummaged around in his large sleeve and drew out a little, lizardy animal. The explorers all leaned forward to take a closer look. It was bright orange in colour, with webbed feet and a green crest on top of its head. Ursula thought it looked rather like a miniature dragon, except that it didn't have any wings.

'This is my own dear pet dizard, Pog,' Rudolpho said. 'I'd like you to take her with you on your quest to stop the Collector. She'll be no trouble. In fact, dizards spend about ninety per cent of their time asleep. Once you find Stella, Pog knows what to do about the cuffs and will break them to free the ice princess.'

'Thank you,' Jai said, looking relieved. 'I thought you were going to direct us to some island where we'd have to capture a wild dizard or something. It'll be much simpler to take yours.'

He held out his hand but Rudolpho suddenly hesitated.

'There's just one other thing,' he said. 'Pog is . . . well, I rather dote on her. She's very dear to me, you see, and I hope you will do all you can to take care of her and keep her safe. I know she's only a pet but—'

Jai held up his hand. 'Say no more,' he replied. 'I completely understand. I myself once owned a marvellous and much-loved seafaring cat by the name of Biscuit.'

In fact, Jai had been so bereft when Biscuit finally died of old age that he was writing a biographical tribute to her. Ursula had seen him working on it most nights – when he wasn't engaged with polishing his medals or tending to his pet plankton. It currently ran to some three hundred pages and Jai insisted he'd still only recorded a mere fraction of Biscuit's achievements and accolades so far.

'Pets are part of the family,' Jai went on. 'I promise

we'll take very good care of Pog and return her to you safely.'

'Thank you,' Rudolpho said, looking relieved. 'She likes to sleep in a sock hung up at the end of the bed. And she'll only eat smoked caviar, I'm afraid – I've brought a large jar to keep her going.'

He reached into his sleeve for the jar and held it out, along with the dizard itself.

'Thank you, Rudolpho,' Mrs Parnacle said. 'If you return to the corridor, someone will escort you to your room.'

The wizard wished the explorers luck, gave Pog one last wistful look and then went out into the corridor.

'I hope he won't be in prison for too long,' Max said, gazing after the wizard. 'He was only trying to save his granddaughter, after all.'

'That's for a mermaid tribunal to decide,' Mrs Parnacle said. 'However, if he's telling the truth about the handcuffs, and if the dizard proves useful, then I'm sure that will go some way to alleviating his sentence. Now, I know you'll be eager to be on your way, but first I have a couple of final gifts to offer you.'

She swam into the corner and tugged a large treasure chest over to them. Ursula had rather hoped for more magical ice cream, so she was disappointed when the headmistress opened the lid to reveal a load of textbooks.

'I understand you are extremely behind on your mermaid education,' Mrs Parnacle said, fixing Ursula with a stern look.

'I've been practising my magic,' Ursula replied, trying not to sound defensive. 'I can call the water horses now, and fire the royal trident, and I've been singing my scales and—'

'That is good,' Mrs Parnacle said. 'But these books will help you develop further if you study them carefully. Most especially, there is a puppet set here to help you practise your persuasive singing.'

Ursula peered into the trunk and saw that there were indeed several puppets folded up inside a little fish tank at the bottom.

'I imagine you've been reluctant to practise controlling people with your singing, and rightly so,' Mrs Parnacle said. 'That particular mermaid skill is not something to be taken lightly. Puppets are used in all mermaid schools as an aid to help young mermaids hone their skill without actually manipulating anyone for real. The book will explain how to use them but basically the puppets have a strong will of their own. If you can successfully manipulate one of them, then you should be able to control a person too.'

Ursula had never liked the thought of using her mermaid skills in this way. It was one of the reasons she had shied away from her mermaid magic for so long, but she understood that she had to use every weapon available to her in the fight against the Collector, so she thanked the headmistress as politely as she could.

'There's one other thing,' Mrs Parnacle said. 'I don't know if you're aware, but we have a vast number of magical pearls here at the academy. It's thought to be one of the largest collections in the world, in fact, and I don't just mean commonplace specimens like the singing pearl. We also have some extremely rare ones ... like the pearl I'm about to give you now.' She took a silver box decorated with swirls of painted coral from her desk. 'You might as well know there was much discussion among the staff about whether or not to allow you to borrow this,' Mrs Parnacle went on. 'Not everyone was in favour but, ultimately, we put it to the vote and those of us who wanted to give it to you were the victors.'

She opened the lid and the explorers leaned forwards to peer at a pearl nestled within a bed of silk. It was grey in colour but when Ursula looked more closely, she saw that the greyness seemed to swirl and dapple within the pearl, moving about like ribbons of fog. And every now and then, when the fog parted just the right way, a tiny shape could be glimpsed within the jewel. It was hard to tell what it was because it was so small, but Ursula thought she recognised the outline and was just about to say something when Max beat her to it.

'Is that . . . a *ship*?'

'It is,' Mrs Parnacle replied. 'A ghost ship, to be precise. The *Jolly Rosa*.'

Ursula was amazed. She'd heard of a ship inside a bottle before, but never a ship inside a pearl.

'What does it do?' she asked.

'There's a full explanation in one of the books I gave you,' Mrs Parnacle said. 'But in short, if you all put your hands around the pearl and speak the ship's name three times, then you'll find yourselves on board. I ought to warn you that travelling by ghost ship is a . . . surreal experience, but because it's a ghost vessel it's not limited by the laws of physics. It can travel underwater, float through the sky, appear and disappear into fog and so on. It might offer you a hiding place or an escape if you need one. Be careful, though. The crew of a ghost ship are . . . well, they can be unpredictable, and this one especially so because they're—'

But that was as far as she got before an alarm sounded within the school.

'Drat!' Mrs Parnacle snatched up a telephone on her desk and dialled a number. A moment later she said, 'Hattie? What's going on? Yes ... Yes, all right. Proceed as planned.' She put the phone down and turned to the explorers. 'You've got to go,' she said. 'Sea gremlins have been spotted near the academy. We think Scarlett might have had them following the fire wizard.'

'Will you be all right—?' Jai began.

Mrs Parnacle waved a hand. 'Oh, we can deal with a bunch of sea gremlins easily enough. But it's better if they don't realise you're here. The less Scarlett knows, the better.'

The explorers agreed, so they waved a hasty goodbye to Kiran, promised to bring his voice back if they could, and then they took the treasure chest and the ghost-ship pearl and raced back to the *Blowfish*. Once on the bridge, they could see the sea gremlin submarines on the radar, so they hurried to the controls, brought the *Blowfish* to life, and soon the submarine was cutting through the water at full speed ahead.

CHAPTER THREE

A week later, Ursula was on the bridge with Genie. They were both still wearing their pyjamas – Ursula's were covered in dolphins, while Genie's sported various terrifying sea monsters – along with fluffy seahorse slippers. Genie also wore a nightcap she'd made herself that had little bobbly sharks knitted all over it. Bess was sprawled on the bridge with them, or at least as much of her as would fit. A large part of her floated in the water outside the submarine but the room was filled with her tentacles.

'Bess, could you shift a little?' Ursula asked. 'Your tentacle is blocking my page.'

Ursula and Genie had gathered together a stack of books from the library and were attempting to find some information about the Nebula Sea. Their calculations showed they ought to be getting very close and should arrive any day now, but hardly anything was known about it. Ursula and her friends had found references to the Nebula Sea a few times in some of the old travel journals, but the people on those expeditions had only mentioned the sea in passing, saying it was not possible to travel into, without giving any explanation as to why.

'It's like they just take it for granted that we already know the reason,' Ursula said, turning another page in frustration. 'But why wouldn't it be possible to travel into the sea if you were in a submarine?'

'I guess we'll find out soon enough,' Genie replied. 'These journals are all pretty old, though. Maybe there are strong currents or something and the submarines back then couldn't cope with them? The *Blowfish* is bound to be able to. I mean, if it can cope with the Bone Current, then it can cope with anything.'

'It didn't exactly *cope* with the Bone Current,' Ursula pointed out. 'We got swept away by it.'

'Oh yes, that's true,' Genie replied. 'But it worked out in the end, didn't it? Because we'd never have rescued Julian otherwise.'

Ursula sighed. It had certainly been wonderful to rescue their fellow Ocean Squid explorer, long thought dead, and to reunite him with his brother Ethan, but still, it was hard not to be a little frustrated by Genie's persistent optimism at times.

'How is your singing practice coming along?' Genie asked now.

'Pretty good.' Ursula put the book down and turned her attention to the tank on the floor beside her.

It looked rather like an aquarium except that it had puppets in it instead of fish, and the puppets were all different types of sea creatures, ranging from crabs to dolphins to sea horses.

'They're ranked by difficulty,' Ursula explained. 'The crab is the easiest to manipulate and the seahorses are the most difficult. I can manage some of them now, but not the seahorses yet.'

She sang a few notes of a song and the puppet crab immediately began scuttling up and down inside the tank. When she turned her attention to the dolphin, she only managed to get it to perform a single leap before she lost control of the magic and the dolphin crumpled into a heap in the tank.

'You'll get there soon,' Genie said confidently.

Ursula didn't particularly enjoy practising, but she knew she had to hone her skills in case they could help her friends. She was about to say something else about the puppets when some movement through the viewing portal caught her eye.

'What's that?' she asked, pointing. 'There's something glittering up ahead, look.'

They got Bess to shift all her tentacles out of the way

and then they went to stand close to the glass. Up ahead of them, the entire ocean seemed to sparkle.

'It's beautiful!' Genie exclaimed. 'It's got to be the Nebula Sea. One of the explorers in the journals said something about it twinkling like outer space, didn't he?'

Ursula agreed. 'We should stop the *Blowfish*,' she said.

The four explorers had decided that when they reached this point, they wouldn't press on until they were all together on the bridge. Besides which, it didn't seem right to delve into such a mysterious and uncharted sea while wearing seahorse slippers and dolphin pyjamas. So Ursula went to the controls, killed the engines and engaged the stabilisers to keep the submarine stationary in the water.

Up closer, she and Genie could tell this was unlike any sea they had encountered before. For one thing, it was a lot brighter because there were dozens of pointy little objects, like tiny stars, floating in the water, and these gave off the glittering light they had seen. Beyond them, there were also glowing clouds of pink and blue. It was completely unlike the usual dark oceans they were used to.

Genie picked up the intercom and sent a message to the boys. 'Are you two seeing this?'

Jai picked up at once. 'It's extraordinary!' he exclaimed. 'Those are star plankton out there! One of the rarest types in the world! They're—'

'Do we really have to spoil this moment with a lecture about plankton?' Max's voice came through.

Jai was fascinated by plankton and, thanks to his photographic memory, knew seemingly endless facts about them that he was always very keen to share.

'Just come and join us on the bridge,' Genie said, rolling her eyes. 'You can tell us about the star plankton then.'

Max and Jai arrived a few moments later. They all admired the view for a while before Ursula said that she and Genie ought to get dressed so they could continue with their voyage.

'Why are you even wearing your pyjamas on the bridge?' Jai asked with a disapproving look. 'It isn't regulation. As the acting captain, I ought to—'

'The longer you delay us, the longer it will take to get ready,' Ursula pointed out. 'We'll be right back.'

It only took a few moments for them to change into their explorers' robes – and for Genie to don her cowgirl boots, kraken T-shirt and a narwhal hat – before returning to the bridge. They were all feeling excited about entering the Nebula Sea and it seemed that everyone held their breath as they started up the engines. The *Blowfish* moved forward through the water – but it only went a short way before it suddenly stopped with a horrible juddering motion.

'What's going on?' Jai asked. 'It feels like we just butted into something, but there's nothing there.'

Ursula looked down at the instrument panel. 'It doesn't make sense,' she said. 'The engines are running normally.'

They tried increasing the power slightly, but that only made the submarine groan loudly, so they altered the course and attempted to enter the Nebula Sea from a different direction, but the same thing happened again.

'It's as if there's some kind of invisible force field keeping us out,' Max said.

'Perhaps we should go out and take a look?' Ursula finally suggested. 'We might get more of an idea what the problem is.'

The explorers always worked outside the submarine in pairs, so Ursula and Jai headed to the swim-out hatch together. A few minutes later they floated in the water beside the submarine, Ursula in her mermaid form and Jai in his diving suit. Bess was waiting for them there too and drifted along in their wake as they swam past the *Blowfish* and right up to the edge of the Nebula Sea.

It glowed and sparkled around them with all the twinkling light from the star plankton, but when Jai and Ursula tried to swim further, they met the same problem as the submarine. There was no current or obstacle that they could see, yet some sort of invisible force field kept them from entering. The barrier didn't seem to affect Bess who passed through as easily as she moved through solid walls. But Bess could hardly return Stardust City by herself, so Ursula and Jai went back to the *Blowfish* in defeat and joined the others on the bridge.

'It doesn't make any sense,' Max said, frowning out of the porthole. 'There's nothing there but plankton.' He glanced at Jai. '*Could* it be something to do with the star plankton? Do they have, I don't know . . . repelling properties or something?'

'Oh, so *now* you want to know about plankton,' Jai said with a bit of a huff.

'Not especially,' Max replied. 'I mean they never seem to actually *do* anything. But if they're responsible for what's happening here then perhaps your encyclopedic knowledge might actually come in useful for something.' He flashed Jai a grin. 'Come to think of it, this must be quite an exciting moment for you.'

They all looked at Jai hopefully but he shook his head. 'Star plankton can't repel anything. They can do lots of other interesting things, though,' he added defensively.

'Name one,' Max replied at once, folding his arms over his chest.

'Well, at night they go up to the surface of the sea to feed on phytoplankton, which is actually the largest migration on our planet, so—'

He was interrupted by Max letting out a very loud and drawn-out yawn. 'Oh, I'm sorry,' Max said. 'Were you still talking?'

Jai scowled at him. 'I suppose you think robots are far more interesting?'

'*Everyone* thinks robots are more interesting,' Max replied. 'Because they can actually *do* things.' He dug into his pocket and produced a tiny robot crab. 'This one, for example, can cut your hair in any style you like, including shave fades.' He gestured at the shark image that was shaved into the side of his head. 'Sharks, squids, kraken, you name it. But if you want to be very boring about it then I could program it to shave a plankton for you?'

Jai instantly took a step back, looking horrified. 'Absolutely not! That hairstyle isn't regulation, and even if it was, I'm not letting a robot crab anywhere near my head!'

'Can we just stick to the matter at hand?' Ursula asked, gesturing towards the porthole. 'If we can't travel into the Nebula Sea then we can't return Stardust City.'

'There's got to be *some* way,' Genie said. 'After all, one of the Collectors before Scarlett stole it in the first place.'

'Could we try putting the engines up to full power?' Max suggested.

Ursula shook her head. 'We'd risk damaging the *Blowfish*.'

'I know!' Genie said. 'How about we use the ghost-ship pearl?'

Everyone turned to look at the box that had been carefully placed beside the pickled parrot charm in the corner. Genie walked over to flip open the lid, and there was the grey pearl with the tiny ghost ship just visible within.

'Bess passes through the barrier, doesn't she?' Genie went on. 'And Mrs Parnacle said that the ghost ship isn't governed by the laws of physics. If it can fly through the air, then perhaps it can travel into the Nebula Sea?'

'Perhaps,' Jai agreed. 'I would have preferred to

take the *Blowfish*. We know we're safe in it. And Mrs Parnacle didn't get the chance to finish telling us about the ghost ship, except that the crew could be unpredictable ...'

'She wouldn't have given it to us if it wasn't safe, would she?' Max pointed out. 'And we're kind of out of options here.'

'What do you two think?' Jai asked.

Ursula was a little wary of the ghost ship too, but agreed with Max that they had no other choice. Genie agreed as well, so Max reached eagerly for the pearl.

'Hold on.' Jai held up his hand. 'I don't think we should just go rushing in like nitwits. Mrs Parnacle said we'd be transported on to the ship, so we should think about what we might need to take with us and pack a bag each. We'll need our expedition flag too, of course. And I have to leave plenty of food for my pet plankton. After all, we don't know how long we'll be away.'

The others saw the sense in this so they agreed to meet back on the bridge with their bags in half an hour. Ursula had never packed for an expedition before and she thought very carefully about the things she ought to take. Eventually, she decided on several bars of mint cake, a ball of string, her lucky spanner, the puppets from the mermaid school and also her trident. There wasn't room for the trident in her bag, of course, but she tucked it under her arm.

When she met the others on the bridge she saw that Max had his robot duck, which included a freezer compartment for some of the mermaid ice cream, and also shot out stink-berries – one of the vilest-smelling substances known to man – from its beak. Jai had his harpoon gun and Genie carried Pog, who'd decided it was too early to get up and was still asleep in her sock. They all carried their own bags too – a black satchel emblazoned with the Ocean Squid crest – and Ursula hoped they'd used the space wisely.

'Are we ready?' Jai asked.

Everyone nodded, so he reached for the grey pearl and carefully scooped it from the box. He closed his palm around it and the other three placed their hands on top of his. Then they took a collective deep breath and spoke the ghost ship's name three times out loud.

'*Jolly Rosa, Jolly Rosa, Jolly Rosa.*'

At once the most ferocious wind whipped up, even though they were standing inside. It was like suddenly being caught inside a storm – their cloaks and hair flew out around them, and the pages of the nearby monster guides and sea almanacs fluttered so much that a couple of pages were even tugged free. The air was filled with the scent of salt, barnacles, spilled rum and bedraggled parrots. And then, in the blink of an eye, the explorers were pulled right off the bridge of the *Blowfish*, as if some invisible hand had snatched them up. The submarine vanished and a mighty galleon sprang up in its place – completely unlike any ship they'd ever seen.

CHAPTER FOUR

The explorers all staggered slightly as their boots made contact with the deck. It was hugely disorientating to find themselves suddenly in a brand-new place, especially as the wooden planks seemed to tilt beneath their feet, and it was only by clutching on to each other that they managed to remain upright.

Ursula looked up and immediately saw great sails looming above them, hanging in tattered shreds. They were grey and so was everything else – the deck, the rigging, the rails. The ship looked as if it ought to be at the bottom of the sea. There were barnacles attached to every surface and dripping lengths of seaweed dangling from rigging, and even a couple of starfish clinging on to the ship.

They were still just outside the Nebula Sea – the explorers could see it sparkling a short distance away, while the *Blowfish* sat stationary in the water behind them. And even though they were on a boat, they were still underwater – the dark sea pressing against them on all sides. The water didn't actually touch them though, and they weren't at all wet. Instead, they breathed a strange, thin air that tasted of the salty ocean. It was like being on the deck of a ship at night-time, but it was still disconcerting to the explorers to know they were many miles under the sea with no diving suits or any other means of protection.

It was hard to think about any of that when faced with the *Jolly Rosa*'s crew, however. They were gathered on the deck, staring curiously at the explorers and they were clearly all ghosts – the explorers could see right through their transparent bodies. They were all women and they were all pirates. Or at least they had been when they were alive.

Ursula saw a lot of magnificent hats with large feathers, as well as cutlasses and even ghost parrots. The pirates wore a lot of jewellery too, with medallions in the form of sea monsters, skulls and galleons. Ursula felt a flare of alarm. No one had told them this was a pirate vessel. They'd had some experience with pirates back on Pirate Island, none of which had been particularly good.

A pirate with an especially splendid purple velvet hat stepped forward and opened her mouth to speak, but Max beat her to it.

'How many different types of you are there?' he asked. 'First we meet pirate fairies and now it's ghost pirates! Next you'll be saying there's dog pirates and chipmunk pirates and gnome pirates too.'

'Naturally,' the pirate with the purple hat replied. She had a mass of curly black hair spilling from beneath her hat and intelligent green eyes. She was as transparent as the rest of them, but the explorers could still make out colours and her velvet coat was the same shade of purple as her hat. Her trousers and boots were black, and her buckles and buttons were shiny gold. 'Gnomes are uncommonly fierce and make particularly good pirates,' she went on. 'We have many pirate dogs on board the *Jolly Rosa* as well as a pirate duck. No chipmunks though.'

Ursula noticed that there were, indeed, several dogs amongst the crew, all wearing their own pirate hats.

'I wouldn't try to touch the duck, by the way,' the pirate went on. 'She's incredibly bad-tempered. But why have you summoned us? Some sort of expedition, is it?' Her eyes took in their explorers' cloaks.

'We're from the Ocean Squid Explorers' Club,' Jai said. He looked wary and Ursula guessed he was uncomfortable being around so many pirates, not yet sure whether or not they could be trusted. 'We . . . well, it's a long story but we want to travel into the Nebula Sea. We need to return a fairy city there.'

The pirate jerked her thumb at the sparkling sea nearby. 'Is that it?'

'Yes. For some reason our submarine won't go into it. It's like it's surrounded by some kind of force field.'

'Don't worry about that – the *Jolly Rosa* will sail through well enough,' the pirate replied.

'So you'll take us then? Just like that?' Max asked suspiciously. 'Aren't you even going to ask for a payment of some kind?'

The pirate smiled. 'Certainly, but not from you. Haven't you ever travelled by ghost ship before?'

The explorers shook their heads.

'Well, it's like this,' the pirate replied. 'Our ship went down a hundred years or so ago during a squid battle. We all drowned.' She shrugged. 'I wish we had been blessed with a little more time, but it was a glorious way to go. And it wasn't the end of our adventures because we had a ghost medallion on board, which meant the ship continued to exist in the spectral realm in the form you see it now. We sail the ghost sea, mostly, but we also drop the occasional ghost ship pearl back into the living world.' She looked at the one still held in Jai's hand. 'That's from the mermaid academy, I believe? We have an arrangement with them to take on passengers at times. They pay us for the service. Pirates are always looking to make more money, you know, even in death. I'm Rosa Knightly, by the way.' She offered them a bow. 'Ship's captain.'

'Rosa Knightly?' Genie looked startled. 'But I've heard about you. They used to call you the Pirate Queen! Weren't you a princess or something like that? Before you became a pirate, I mean?'

'Hardly!' Rosa replied, laughing. 'Oh, I had a title, but I was just a lady. Nothing so grand as a princess. Besides, I like to think they called me the Pirate Queen because of how very successful I was at it rather than my boring background. You'll get to know the rest of the crew as we go along.'

'But is it *safe* for living people to travel on board a ghost ship?' Ursula asked. She remembered Mrs Parnacle's half-spoken warning and still felt a little nervous.

'Safe?' Rosa asked. 'Well, of course. I mean, as safe as anything ever really is at sea. I can't guarantee you won't be dragged overboard by an angry sea monster or fall into a whirlpool and drown, but you'll be safe enough on the ship itself. The ghost medallion will cast its magic over you if you're on board, so anything the ship passes through, you'll pass through too. Well, what do you say? Shall we set sail for this Nebula Sea of yours?'

Jai looked back longingly towards the *Blowfish*. 'I don't suppose there's any way of taking our submarine with us, is there?' he asked.

'Not unless you've got a pirate fairy on board who could shrink it small enough to fit in your pocket,' Rosa replied.

They all thought of Zara and wished she was still part of their crew, but as the pirate fairy who'd accompanied them on their last mission had long since gone, they had no choice but to leave the *Blowfish* where it was and hope that it would be all right. The pirate crew went to their various posts and the explorers all hurried over to the rails to watch as the *Jolly Rosa* turned towards the Nebula Sea. There was no wind underwater, so Ursula guessed she was being moved by something more than her sails as she glided majestically forward. As Rosa had promised, the ship had no problems at all passing through the barrier, and soon they were in the Nebula Sea.

The explorers gave Rosa the coordinates for Stardust City and she plotted a course, estimating that they should reach the correct spot in about two weeks. There was sparkling star plankton all around them, making it feel more like they were in outer space than underwater. Genie told them that the blue-and-pink clouds they passed were whale burps, which meant there must be whales in the sea somewhere nearby too. They didn't see any, however, and after half an hour or so of sailing, one of the crew approached and asked if they'd like a tour of the ship.

They were about to go below decks when Bess gave everyone a fright by suddenly appearing right there beside them, tentacles sprawling everywhere and huge eyes blinking around her curiously. The crew let out shouts of alarm and all went running for their harpoon guns, but Genie quickly explained that Bess was a shadow kraken.

Rosa gave her a shocked look. 'Kraken whisperer, eh? I've never heard of such a thing.' Her eyes narrowed slightly. 'Doesn't quite seem natural. You must be a mighty strange sort of person. I suppose that's why you're carrying that old sock around?'

Genie looked down at the sock. 'Oh. No, there's a sleeping dizard in there.'

'Even stranger,' Rosa said. 'I don't like it. You might have said something before. I'm no fan of surprises.'

'Why does it matter to you anyway?' Max asked. 'Even a real kraken couldn't destroy a ghost ship or kill an already dead crew.'

'Perhaps not, but old habits die hard,' Rosa replied, frowning at Bess. 'Sea monsters and pirates have been enemies for centuries. Look, is there anything else I ought to know about you lot? Or your expedition?'

Ursula would have felt tempted to stay quiet about the Collector, but Jai was too honourable for that and explained all about the Phantom Atlas Society.

'It only seems right to warn you that Scarlett might be able to capture a ghost ship inside one of her magic snow globes,' Jai said.

Rosa shrugged. 'Even if she managed it, we'd still be able to use one of our own ghost pearls to slip back to the ghostly realm. That's the one place the four of you wouldn't be able to accompany us though, so for your sake I hope it doesn't happen.'

The explorers hoped so too. None of them fancied being stuck inside a snow globe, or worse, suddenly adrift deep underwater without the protection of the ship and its ghost medallion.

'Don't look so glum,' Rosa said, smacking Jai on the back. 'If you go with my first mate Jules, she'll show you around below decks and you'll probably be just in time for the pirates' afternoon tea too.'

'Afternoon tea?' Max suddenly looked a lot more

cheerful. 'You mean it's not just grog and stale ship's biscuits?'

Rosa turned away from them with a smile. 'Not on this ship,' she said.

The explorers went with Jules, a red-headed pirate with a scarlet coat and an octopus ear cuff, who led them down below. Back at the Ocean Squid Explorers' Club, Ursula had mostly worked on submarines, but she'd been on expedition ships from time to time too. The *Jolly Rosa* was nothing like any of them. The explorer galleons were all kept scrupulously clean and contained a lot of polished brass and gleaming wood and paintings of famous explorers.

But the inside of the *Jolly Rosa* was as covered in barnacles and seaweed as the deck had been. They even spotted several startled crabs scuttling back and forth. There were a few paintings of fearsome-looking pirates and even fiercer octopuses. The portholes were so dirty that it was hard to see anything out of them and the whole place smelled of brine and rot, as if the ship was decomposing on a seabed – which, Ursula supposed, the real *Jolly Rosa* actually was. It was a disconcerting reminder that they weren't on a real vessel at all.

The other difference was that while explorer ships were strictly organised and disciplined, the pirate ship had mess spilling from every doorway in the form of loose gold coins, parrot-grooming equipment, rolled-up treasure maps and other bits and pieces.

Jai was appalled. 'Aren't you worried something will get damaged?' he asked, carefully moving an old treasure map to one side.

Jules shrugged. 'Nothing can really be damaged,' she said. 'It's not actually here – just an echo of what we had on the original ship.'

'Even so . . .' Jai looked around him. 'They're solid enough to be trip hazards. And don't you want to live in a clean, orderly place? Captain Filibuster says that any place that's clean and orderly is—'

'Boring as all heck!' Jules cut in.

Max laughed and Jai looked mildly offended but said nothing. Captain Filibuster was a very famous explorer who had written numerous guides to exploring and expeditions. Max had made no secret of the scorn he felt towards these volumes, but Jai had collected the entire set and knew them all from cover to cover – including the notoriously hard to come by *Captain Filibuster's Guide to Bathyspheres and Bobble Fish*.

'I'll show you where you'll be sleeping first,' Jules said, leading the way down a corridor.

The explorers were used to their own luxurious bubble

rooms on board the *Blowfish*, but the dormitory Jules showed them was shared by around twenty members of the crew at any one time. They all slept in simple hammocks strung up from the ceiling. A few pirates were in there now, snoring loudly with their boots still on, and there were a couple of pirate dogs curled up in the hammocks too. The whole place smelled of pirate feet.

A look of dismay flashed briefly over Jai's face before he mastered it and thanked the pirate politely.

'We don't have set hammocks,' Jules said. 'You just take any one that's going free. And you can chuck your stuff in the corner if you like.'

'Thank you, but an explorer must carry their possessions with them at all times,' Jai replied. 'It's one of our rules.'

This wasn't true, but Ursula assumed he didn't want to leave their bags unattended in case the pirates got too interested in them.

'Suit yourselves,' Jules replied with a shrug. 'Come on, let's get to the galley before the pirate tea is all gone.'

They followed her to an enormous room with long wooden tables stretching its length. Several large chandeliers hung from the ceiling, shaped like octopuses, their long tentacles coiled around dozens of flickering candles. Like the rest of the ship, it didn't look as if anyone had ever cleaned in here. There were all kinds of food stains on the tables, sticky patches on the benches and spilled drinks on the floor. Several pirate dogs chewed discarded bones.

It was all rather noisy and chaotic, but Ursula had to admit that the tea itself looked wonderful. Spread out along the tables were chocolate pirate ships, bright-green marzipan parrots and sugar skulls, along with candy dolphins and treasure chests made of fudge. As well as the sweet things, there were large platters piled high with hot dogs and bacon butties, and the smell of cooked meat made all their stomachs rumble.

'This is more like it!' Max exclaimed. 'Where do I sign up for being a pirate?'

Jai shot him a disapproving look, but when Jules invited them to help themselves, he was as keen to dig in as all the others. They piled their plates up high with hot sandwiches and sticky treats before finding a seat and settling down to enjoy their meal. The food was as delicious as it looked and the explorers all went up for second helpings. Max was even about to go for a third when, all of a sudden, they heard a commotion up on deck, and then there was the sound of alarm bells ringing throughout the ship.

CHAPTER FIVE

The pirates all abandoned their food and hurried from the room with the explorers close behind them. They had no idea what the bells might mean, but they knew it was unlikely to be anything good.

'What could be making them sound the alarm anyway?' Ursula wondered. 'Didn't Jules say that nothing on the ship could really be damaged?'

'Perhaps it's just a drill?' Genie suggested hopefully.

They frequently had all manner of safety drills back on the *Blowfish*. Sometimes it seemed like Jai was forever blasting them awake with an alarm in the middle of the night.

'I'm not sure pirates are the type to go in for drills,' Max said.

They snatched up their things and arrived on the deck somewhat breathlessly, still half hoping that this might be nothing more than a safety exercise. But Max had been right – pirates only sounded the alarm in a genuine emergency. The explorers had seen some startling sights since setting off together but nothing quite compared with this. In the water up ahead was the most gigantic shark, bathed in the shimmering glow of the surrounding star plankton.

It was a colossal dinosaur of a creature – as big as a kraken – with cold, dead eyes and a sleek, muscular body. Ursula felt her heart plummet into her boots at the sight of it. It was so massive that it was hard to take in all at once, but it would easily be able to swallow up the ship in one gulp. And it had clearly seen them. Its black eyes, each the height of a person, were fixed on them hungrily as it rushed closer through the dark water, moving with astonishing speed for something so big. In a matter of minutes, it would surely be upon them.

'All hands!' Rosa was bellowing. 'All hands to the sails!'

The pirates raced to the masts, hurrying to drag down the tattered grey sails as the explorers ran across the deck to Rosa.

'What's going on?' Jai asked. 'I thought the shark couldn't damage the ship?'

Rosa gave him a pitying look. 'It can't,' she said. 'But if it swallows us whole then we'll have to use the pearl to return to the ghost realm. Which means you four will be left behind in the shark's belly and we won't get paid for transporting you.'

Ursula stared at the shark in horror. It had already halved the distance between them in the water. Bess had appeared beside the *Jolly Rosa* and was doing her best to flail her tentacles about in a menacing fashion, but past experience had taught the explorers that animals could sense Bess was a shadow creature with no physical substance, so the shark was unlikely to pay her much heed.

'It's one of those annoying rules the mermaids insist on,' Rosa said with a shrug. 'No payment for dead passengers.'

'What can we do to help?' Jai gasped.

'Grab a rope,' Rosa replied. 'And help haul the sails. The flying ones are especially heavy.'

The explorers didn't know what she meant by that, and it was hard to work out how changing the sails would help, but now didn't seem the time for asking questions. There clearly wasn't a weapon on board that would be any use against a monster of that size, so they could only trust that Rosa knew what she was talking about as they raced over to the nearest mast. The pirates had swapped the grey sails for equally tattered blue ones and were all tugging on the ropes to haul them up. The explorers threw their belongings into a corner and then hurried to help, heaving with all their might on the ropes.

The sails were unexpectedly heavy and Ursula's arms and back were on fire with the effort, but she summoned up every last ounce of her strength. She knew for a fact that several explorers from the Ocean Squid Explorers' Club had met their ends by being gobbled alive by giant sharks, and that it was in fact considered one of the most glorious ways for an Ocean Squid explorer to go. But she *really* didn't want this happening to her just the same.

The blue sails finally settled into position, and at once the ship stopped going forward and began to rise straight up instead, moving quickly through the water, with Bess trailing along behind. The explorers hurried to the railings and saw that the colossal shark was still swimming straight for the spot where they had been. Ursula guessed it must not have very good eyesight and couldn't tell they'd moved. She was just about to breathe a sigh of relief when Rosa bellowed, 'No slacking! It'll figure out where we've gone soon enough. We need full power! Full power!'

Ursula looked around, expecting to see pirates

scrambling up the masts and doing something with the ropes, but it seemed that Rosa had been talking to the ghost parrots instead. The air around them became filled with feathers as the parrots soared up to the crow's nest, where they settled and began shouting out pirate curses in their high-pitched squeaky voices. The *Jolly Rosa*'s speed increased at once, and Ursula saw hundreds of tiny bubbles race past them as the ship rose faster and faster towards the surface.

But Rosa had been right about the shark. It quickly realised where the ship had gone, and charged through the water after them. When the explorers peered over the railings they were met with the horrifying sight of the shark's head, its hungry black eyes filled with grim determination. It completely ignored all of Bess's attempts to distract it, and finally the shadow kraken gave up and materialised on the deck to curl her tentacles protectively around Genie instead.

'What can we do?' Ursula yelled at Rosa.

The pirate gripped the rails beside them with a grim look. 'At this point?' she said. 'Pray.'

They were rapidly nearing the surface. Ursula could tell because of the way the water lightened around them, turning from black, to dark blue, to pale aqua as the sun's rays rippled through. But they weren't moving

quite fast enough. They could see that the shark was catching up with them.

'Drat,' Rosa muttered. 'We're all out of parrots. Sorry, kids. It's a grisly way to go but—'

'Can't we fire the cannons at it?' Max gasped.

'No point,' Rosa replied. 'We're a ghost ship, remember? The cannon balls would just pass straight through. They wouldn't be enough to kill it anyway.'

'But we don't need to kill it,' Genie said from somewhere within Bess's writhing tentacles. 'Just slow it down. Ursula, your trident!'

Ursula looked across the deck to where the explorers had left their things, including her trident. The last time she had used it to try to save them back at Skeleton Cove she had lost control and put them all at risk, almost losing Genie in the process. She was afraid to wield it again in case the same thing happened, but she'd been practising with it since then and was surely more in control of it now than she had been before.

Jai met her eyes. 'We've got nothing to lose,' he said. 'Come on.'

They hurried over to pick up their weapons, then stood shoulder to shoulder at the rails. Jai raised his harpoon gun as Ursula lifted her trident, realising as she did so that her hands were suddenly sweating.

Rosa saw what they were doing and let out a rather insulting laugh of disbelief.

'You're not serious?' she scoffed. 'There's no way those will do anything. A harpoon will just bounce off its thick skin for a start.'

'I'm not aiming for its skin,' Jai said, hoisting the gun to his shoulder.

He was known for being one of the best shots in the Ocean Squid Explorers' Club and the others held their breath as he took aim and let loose the harpoon. It raced through the water and struck the shark right in its eye. At the same instant, Ursula pointed the trident and sent a bolt of shining lightning directly into the shark's other eye.

The creature gave a bellow of pain so loud that it sent ripples through the ocean around them, but it didn't slow down even a little bit – if anything, it just seemed more determined than ever. Ursula was about to blast it again when the *Jolly Rosa* suddenly burst up from beneath the surface, casting glittering diamond drops of spray in a great explosion around them. The sun seemed blindingly bright after the darkness of the sea and Ursula could barely look at the water because of the glare.

The ship continued to fly upwards, straight into the

sky. For a moment, Ursula thought they had done it, but the next second the shark broke the surface of the water too, its gigantic head rising up perilously close beneath the ship. Water poured down its sleek grey skin as it opened its jaws wide, revealing terrifying rows of massive ivory teeth. It let out another bellow, and Ursula's eyes watered with the fetid stench of rotting fish.

They could no longer see its eyes, but Ursula was about to try shooting it with the trident again anyway when Max said, 'Here, let me!'

He hoisted his robot duck on to the rails and pressed a button on its side. At once, a stink-berry shot from the duck's beak and sailed straight down into the shark's open mouth. The berry was so infinitesimally small that it was like hurling a pebble into a canyon and it was quickly lost from their sight. But it must have exploded against the shark's tongue because the creature suddenly roared in disgust and fell back into the sea with a splash so huge it sent a mighty wave crashing over the top of the ship. The force field in place around the galleon meant that the water didn't touch them, but they saw it falling down in a sparkling sheet. When it ended, the shark had disappeared back beneath the sea, and in another few moments the *Jolly Rosa* had risen into the sky like a dirigible, finally high enough to be safe.

'Good Lord!' Rosa stared at the explorers in admiration. 'What the heck was in that duck?'

'Stink-berries,' Max replied, wiping the sweat from his brow. 'They're one of the most potently horrible things known to man.'

'Well!' Rosa seemed momentarily lost for words. Then she shook her head and slapped Max on the back. 'I've seen some close shaves in my time but that was something else. Good for you! It would have been a great pity if you had all ended up as shark steaks. Mighty impressive! No wonder you explorers are always meeting sticky ends.'

'Not *always*,' Genie replied. 'Some explorers live to a grand old age.' She smiled at her friends. 'Well done, everyone. That was incredible.'

She threw her arms around Ursula, who reached out to draw Max and Jai into the embrace too. They'd faced up to a giant shark and lived to tell the tale. It was an adventure worthy of any flag report and they all felt an immense sense of pride at surviving the ordeal.

'You can stop that hollering now!' Rosa shouted up at the parrots.

The birds fell silent and left the crow's nest, flying down to their various perches. At once the *Jolly Rosa* ceased accelerating upwards and floated serenely above the sea instead. The water glittered a beautiful jewel-bright blue and it seemed the shark must have retreated back into the depths because they could see no dark shadow moving beneath the surface.

There was no land in sight either – only a great expanse of ocean as far as the eye could see. Ursula could immediately tell that they were still in tropical waters because the sun beamed down strongly, evaporating the spray from the deck. The air had a summer scent that reminded her of warm sand, cold ice cream and swaying coconut palms.

'There's a new blue streak in your hair,' Genie pointed out.

Ursula ran her hand through it and saw that another blue streak had indeed appeared. She'd noticed her hair changing colour when she practised her magical singing with the puppets too and knew that soon there would probably be no black left in it at all. This would have been a big problem if she'd been trying to hide her mermaid heritage, as she once had to, but now that it was no longer a secret it didn't matter, and Ursula rather liked the blue and purple colours.

'Suits you,' Max said with a smile. Then he rubbed his stomach and went on, 'Maybe it's all the adrenaline, but I'm starving. I could easily eat three more of those bacon butties.'

Jai frowned. 'Me too,' he said. 'I feel like I've hardly eaten at all.'

'Well, technically speaking, you haven't,' Rosa said.

The explorers all turned to look at her. 'What do you mean?' Ursula asked.

The pirate shrugged. 'We only have ghost food on board,' she said. 'Whatever you eat will fade from your bodies after an hour or two.'

'You mean ... there's no food here for us?' Jai asked, looking alarmed.

'It's a ghost ship,' Rosa replied. 'What did you think you'd be able to eat on it? It's the same for the drinks, I'm afraid. All the ginger beer, grog, water and so on will eventually vanish.'

Jai cast the others a worried look. 'Did any of you pack food?'

'A few bars of mint cake,' Ursula said.

The others had mint cake too, along with some tins of spam, and of course there was the Ocean Discovery ice cream in the robot duck, but their total supplies wouldn't keep them going for more than a day or two. And none of them had brought any water. Genie had used most of her bag space to bring hat-making supplies and polish for her cowgirl boots, and Max had mostly packed his robotics equipment.

'What were you two thinking of?' Jai groaned. 'Those things won't help us much on an expedition.'

'Am I losing my hearing?' Max asked. 'Because it sounded like you just suggested my robots won't help us – mere minutes after Ducky saved us all from a gigantic shark. Besides, you're one to talk, seeing as you've packed the book you're writing about your cat. Are you ever going to finish that thing?'

'Biscuit achieved a lot of notable things when he was alive—' Jai began.

'Nobody cares!' Max interrupted in a burst of impatience. The next moment he shook his head and said, 'Look, I'm sorry. I'm sure Biscuit was an excellent cat. But there comes a point when you have to just ... let go of the past. Anyway, Biscuit isn't going to help us much in our current predicament, is he?'

'We'll just have to find food and water somewhere along the way,' Genie cut in, frowning at Max.

Ursula felt a deep stirring of unease. There was nothing ahead of them in any direction except the ocean. And since this was an unexplored sea, they had no idea how far away the next bit of land might be. In fact, they really knew nothing about the Nebula Sea at all. And when they asked Rosa if she had any idea, the pirate only laughed.

'This is your expedition,' she pointed out. 'Not mine. I'd never even heard of the Nebula Sea before you brought us here. But the gigantic shark monster doesn't exactly make a great first impression, does it? Don't you lot do any kind of research before blundering in somewhere? And to think they call pirates reckless! I'll stick someone on watch in the crow's nest. Hopefully there's land around here somewhere with a cow or something on it that you can eat.'

She wandered off, still laughing.

'We'll figure out something,' Jai said, although he looked very worried.

'The other explorers' clubs do this all the time,' Genie added. 'They don't have submarines so they can't carry as many supplies with them, and they have to find food as they go.'

'That probably involves quite a lot of hunting with spears, though,' Max pointed out. 'Do any of you have any idea how to hunt? Because I certainly don't.'

They all shook their heads.

'I don't want to hurt a cow anyway,' Genie said. 'Maybe we won't have to? I read Stella's flag report from their first expedition; when they went to the Icelands they discovered a magic goose that lays these golden eggs. They contain whatever food the person would most like to find inside. There's even a pudding course.'

'Well, that was extremely fortunate for them,' Max replied. 'But I don't think we're likely to discover any kind of goose – magical or otherwise – in the middle of the ocean. I suppose we could always eat Pog's food – someone packed her caviar, right? And if we get really desperate, we could always eat Pog herself.'

Jai looked aghast. 'We are *not* eating the dizard!' he exclaimed. 'I made a vow to Rudolpho to take good care of her and keep her safe.'

'I was only joking,' Max replied. 'Keep your shirt on. It doesn't look like there's much meat on her anyway. But it doesn't change the fact that we're going to run out of food soon.'

'We've foraged for water before,' Jai pointed out. 'We'll find a way to top up our provisions. It's either that or ask Rosa to turn the ship round and take us back to the *Blowfish*.'

Nobody much cared for the idea of doing that. They'd be right back where they started then, and they all agreed that the sooner they could return the galaxy fairy city, the better. They would just have to hope that land appeared before too long.

In the meantime, the explorers tried to settle into life on the pirate galleon. As they had already begun to realise, it was a noisy and chaotic place and there didn't seem to be any routine or structure on board at all. There wasn't an awful lot of work for the pirates to do when it came to sailing the ship because it was powered by a ghost wind. Jules explained that different sails were used depending on which direction they wanted the ship to travel. Grey took them straight ahead and blue took them up – as they had seen when the shark attacked. Green sails took them down and purple sails meant sideways. If they wanted to increase their speed, they sent the ghost parrots up into the rigging to shout curses, which whipped up the ghost wind. In the absence of any work to do, the pirates spent a lot of their time feasting and merry-making, and this went on throughout the first night on board, making it very difficult to sleep.

The next morning dawned bright and cheerful, and Ursula was surprised to wake up to sunlight forcing its way through the ghost ship's dirty portals. Day or night, it was always dark on board a submarine and waking to sunshine was something she really missed. Her stomach rumbled with hunger though, and it didn't help that she could smell the pirate breakfast of eggs and bacon drifting up from the galley.

The other explorers were awake too and they all agreed they wouldn't try to eat any of the pirate food as it only made them even more hungry when it inevitably faded away. Instead they went on deck to enjoy the sunshine and to share out a miserly breakfast of two squares of mint cake each.

'We have to ration ourselves,' Jai insisted.

'It doesn't look like Pog's rationing,' Max pointed out in a grumpy tone.

The little dizard was beside them, chomping through a huge heap of caviar, eating with such greedy speed that she frequently had to stop to belch.

'She doesn't need to,' Jai replied. 'Rudolpho provided her with enough food to last the journey.'

Max rolled his eyes and muttered something about how the dizard could share some of her food, but Jai wouldn't hear of it. The care of someone's pet was at stake and so it was now a matter of honour to him.

'If I'd ever trusted someone enough to look after Biscuit I would have been outraged if they hadn't done it properly,' he said.

'You're always banging on about that cat,' Max replied. 'Why haven't you got another one by now?'

Jai flinched. 'No other cat could replace him.'

'Well, it doesn't need to replace him, it just needs to be another cat for you to love,' Max pointed out.

'That's what I keep telling him,' Genie said. 'Jai's so good with cats – he should definitely get one.'

'That's it then,' Max said. 'Once we've found Scarlett and stopped the Phantom Atlas Society, I'm getting you a kitten.'

'Don't be ridiculous,' Jai replied. 'Anyway, we've got more important things to think about right now. Like—'

But before he could go on, there was a shout from the crow's nest – two words they had all been hoping to hear:

'Land ahoy!'

CHAPTER SIX

A short while later, the explorers stood at the rails and gazed down at the island beneath them. It had all the features of a tropical paradise, with golden beaches, swaying palm trees and cascades of glittering waterfalls. The foliage was dense so they couldn't see what lay beneath, but the island looked quite mountainous and seemed peaceful.

'Looks safe enough,' Rosa observed. 'Hopefully you're in luck and there aren't any wild boar or similar prowling about. Shall we set you down on the beach?'

The *Jolly Rosa* swapped its sails to descend until it was hovering just over the sand, and then the explorers used the rope ladder to climb the rest of the way. Jai had brought his harpoon gun and Ursula had her trident, although the thought of actually hunting anything with it appalled her. She'd never really considered how lucky she was to be in the Ocean Squid Explorers' Club with a submarine full of food, ice-cream sundaes and popcorn, but now she wondered how the other clubs ever managed to get anything done when they were forced to scrounge for food all the time.

Once it had dropped them off, the *Jolly Rosa* retreated a little way and settled itself down on the sea, bobbing gently upon the calm surface. The explorers walked along the beach until they found a path leading into the jungle. Ursula felt a bit on edge after what Rosa had said about wild boar, but they saw no sign of any large beasts as they walked further inland. In fact, there seemed to be very few animals at all. Ursula had expected to hear the call of birds in the trees and to see leaves rustling as smaller creatures scampered by. But there weren't even any mosquitoes in the air.

'This is odd,' Max said. 'I thought there'd be more life here.'

'Maybe there is some sort of dangerous predator on the island, after all,' Jai said, looking worried. 'Everyone keep a sharp eye out.'

They soon arrived at their first waterfall, which gushed over the edge of a hill and straight into a small lake. The explorers hurried over eagerly, hoping this might be fresh water they could take back with them to drink, but when they got closer, they saw that it didn't look quite right.

'It's yellow,' Max pointed out, wrinkling his nose. 'Maybe it's a toilet for whatever's living on the island?'

'It doesn't smell like a toilet,' Genie said, sniffing the air. 'It smells sweet and . . . lemony.'

'It's fizzing too, look.' Ursula pointed. 'I thought it was just frothing where it had fallen from a height, but it's fizzy here in the shallows as well.'

Now they looked closer, they saw that tiny little bubbles streamed up all around the pool.

'Well, there's only one thing for it,' Max finally said. 'Someone's going to have to be brave enough to have a taste. I just really hope it's not wild boar wee.'

He bent at the edge of the lake, scooped up a handful of liquid and drank it from the palm of his hand while the others watched nervously. Then he looked up at them and grinned. 'It's lemonade,' he said.

Everyone immediately crouched down to try it. Max was right. It wasn't water at all, but cold, fizzy, delicious lemonade that bubbled pleasantly over Ursula's tongue. Bess materialised alongside them and seemed to very much enjoy drifting around in the lemonade pool until the fizziness of the water made her sneeze. Ursula had never seen a kraken sneeze before and it was such a loud, explosive sound that she almost jumped out of her skin.

'Well, that's one way to announce our presence,' Max remarked. 'Not that there appears to be anything here to announce it to. Not even any birds to be startled out of the trees.'

'If the other ponds and lakes on the island are lemonade then I guess it explains why there are no animals here,' Jai said. 'They all need water to survive, even the insects.'

'Let's just hope we find a plant with some edible berries or something then,' Max replied.

The explorers left Bess paddling beneath the waterfall and made their way deeper into the island. They quickly discovered that the lemonade waterfalls weren't its only unusual feature – they also found a pond full of cherryade and another waterfall of cream soda.

'This is great!' Genie beamed. 'We can get some of the empty rum casks from the *Jolly Rosa* and fill them up.'

'It's not ideal for our teeth but I guess it's something,' Jai agreed.

'Now we just need to find some food,' Ursula said.

She'd been keeping her eyes peeled but so far she hadn't seen a single fruit or mushroom. When Max gave a sudden shout of excitement, she hoped he'd found food, but instead he said, 'Look, a paw print! There's animal life here, after all!'

They all gathered round and saw that he was right. In the earth before them was a set of gigantic paw prints.

'They look just like Biscuit's,' Jai said. 'Only much, much bigger.'

'Oh good,' Max said. 'Perhaps we'll find you a kitten here?'

Jai shook his head. 'Look at the size of them,' he said. 'Those prints belong to a leopard or a tiger or something.'

Ursula felt her insides cramp with worry. It had been bad enough when Rosa had suggested wild boar, but a tiger-infested jungle was even worse.

'Well, at least it means there must be food here,' Genie pointed out. 'The leopards, or whatever they are, must be eating something.'

Ursula tried to feel heartened by this but it was difficult to be anything other than worried about the giant wild cats, especially when the explorers ventured further into the jungle and began to notice other signs of them. The undergrowth was flattened in places and they spotted several piles of big-cat droppings and even a whisker.

'It's huge,' Jai said, picking it up. 'And it's sparkling. Did anyone ever hear of a cat with sparkling whiskers?'

The others shook their heads. They only spoke in whispers now and mostly moved through the jungle in silence, which meant they were very aware whenever a twig snapped or leaves rustled nearby.

'Did you see that?' Max suddenly asked.

'What?'

'There was something there in the bushes.' He pointed. 'I just saw it for a moment – a big white shape.'

'Perhaps it was one of the wild cats,' Ursula said. She strained her eyes into the foliage but couldn't see anything.

'It wouldn't have been white,' Jai replied.

'Unless it was a snow leopard,' Genie pointed out.

Max frowned. 'Why would a snow leopard be on a tropical island?'

'Look, perhaps we should turn back?' Ursula said. 'Just concentrate on getting the soda on to the ship and find food somewhere else? We might end up getting hunted if we stick around here. Hopefully there are other islands nearby that don't have giant cats prowling about.'

'All right,' Jai said. 'I guess something to drink is the most important thing anyway.'

The explorers turned around, intending to return by the same path, but then they all froze rigid in shock. The way ahead was blocked by an enormous sabre-tooth tiger with massive, curved canines stretching out from its fearsome jaws. These teeth – just like its whiskers – sparkled. And this wasn't the only remarkable thing about it. Instead of the usual black and orange stripes, this tiger was white with pale silver stripes and its eyes were deep blue. It stared at them with a cold, fierce, hungry look and its lips slowly rose in a snarl.

CHAPTER SEVEN

Ursula stared at the tiger and felt as if her heart was doing a hundred beats per minute.

'Just . . . keep very still,' Jai whispered. 'Perhaps it will go away and we won't need to hurt it . . .'

But the tiger was already stalking down the path towards them, its hackles raised in a way that looked truly ferocious.

'If you don't shoot it, I think it's going to eat us,' Max said grimly.

Jai groaned. The Ocean Squid Explorers' Club – just like the other clubs – was full of stuffed specimens of wild animals that other explorers had killed and brought back home with them, but Ursula knew that Jai wanted to explore in a different way from what had gone before, and that he had no wish to harm the tiger. Their own safety had to come first though, so he reluctantly raised the harpoon gun to his shoulder and started to take aim.

At the same moment, there was a rustle in the trees behind them and a second tiger stepped out, looking every bit as strong and ferocious as the first one. Ursula turned towards it, pressed her back against Jai's and raised her trident. Like the others, she had no wish to hurt the tigers, but what else could they do?

'Ready?' Jai whispered to her as the giant cats padded slowly closer.

Ursula nodded. 'Ready.'

But then there was more rustling and three other tigers prowled out from the undergrowth, their ice-blue eyes fixed on the explorers, their sharp teeth bared. The children were surrounded and the trident in Ursula's hands began to shake as her hands trembled.

'Five is too many,' Jai muttered. 'We'll never take them all down in time.'

Ursula knew he was right. Even if she and Jai were lucky and managed to stop a tiger each on their first try, the other three would be upon them at once. Sensing the danger, Bess appeared beside them and waved her tentacles, but the tigers barely glanced at her.

Ursula's mind raced for a solution. She'd heard of explorers in the Jungle Cat Explorers' Club being killed by sabre-tooth tigers in the middle of hot jungles, but she'd never thought it would happen to someone in the Ocean Squid Club.

'Any ideas?' Max muttered to Jai as the tigers padded closer. 'Come on, you're the wonder boy, aren't you? Back home it seemed like you were always getting medals and accolades for firing impossible shots with arrows and rescuing teammates from certain death.' A note of desperation had come into Max's voice. 'If anyone can thwart five sabre-tooth tigers and live to tell the tale then surely it's Jai Bartholomew Singh?'

'I'm thinking, I'm thinking!' Jai muttered.

'Well, think faster!' Ursula said. 'Because any minute now they're going to—'

'Wait! I have an idea!' Jai dropped the harpoon gun and rummaged in his pockets, finally drawing out a bag of what looked like tiny biscuits. Everybody stared.

'Are those . . . *cat* treats?' Max asked, looking aghast.

Jai looked a little sheepish. 'I couldn't bring myself to throw them away,' he said. 'They were Biscuit's favourite, you see. These treats are made from special cat chocolate and—'

'You've lost your mind!' Max exclaimed. 'There's no way that's ever going to work! You'll get your hand bitten off if you try to—'

But then abruptly he went silent because Jai held

out his hand to the nearest tiger, palm upwards, with a single cat treat resting there. And instead of biting his hand off, as the other explorers all feared it surely would, the tiger suddenly stopped snarling, sniffed at the treat, and then flicked out its big pink tongue to lap the biscuit straight from Jai's palm. The next second, it began to purr – a deep, rumbling sound that made the ground beneath their feet tremble slightly. The other tigers stopped snarling too and crowded around Jai eagerly as he dished out more cat biscuits. The explorers stared, hardly able to believe what they were seeing.

'This . . . this is ridiculous!' Max protested. 'A little bag of cat treats shouldn't have worked on whopping great tigers! You ought to be tiger meat!'

Jai shrugged. 'I thought it was worth a try. Biscuit loved them. In fact, that's how he got his name. You see, he—'

'Never mind about that right now.' Max cut him off. 'It's the most incredible luck but I'm not counting it as one of your heroics. Something this stupid doesn't get to count.'

Ursula could hardly believe it either. Not only had the tigers stopped snarling, but a couple even butted their huge heads against Jai in an affectionate manner, as if they were house cats.

'Jai's always been good with cats but what happens when the treats run out?' Genie asked quietly. 'Will they still be friendly towards us then?'

No one had any answer to this, but the bag of cat biscuits hadn't been full to begin with and it didn't look as if there were too many left.

'Perhaps we should start making our way back down the path,' Jai suggested. 'Slowly. I'll try to eke the treats out in order to—'

But that was as far as he got before an exasperated voice behind them said, 'What's going on here? Are you feeding the tigers? More importantly, *how* are you feeding them? They're only supposed to accept food from us. And is that a *kraken* floating over your heads?'

The explorers turned around and saw a little group of trolls on the path ahead. For a moment, Ursula thought they were ice trolls because they all had a shock of white hair that sparkled in the sunshine, and the tufts poking out of their ears and fluffing from the end of their tails were all white as well. But surely ice trolls wouldn't be living in a tropical jungle? They were quite tall for trolls too – as tall as adult humans – with lanky frames and very long noses. They all wore dungarees and they all looked extremely cross. One of them snapped his fingers and the tigers immediately left the explorers to return to them, licking their chops and looking a little sheepish.

'Good day,' Jai said, immediately launching into the speech he knew by heart from *Captain Filibuster's Guide to Expeditions and Exploration*. 'We are members of the Ocean Squid Explorers' Club and we have travelled a long way to—'

'Never mind all that.' One of the trolls cut him off. 'You haven't answered my question. How is that kraken floating in mid-air? And how did you tempt the tigers? Sugar-tooths don't normally take kindly to strangers.'

Max frowned. 'Don't you mean sabre-tooth?'

The troll glared at him. 'I think I know what type of tigers I own, boy.'

'Please excuse us,' Jai said. 'We didn't mean to cause any offence.' He gestured at Bess and said, 'She's floating in the air because she's a shadow kraken. And I just offered the tigers some of my old cat's treats, that's all. None of us have ever heard of a sugar-tooth tiger.'

'They're a cousin to the sabre-tooth,' the troll replied, still squinting at Bess suspiciously. 'Only they eat sweet things rather than meat.'

'Oh. Well, they're very handsome,' Jai said. 'And does that mean . . . Are you sugar trolls?'

'What else?' the troll replied.

Ursula racked her brain, trying to recall any knowledge she might have about sugar trolls. She'd heard of mountain trolls, cave trolls, woodland trolls and even sea trolls, but she couldn't remember ever hearing of sugar trolls before.

Jai took a cautious step forward on the path. 'We're very pleased to make your acquaintance,' he said. 'There are many in our world who think that sugar trolls are only a myth.'

'We could say the same for you,' the troll replied, eyeing their explorers' cloaks warily. 'We've all heard talk about the explorers' clubs – humans who go poking into corners of the world that aren't their own, helping themselves to anything they find there, killing animals and stealing plants to take back with them.' His long fingers clenched into fists. 'You may have managed to cast some kind of magic spell over our tigers, but don't think we'll allow you to strip our island bare without a fight.'

'Oh no!' Jai hurried to say. 'Please, whatever you might have heard about the explorers' clubs, we would never take anything without your permission. We want to be different kinds of explorers from those who have gone before us. Absolutely no more stealing or pillaging. We *did* come here looking for food and water – we're running desperately short, you see – but I hope we can reach an agreement to pay you for whatever you might be prepared to sell us.'

'We labour hard over our food,' the troll replied. 'And I can't imagine an explorer would have anything we might want. What if we're not prepared to sell you anything?'

'Then we'll leave,' Jai said simply.

The trolls all narrowed their eyes in suspicion. 'Just like that? You won't try to take anything from us by force?'

'Absolutely and categorically not. I give you my word,' Jai promised. 'Like I said, we want to do things differently. With honour. If you don't want to trade then we'll leave right away and look for food somewhere else. You see, our expedition is quite urgent. We're on our way to return Stardust City to its rightful place in order to—'

'Hang on!' the troll exclaimed. 'Did you say you have Stardust City? Home to the galaxy fairies?'

The trolls looked so eager that Jai became suddenly wary. 'Yes,' he said. 'We rescued it from the Phantom Atlas Society and it's been entrusted into our care. It's not available for trade, though. In fact, we don't even have it on us. It's—'

But that was as far as he got before the trolls hurried forward to embrace the explorers in excitement. Ursula found her nose being tickled by one of the troll's tufts of ear hair. To her surprise, the troll smelled of freshly baked cake and sticky jam tarts, which wasn't a scent she expected a troll to have.

'But that's wonderful!' one of the other trolls exclaimed. 'Wonderful! The galaxy fairies are dear friends of ours. They often used to visit our island in one of their rockets before continuing on their journey to outer space.'

'So the fairies really could travel into space then?' Genie asked, sounding impressed.

'Oh yes! You ought to have seen their rockets – a whole fleet of them gleaming silver in the sunlight. They were quite a sight to behold. And they often used to bring us back moon dust to put into our moon cakes. Oh, we've missed them dreadfully! It was a dark day when the Collector stole them away. For years we've lived in fear that the Island of Sugar Trolls might be next.'

'We're on a mission to stop the Collector and disband the Phantom Atlas Society,' Ursula said. 'If we're successful, then you'll never need to worry about being stolen away again.'

The trolls looked profoundly delighted by this news. A couple of them even had tears sparkling in their eyes. The commotion had drawn the sugar-tooth tigers over as well, headbutting their troll owners in concern. Bess seemed rather confused by it all, but curled her tentacles around everyone affectionately, keen to join the group hug for a moment before she disappeared once again, probably to return to paddling in the lemonade waterfall.

'It's one of the most important expeditions anyone in the Ocean Squid Explorers' Club has undertaken for decades,' Max said. 'So, you know, if you *do* have any food that you might be able to spare us then it would be greatly—'

'Oh, my dear boy, say no more!' one of the trolls instantly replied. He stuck out a long-fingered hand. Ursula noticed that his fingernails were all white and sparkled as much as his hair. 'My name is Alf and of course we will provide you with food and drink, free of charge.'

'We're more than happy to trade—' Jai began, but the troll wouldn't hear of it.

'Absolutely not! It would be a privilege to assist in any way that we can. All I ask in return is that you pass on our good wishes and fondest love to the galaxy fairies once you set them free, and that you ask them to visit us here at their earliest convenience. We have much to catch up on and many happy times to share. But first, your provisions! I know you're in a hurry, so we won't waste time. Our camp is just beyond the next waterfall. Follow me.'

The explorers set off with the trolls and the sugar-tooth tigers, delighted by how their luck had changed. Along the way, they told the trolls all about Scarlett Sauvage and how her hideout had been discovered – although Jai didn't join in much as he was too busy playing with the tigers. Ursula had never seen him with a cat before, but it was clear from how his eyes lit up around them that he was overjoyed to be near one again, even if it was a gigantic beast.

Soon enough, they passed the waterfall the trolls had spoken of, and then found themselves deep in the heart of the island's jungle.

'Here we are,' Alf said. 'Our camp.'

Ursula couldn't work out what he was talking about at first. There didn't seem to be anything up ahead except more jungle. But then she followed the troll's upward gaze and realised there was an entire village of tree houses suspended above their heads. Only they weren't made from sticks and planks of wood – instead they sparkled white in the sunshine and Ursula realised they were constructed from sugar. There were rope ladders strung between them, connecting one tree to another, so that it seemed like there was an entire village up in the treetops. The tree houses themselves were grand affairs, with turreted roofs, like miniature castles, and some of them even had little drawbridges and sugar gargoyles perched upon the turrets.

Several small lakes glittered beneath the tree houses, and Ursula realised that these must all be different-flavoured sodas because they ranged in colour from cherryade pink to bubblegum blue. A pulley system of tumblers on ropes trailed down from the tree houses towards these in a constant circle, so that refilled drinks were always being sent back up to the trolls, several of whom had already come out on to the bridges to stare curiously down at the explorers. Ursula saw that there were more sugar-tooth tigers here too. Some of the giant cats were stretched out at the edge of the soda lakes, while others lazed on the branches of the trees themselves. Hundreds of lanterns dangled from the boughs, and Ursula thought it must all be incredibly pretty after nightfall.

'Under normal circumstances, we'd love to invite you to a troll feast,' Alf said. 'Of course, you won't have time today, but perhaps once you've successfully completed your mission you might return to the island and allow us to provide a feast in your honour then?'

'We would be delighted,' Jai replied. 'Thank you.'

'Come up to my home for now,' Alf said. 'And I'll supply you with what you need.'

He led the way over to a tree and the explorers followed him, climbing up the ladder attached to its side. Before long, they'd reached the front entrance to his tree house and stepped into a large, circular kitchen. There was an array of treats on the countertop, including cherry tarts and an entire fudge cake. Pretty curtains hung at the round window, and a wooden table and chair set took up a large part of the floor, while another ladder led to the house's upper floors.

When Jai made a strangled sound of delight, Ursula thought at first that he was charmed by the troll's lovely home, but then her eye fell on the tiger sprawled on a nest of blankets on the other side of the table. The blankets seemed to wriggle about a bit and that's when she realised that the tiger had a litter of cubs with her.

When they saw they had guests, several of the cubs gambolled over to the explorers, nudging their hands playfully and rolling over in order to have their bellies rubbed. Jai couldn't have looked more delighted as he crouched down to stroke them, and before long he had several tiger cubs piled on top of each other in his lap, all purring contentedly.

The sugar troll went over to the mother tiger and stroked her head affectionately. 'This is Bianca,' he told them. 'She's one of the finest sugar-tooth tigers I've ever owned. There were twelve cubs originally, but some of them have already gone to their new homes. Anyway, let me fetch those supplies for you.'

He disappeared up the ladder to the upper floor and returned a moment later carrying a picnic basket. It was made from wickerwork and lined with a blue-and-white checked tartan cloth. It was a lovely-looking object but the explorers were all a little crestfallen at the sight of it because of its size. It might perhaps provide one reasonable meal for the four of them if the food inside was tightly packed, but it wasn't going to stretch to any more than that.

'Er ... thank you,' Jai said. 'That's very kind. It is likely to be quite a long expedition though, so I wonder if it might be possible for us to purchase a few more picnic baskets from you?'

Alf grinned. 'Don't worry,' he said. 'One will be plenty.'

Ursula started to wonder whether perhaps sugar

trolls had extremely tiny appetites and maybe he didn't realise how much a human typically ate?

'It's just that we normally need three meals a day,' she said, trying to clarify.

Alf looked instantly shocked by this. '*Three?*' He shook his head. 'Good grief. Well, this basket will be more than enough for you then. It's designed for a family of four sugar trolls, and we have at least ten meals a day. Here, look, I'll show you how it works.'

He flipped the lid open and the explorers leaned forward to see an array of tasty-looking food inside – mostly cakes and desserts – along with flasks of drink. Alf proceeded to take everything out and lay it on the table. To their surprise, the food kept on coming, long after they thought the basket should have been empty. It was as if there was no bottom to it. Finally, the basket was empty except for a few crumbs, so Alf closed the lid. He flipped it open the next moment and, to their amazement, the picnic basket was full again.

'That's amazing!' Max exclaimed. 'A bottomless picnic basket is even better than that magic goose the Polar Bear explorers found!'

'It's not quite bottomless,' Alf replied. 'You can get ten meals a day out of it, but then you'll have to wait until the next day.'

'Ten meals are more than enough,' Jai said. 'Thank you. Is there anything we need to do to keep the basket full?'

'Nope, it runs on troll magic,' Alf said. He closed the lid again and handed the basket to them.

The explorers thanked him and said they should be on their way, although Jai seemed very reluctant to leave the tiger cubs. Finally though, they said goodbye to Alf, descended the tree and began to follow the path out of the troll village. They were slightly delayed when Max realised he'd left his robot duck behind and went back to retrieve it, but he soon caught them up and a short while later they were waving at the *Jolly Rosa* from the beach.

While they waited for the ship to pick them up, they realised that the beach wasn't actually made from sand at all, but biscuit crumbs. They were buttery and delicious and the explorers couldn't resist eating several handfuls before returning to the *Jolly Rosa*.

Once they were all on board, the ship set sail and then Jai, Ursula and Genie set out their picnic on the deck. Max had disappeared below, but he returned a moment later and tapped Jai on the shoulder.

'Here, I got you a present,' he said.

'What pr—' Jai began, but then Max dropped a tiger cub in his lap.

The others all stared in astonishment as the cub snuggled into Jai's cloak and looked up at him with big blue eyes.

'I didn't really forget my duck,' Max said, plonking himself down next to Ursula. 'I just went back to ask Alf if I could buy a cub as he'd said they were looking for new homes. Though it was the same as the food in the end. He wouldn't let me buy one; only insisted I took one for free.' He looked at Jai. 'I know the tiger isn't Biscuit, but anyone can see that you need a new pet cat. And I'm sure you'll love this one in a different way.'

'A sugar-tooth tiger isn't exactly a cat,' Jai replied, although he looked delighted as he scratched the cub's ears.

Max shrugged. 'A tiger seems like a fitting companion for a hero and explorer of your stature,' he said, only half sarcastically. 'Especially one with so many medals.'

'A pet is a great responsibility, whatever type it is,' Jai said, ignoring the dig about his medals. 'You probably shouldn't have got this one without consulting me ... But I'm glad you did. Thank you.'

His arm was wrapped around the cub and he couldn't hide the joy from his face.

'You're welcome,' Max replied. 'She's a girl, by the

way. Alf said her name was Jewel. Apparently sugar-tooth cubs have one sugar mouse a day for breakfast, lunch and dinner. He gave me a big bag of them. Oh, and he said they grow quickly – much faster than regular cats – so don't be surprised if she's taking up all the room soon.'

Ursula was glad that Max had done such a nice thing for Jai, and the explorers enjoyed the rest of their picnic in companionable silence, looking forward to whatever lay ahead, while the Island of Sugar Trolls grew smaller and smaller behind them.

CHAPTER EIGHT

The next two days passed by uneventfully. The *Jolly Rosa* continued to sail further into the Nebula Sea and the explorers settled into the rhythm of life on board a pirate ghost ship. It didn't come naturally to any of them. The pirates kept no set schedules and seemed to spend most of their time feasting, carousing and poring over a vast collection of treasure maps. Even in their ghostly state, they seemed obsessed with discovering more and more treasure. It was a chaotic, noisy existence, especially with all the pirate dogs and the pirate duck running around.

The pirate duck was fond of waddling up and down the corridors, and they learned that her name was Mabel. Rosa hadn't been exaggerating when she'd warned them not to touch her. Mabel was *extremely* bad-tempered and seemed very cross not to have the ship to herself. She'd quack angrily at anyone who so much as walked past her, although she seemed to take something of a shine to Max's robot duck and would often snuggle up against it.

Jai found the mayhem particularly hard, but they all longed for the cleanliness and serenity of the *Blowfish*. They checked the pickled parrot charm each night too. It had lost a few more silver feathers and everyone was anxious about how much longer the charm might protect them. In an effort to distract themselves, they all retreated into their various pastimes. Jai laboured over his memoir about Biscuit with Jewel curled around his neck like a purring scarf. Genie created a new assortment of hats. Max tinkered with a robot terrapin he'd been working on, delighted that he'd finally created something with laser-beam eyes. And Ursula brought out the puppets to practise her magical singing.

The ghost pirates didn't seem at all sure about this, and Rosa was most unhappy to learn that Ursula was half mermaid. Accepting payment from mermaids for taking people aboard was one thing, but none of them had ever expected a mermaid to travel by ship. After all, pirates and mermaids had long been foes and so Ursula always tried to find a quiet corner of the ship in which to study. Her work paid off though because she soon found she could manipulate the dolphin into doing several leaps in a row.

Another day passed and on the morning of the sixth day after joining the crew of the *Jolly Rosa*, the explorers were all in their hammocks sleeping peacefully when there was a great crash. The ropes holding up Jai's hammock had stretched and broke. He tumbled to the ground and the others jerked upright in their own hammocks, trying to work out what was happening.

Jai was lying in a heap on the floor, tangled in the net of his hammock with something huge sprawled on top of him. It took Ursula a moment to realise that the something was Jewel. The little tiger had taken to sleeping curled up in the hammock with Jai and last night was no exception. She'd been an ordinary-sized cub then, but now, all of a sudden, she was a full-size tiger, as big as the ones they'd seen back on the Island of Sugar Trolls. Jewel still acted like a cub though, gambolling playfully around Jai as he propped himself upright.

'Wow!' Max gave a low whistle. 'Alf said they grow fast, but I didn't think he meant as quickly as that! Are you OK?'

He reached down to help Jai struggle to his feet but was almost immediately flattened again when Jewel threw herself at him affectionately.

'Hey!' one of the pirates said from the other side of

the room. 'What's all this? You can't have a tiger in here! Chain it up on deck where it belongs.'

'I'm not chaining her up!' Jai said, aghast. 'She's not dangerous – she's a sugar-tooth, and only a baby.'

'Huh!' the pirate grunted. 'Some baby! We'll see what the captain has to say about this.'

The pirate stomped off to complain to Rosa, but it seemed that the agreement they had with the mermaids meant that any guests were allowed to bring pets with them – with the exception of carnivorous cabbages, which were on the banned list.

'Why would anyone have a carnivorous cabbage as a pet anyway?' Max asked.

Rosa shrugged. 'Don't ask me. It takes all sorts. I knew a man who kept a murderous carrot as a pet once. And there was another who doted on his vengeful radish until the thing finally did him in. Don't even get me started on the Island of Wrathful Grapes. No treasure is worth venturing there again, no matter how many gold coins are meant to be stashed in the mountains.'

And so Jewel was allowed to stay with Jai, which was probably for the best because she seemed absolutely devoted to him already and it would have taken a great deal of persuasion to prise her from his side.

'It was like this with Biscuit too,' Genie said as she put on her jellyfish hat. 'Sometimes I think Jai should have been born a cat whisperer.'

The pirate crew quickly got used to Jewel, especially as she spent most of the time on deck with the explorers. The children were all keen to see what was coming up next. There hadn't been much land sighted since the Island of Sugar Trolls, but later that day they saw strange lights flickering beneath the surface of the sea. And because this was a ghost ship, they were able to dive beneath the surface as easily as if they were on a submarine. The crew hoisted the green sails and the ship immediately began to descend. It was odd watching the water close over their heads, surrounding the ship as if it were inside a bubble.

'Ghost ships might be the perfect form of transport for sea exploration,' Max said. 'Since they can sail, fly and dive. Maybe the Ocean Squid Explorers' Club should look into getting some?'

'I still prefer submarines,' Jai and Ursula both said at the same time.

The ship was fully submerged now and they finally saw what had been creating the glow beneath the waves. They were surrounded by dozens of silver seahorses, but they were unlike any seahorse Ursula had ever seen before. They were silver in colour and they sparkled, casting glittering diamonds of light into the water all around them.

'Oh, these must be galaxy seahorses!' Genie exclaimed. 'We can't be too far away now. Galaxy seahorses often live in the same waters as galaxy fairies.'

They continued to sail underwater and the seahorses stayed with them for a while, peering at the ship curiously as it glided by. When the ghost ship dived deeper, they saw moon coral on the seabed, shining with a soft silver light. In fact, everything in this part of the sea seemed to be silver – the water, the sea creatures, even the bubbles.

'It's like being in space,' Ursula said.

'Look!' Genie leaned over the rails. 'What's that down there?'

They followed her pointing finger and saw that there was a miniature building perched on top of a tower of moon coral nearby.

'It's a stable,' Ursula said, noticing the words painted on the exterior: *Galaxy Seahorse Stable*.

'It must have belonged to the fairies,' Genie said. 'It looks deserted now, though.'

It certainly seemed as if the stable hadn't been used in years. They could see through the windows that it was empty, with just a few miniature saddles hanging from hooks. As the *Jolly Rosa* continued on, they spotted more evidence of fairy life, all of which now lay abandoned. There was a little fairy hotel surrounded by an overgrown sea garden. And a tiny, rusting fairground covered in seaweed and barnacles.

'Perhaps this was where the galaxy fairies used to come when they wanted to get out of the city?' Ursula suggested.

It was sad seeing the fairy places deserted like this, with nothing but eels and stingrays gliding past, but at least they knew they were heading in the right direction. They continued to sail underwater and soon saw that this part of the sea was teeming with life. Everywhere they looked there seemed to be an abundance of jellyfish and turtles and crabs, but they were all slightly different from the types they'd seen before. The turtles had dusty, moon-coloured shells, while the jellyfish glittered as if they were full of space dust and the crabs were a peculiar luminous white.

And there were some creatures there that the explorers didn't recognise – many-tentacled things that were not jellyfish, octopus, kraken or squid, but something else altogether. A few of them had electric-blue tentacles and no eyes that they could make out at all.

'They look more like aliens than sea creatures,' Genie remarked. 'Maybe that's why they call this the Nebula Sea? It sometimes seems closer to being in outer space than being at sea.'

Ursula thought Genie was probably right, and indeed the sea became increasingly space-like the further they travelled. A couple of hours after the fairy buildings, they saw what could only be described as a meteor shower up ahead – shining bright lights that looked just like shooting stars with their glittering tails flashing through the water in perfect arcs. Ursula thought it was incredibly pretty, but Rosa seemed suspicious.

'I never heard of a meteor shower underwater before,' the pirate captain said, looking distrustfully at the display. 'In fact, I don't much care for this sea at all. Perhaps we should return to the surface?'

The explorers all protested at once. Since the ghost ship was able to travel underwater, it seemed a great pity to travel above the waves and miss all these strange and peculiar sights.

'All right, have it your own way,' Rosa sighed. 'I still don't like it, though.'

The rest of the pirate crew seemed similarly on edge and Ursula heard several of them muttering nervously to themselves, but the explorers were more used to unfamiliar territory, as well as travelling underwater, and they enjoyed seeing new and unusual things.

But then Ursula spotted something and pointed. 'What's that down there?'

The others tore their eyes from the meteor shower. Directly below was a sight none of them had ever seen before – a kind of spiral with glowing, ruby-red lights that curved outwards like tentacles. In the middle was a dark circle, inky black. It had the look of a really, really deep well and Ursula found herself shivering as she stared at it.

'It looks like a sort of portal,' Jai said.

'I know what you're going to say, but the answer is no,' Rosa said firmly. 'Categorically no. Don't even think about asking me to sail into that thing so you can explore whatever's on the other side.'

Jai shook his head. 'We've got other things to do right now,' he said. 'And anyway, that looks a bit ... well, a bit too alien even for explorers. If it's a portal then we have no idea what's on the other side and, contrary to what you might think, we're not completely foolhardy. We like to have *some* idea about what we're heading into.'

Ursula agreed with Jai about the portal. There was

definitely something strange about it and she suddenly felt she would be very glad to leave it behind.

'Perhaps we should raise the ship to the surface for a while after all?' Jai went on.

'Now you're talking sense,' Rosa replied. 'Finally.'

She called out to her crew, giving the order to hoist the sails to take them up. The other pirates were eager enough to ascend and worked quickly, but once the sails were in place nothing happened. The ship didn't rise. In fact, it seemed to be edging closer to the portal below.

Rosa frowned. 'That's not right,' she said. 'Parrots! Take your positions!'

The ghost parrots all flew to the rigging and began yelling out their curses as they'd done before when they'd been fleeing the giant shark. Only this time it didn't work. The parrots and the sails had no effect whatsoever. The ship wasn't going up – it was continuing to sink.

'Whatever that thing is down there, it's acting like a magnet,' Rosa said, glaring at the portal. 'And it's drawing us in.'

CHAPTER NINE

The explorers watched in a kind of horrified fascination as the ghost ship sank lower and lower towards the glowing red portal beneath. As they got nearer, Ursula saw that the centre wasn't pitch-black after all. There were bright pinpricks of light in it, shining as brightly as stars, as well as a large, cratered object that looked very much like ... Well, it couldn't possibly be, but it looked like a—

'Great Scott!' Max exclaimed. 'Is that a *moon*?'

The explorers all stared at one another in dismay.

'Do you think that portal could lead to *outer space*?' Max asked. He looked half excited and half horrified.

Ursula thought of the strange marine life they had seen so far, the signs of moon dust and stars, and the very name of the Nebula Sea itself, and she felt a sudden rush of fear.

'What if there's no air in space?' she said, panicked. 'I read an article in one of the scientific journals back at the club once that said space exploration would be impossible because there's no air to breathe up there!'

'Don't worry about that,' Rosa said beside them. 'The ghost ship travels within its own bubble, remember? The same magic that allows you to breathe underwater works just as well anywhere else. But I don't like it. I don't like it at all. Space is too big, too strange. Pirates aren't supposed to be messing around in space. We belong in the ocean.'

Yet it appeared that there was absolutely nothing they could do to stop it. The ship was descending towards the portal more quickly now, rapidly picking up speed as it got closer. In another few minutes they were in the middle of the spiral, surrounded by glowing red lights and what looked suspiciously like space dust.

'We're going through to the other side,' Rosa warned. 'Brace yourselves!'

The pirates all hung on to their hats and parrots, while the explorers gripped the railings with white knuckles. There was a jerking, shuddering motion as the ship descended through the portal, glowing bright red for a moment before coming out the other side. Everyone stared in amazement. Max's guess had been correct – they were, quite unmistakably, in outer space, surrounded by the soft, white lights of thousands of stars. Not only that, but there was a large, cratered moon nearby, as well as great clouds of glowing space dust.

Rosa had been right when she'd said that the ship's magic would keep air on deck for them to breathe, but they all felt the icy coldness of space pressing in on them like a physical weight. The ghost ship had only been out there for seconds and already it glittered in a thick coating of frost. It was quite a shock after the balmy warmth they'd enjoyed before, and Ursula wished she had her explorer's cloak with her. There could be no thought of going to fetch it, however. Not when there was so much excitement on deck.

Explorers and pirates alike all fumbled for their telescopes to gaze in wonder at the galactic view, so unlike anything any of them had ever come across before. In some ways Ursula thought that space *was* rather like the ocean. It had that same vastness about it – a sense that it was a ginormous world of possibilities and everything floating through it must be small and insignificant. But they hadn't intended to venture into space and Rosa was keen to get them back to the ocean as soon as possible.

'It's too cold out here for a ship,' she said. 'Even a ghost ship.'

And indeed, Ursula could hear the wood groaning in a disconcerting sort of way, as if it might splinter apart altogether under the strain. Rosa gave the order for the ghost parrots to return to the rigging once again to add extra power, but it was as if the magnetic field around the portal was now repelling them and they were unable to pass back through. Finally, they were forced to give up and allow the ship to drift.

'Well, this is just great,' Max groaned. 'What hope have we got of stopping Scarlett if we're not even on the same planet any more?'

'We've got bigger problems than that,' Jai said, glancing over to where Rosa was talking to some of the other pirates. 'If we can't find a way back, then there's nothing to stop this ship just vanishing into the pearl again, leaving us drifting in space. We need to make a plan and quickly.'

'What about moon dust?' Ursula said, glancing at the nearby moon, glowing pale and silver before them.

'What about it?' Jai asked.

'There's a theory that adding it to fuel makes submarines faster and more powerful. I learned about it from Old Joe and the other engineers. Sometimes, when a meteor or a comet crashes into the world, any moon or space dust is salvaged to add to fuel.

Well, what if we can make it work on board the ship somehow? We could . . . I don't know . . . paint the sails with it, or dip the parrots' feathers in it or something?'

'I remember reading about that too,' Max said. 'In one of my robotics magazines.'

'It's as good an idea as any,' Genie said.

They all glanced towards the moon and noticed that Bess had appeared floating alongside the ship. Even though she had no physical substance, the air was so cold that her tentacles sparkled with frost just like the ghost ship did. She didn't seem at all bothered to be in outer space. In fact, she seemed delighted, waving her tentacles about in excitement. Ursula recalled how Genie had once told her that kraken were in love with the stars and would often rise to the surface of the sea to gaze at the night sky in wonder.

'Come on,' Jai said. 'Let's go and persuade Rosa to take us to the moon.'

They went over to the pirate captain who stopped talking very suddenly when they approached, which didn't fill any of them with confidence about what she might have been saying.

'We have an idea,' Jai told her, 'for how to get back to the Nebula Sea.'

'I'm all ears,' Rosa said.

It took a little while to convince her to sail towards the moon. The pirates all seemed to have a superstitious dread of being in outer space, and Ursula guessed their first choice would be to retreat back into the ghostly world of the pearl as soon as possible. But perhaps Rosa had grown to like the explorers just a little bit – or perhaps she was still thinking of the fee she would get from the mermaids for carrying them safely to their destination. Either way, she agreed to take them to the moon and see if its dust would help them re-enter the portal.

It felt odd sailing deeper into space, and Ursula found that she kept checking over her shoulder to make sure that the portal was still there. What if it closed behind them? Was that a thing that could happen? As far as she knew, no other explorer had ever come across a space portal before, so they really had no idea how it worked, but the idea of being stranded in space was terrifying them all.

The moon seemed to get larger and larger as they approached it, and they saw all the many pockmark craters where it had been hit by meteors and asteroids. Like everything else out here, the chalky surface glittered in an icy coating of frost, but they could see there was plenty of moon dust piled up too. Rosa's crew navigated the ship so it sailed right above the moon, before slowly lowering it to land. Now they only had to work out how exactly to collect the dust.

'How far does the protective bubble around the ship go?' Jai asked Rosa.

'Just around the ship itself,' she replied. 'As soon as you step off the deck, you'll be exposed.'

Jai frowned. 'That's what I thought. I know it's a lot to ask, but might one of your crew be able to—'

Rosa was already shaking her head. 'We're a ghost ship crew. None of us can leave,' she said. 'And that includes the parrots, the dogs and the pirate duck.'

'Pirate duck! That gives me an idea!' Max turned back to the other explorers. 'Ducky could do it.' He pointed at the robot duck currently waddling around the deck, quacking at intervals. 'He doesn't need to breathe air and he can fly there and back on his robot wings.'

The others all thought this seemed like a good idea, so Max called Ducky over and then lifted up a little flap on his back to program the new instructions. Genie went to fetch a glass jar from the galley and handed it to the duck, who clamped it firmly in its beak. Then they all watched with bated breath as it spread its wings and flapped up and over the railings. The next moment it arrived on the surface of the moon and was immediately covered in a coating of frost so thick that it looked as if the duck had been painted white.

It quickly began to shovel up moon dust with its beak and deposit it inside the jar. Soon it was completely full and the explorers began to feel hopeful that their plan would work. The robot duck picked up the jar and spread its wings to return to the *Jolly Rosa* – but just as it lifted off, something popped up from beneath the chalky surface. Ursula half expected to see a little green Martian, or perhaps a space worm of some kind, but in fact this creature looked more like a mole. You could tell it was a space mole though because it had green fur rather than brown, and its large claws and piggy nose were silver.

It gave a funny little squawk of indignation when it saw the robot duck, and this caused several more space moles to immediately pop up from beneath the moon's surface. Then they all charged at the robot duck at once, battering it with their claws and causing it to drop the jar, which smashed apart on the moon's surface. The explorers groaned as dozens more moles popped up to join in the fray, all making a horrible, angry chittering sound. Ducky honked in surprise and annoyance, but fortunately the robot was much stronger than the moles and spread its wings again to return to the ghost ship while Max shouted encouragement from the railings. Ducky flew away from the moon but one particularly determined mole managed to cling on by wrapping its arms around the duck's neck.

Ducky landed on the ship's deck, still honking wildly and jerking around in an effort to dislodge the mole, which only tightened its grip. It was quite hard to intervene because they were both thrashing around so much, bashing into various things on deck and eliciting cries of dismay from the pirates, but finally Genie managed to grab hold of the mole and dropped it over the rails of the ship. That's when they noticed that several more moles were determinedly climbing up the sides of the galleon, baring their teeth in a vicious-looking way, so Jai called out to Rosa for the ship to set sail again. Several moles still clung to the ship as it began to ascend, and they all seemed absolutely furious for some reason, hissing and spitting and lashing out with their claws whenever they got near anyone.

'What is their problem?' Max gasped, using a spare oar to prod one of the moles back over the side. 'Can't they see we're leaving?'

'I guess they're angry that we tried to take some

of their moon dust,' Genie replied. 'Maybe it's really useful or valuable to them or something? We might have just done the equivalent of trying to break into a bank's safe and steal all the money from it.'

'The rules could be different in space,' Jai agreed, using his prosthetic hand to throw off another mole. 'I hope we haven't offended them in some way.'

'Offended *them*?' Max gasped, as he warded off a mole attack. 'I'm feeling pretty offended myself right now.'

'Well, the sooner we get back to our own planet, the better,' Jai said.

'Right,' Ursula agreed. 'We're ocean explorers, not space explorers. Perhaps we should—'

But before she could continue, Max let out an appalled cry. 'The portal!' He pointed at it. 'It's shrinking!'

They all spun round to look, and saw that Max was right. The portal was definitely smaller than it had been when they arrived.

'Do you think we'll fit through it now?' Ursula asked, panicked.

'Even if there was room, we still don't have enough power to do it,' Jai said, looking around in desperation for something that might help them.

'Man, this is too bad for you guys,' Rosa said, leaning against the rails with her arms folded as she gazed at the portal. 'If that portal shuts, we're going to have to travel back into the ghost pearl and leave you here with the space moles, I'm afraid. It's not a nice fate, to be sure, but at least you'll probably freeze to death before the moles can eat you.'

Several of the moles were still on board the ship, still making that horrible chittering noise. And the din from the ones left behind on the moon was even worse. It was hard to hear themselves think over all the screeching, and Ursula wished they would quieten down for a moment as her mind cast about desperately for a solution. The portal was shrinking before their eyes now, and although Rosa had steered a course towards it, it seemed likely that they still wouldn't be in time to pass through. Ursula really, *really* didn't want to end up being eaten by space moles but she couldn't think of any plan that might get them out of this predicament.

'If anyone has any last-minute ideas or heroics, declare them now!' Max gasped, looking pointedly at Jai.

But for once Jai appeared to be all out of ideas and seemed more concerned about his sugar-tooth tiger than anything else.

'Could you at least take Jewel with you?' he begged, looking imploringly at Rosa.

But the pirate captain shook her head. 'No living creature can pass into the ghost pearl. I'm sorry.'

'Everyone be quiet!' Genie suddenly called out, startling everyone. 'Bess is trying to tell me something.'

Ursula realised that the shadow kraken had appeared alongside the ship, waving its enormous tentacles eagerly. Genie's eyes widened, and then she turned to the others so quickly that the tentacles of her jellyfish hat spun out around her.

'She says there's a space octopus behind the moon. It was trying to have a snooze, but the noisy moles have woken it up. It's about to come out and Bess thinks it's heading for the portal. She says she can speak to the space octopus – it's a sort of cousin to the kraken. She thinks it's going to travel back through the portal to take a bath in the sea and might be able to tow us behind it.'

CHAPTER TEN

Rosa looked dubious. 'I never heard of a space octopus,' she said. 'And I don't see any—'

But at that exact moment, the octopus emerged from behind the moon. They saw the glow of it first – an icy, sparkly blue – and then the creature itself drifted slowly into sight. It was about the same size as a kraken, and Ursula thought it was incredibly beautiful – all sparkling blue tentacles and minty-green eyes. There was something undeniably alien about it too. For a start, it had ten tentacles rather than eight, and three eyes rather than two. As it got closer, she also noticed that it had lightning-coloured spirals all over its body.

'It won't make any difference,' Max groaned. 'The octopus isn't fast enough. It's moving much slower than the ship and—'

But that was as far as he got before the spirals on the octopus flashed bright white, it pushed out with its tentacles and shot past them so quickly it was almost as if it had transported itself from one place to another in the blink of an eye. Suddenly, everyone was running around the deck in panic, racing straight for the coils of rope.

A couple of pirates reached them first, hastily snatched up the rope and then hurled it towards the octopus. The first two attempts didn't quite make it, but finally the rope reached the octopus, who immediately wound its tentacles around it in tight knots. In the meantime, the portal was looking dangerously narrow and Ursula worried it might already be too late for them to fit through the gap.

'We need to go *now*!' she cried.

The space octopus flashed that lightning colour once again, and then the ship was zooming so fast behind it that explorers and pirate crew alike were all thrown flat to the deck. The *Jolly Rosa* was hurtled through space at an incredible speed, the ghostly wood groaning in protest. The ruby-red lights of the portal raced towards them, and everything was such a blur of stars, and space, and tentacles that Ursula felt dizzy and would have fallen over if she wasn't already sprawled on the deck.

The octopus zipped through the portal and the *Jolly Rosa* squeezed in behind her, only just about managing to pass through the shrinking space. In an explosion of bubbles, they found themselves back in the Nebula Sea. Moments later, the portal had collapsed entirely, vanishing with a *pop!* that sent ripples through the water.

'Well, I never.' Rosa picked herself up from the deck and dusted herself down with her hat. 'This is exactly why most ships' captains won't allow explorers to travel on board. Too much calamity, and portals, and space octopuses for my liking.'

'Don't forget about the space moles,' Max said, wincing as one of the creatures took a swipe at him with its silver claws. It seemed that a couple had managed to come through the portal with them. Max lunged at his attacker, but it went scuttling off across the deck.

'We don't normally have anything to do with portals and space moles either,' Jai said. 'But I'm glad about the space octopus. Genie, can you ask Bess to say thank you for us?'

Genie did so, and the octopus waved its tentacles in a friendly sort of way before drifting down towards the golden sand of the seabed, presumably in search of a more peaceful spot to continue its nap.

'Will it be able to get back to its home now that the portal has closed?' Ursula asked.

'Perhaps the portals open and close all the time?' Max suggested. 'Another one could be about to appear right this second for all we know. I think we should send the ship back up to the surface before we get sucked into space again.'

'No arguments from me,' Rosa said, already giving the order. 'We won't be descending into this sea in a hurry, I can tell you that, no matter how many lights you see sparkling beneath the surface.'

This seemed like a pretty good idea to the explorers, especially as it took them ages to round up the two space moles, incurring several scratches in the process. By the time they'd secured them both in a large treasure chest, the *Jolly Rosa* was floating on the sparkling surface of the ocean once more, and it was a big relief to everyone to have the bright sun shining down on them and to breathe warm coconut-scented air again. As the ship resumed its course, Max was all for throwing the two moles overboard, but the others protested.

'We can't just cast them into the sea,' Genie said. 'They might not be able to swim.'

'Then they should have thought about that before they stowed aboard and attacked us,' Max replied. 'Look at the dents they've taken out of poor Ducky!'

The robot duck did look a little worse for wear and was still honking indignantly in Max's arms.

'They're only animals,' Jai replied. 'There's a lot they don't understand, and we did invade their home. If anything we have a responsibility towards them now.'

'If you consult the guide written by your precious Captain Filibuster,' Max replied, a little waspishly, 'I think you'll find that your only obligation is to transport them straight back to the club where they can be duly stuffed and put on display.'

'Yes, well.' Jai adjusted his collar. 'Captain Filibuster and I don't agree on *absolutely* everything. Even if I do think he's a great man. And an excellent explorer. But . . . there was a lot he got wrong. Those books were written a long time ago now, after all. And there are certain things we ought to be doing differently.'

'Well said.' Max gave a thumbs-up.

'Like letting girls into the club,' Genie added.

Ursula had seen Jai lobbying for this back at the club, but the president had been distinctly unimpressed. Still, if anyone could change the way things were done, she thought it was probably Jai.

'Who knows?' she said. 'Perhaps one day there'll be a *Captain Singh's Guide to Expeditions and Exploration* to replace Captain Filibuster.'

Jai blushed. 'I don't know about that . . .' he began.

'I think it's a capital idea,' Max said. 'Of course, you'd have to finish writing that book about your cat first.'

'Actually, I've already finished it,' Jai replied. 'Last night.' He reached down to stroke Jewel, who was leaning her huge body against him affectionately. 'You were right,' he said. 'It was time to write the last chapter. I hope one day the book will sit on the shelves of the Ocean Squid Explorers' Club library beside accounts of the other seafaring animals.'

'I'm sure it will,' Max said. 'But we've got to stop the Collector first.'

The explorers decided to keep the moles in the storage hold with the pirates' loot. They seemed happy enough in there, and Genie volunteered to take some food down to them from the sugar troll's hamper each day. They could only hope that troll food would be amenable to them and that they didn't only eat space rock and moon worms.

Disappearing into the portal had been a hairy moment, but after they'd had time to catch their breaths, the explorers all felt rather proud of the fact that they'd ventured into space, and Jai thought it would be a spectacular addition to their flag report when they finally returned to the club.

The next two days passed by uneventfully. Ursula had perfected manipulating the dolphin puppet and moved on to the turtle. When she wasn't practising her singing, she joined the others on deck to take in the passing view. They spotted several islands in the distance but – much as the explorers longed to stop and visit them – they knew they couldn't afford to lose any more time returning the fairy city; the pickled parrot charm was already down to its last couple of silver feathers. It had been more than a week since Ursula was desperate to feel the cold waves against her mermaid's tail, but there wasn't time for this either. Besides which, she was rather nervous about going into the Nebula Sea in case she was sucked into another portal.

The explorers contented themselves with viewing the islands through their telescopes as they sailed past, which only piqued their interest even further. There was one that had coconuts that were bright blue in colour, another had rainbow-coloured monkeys, while yet another had extraordinarily tall buildings that looked as if they must have been ten storeys high at least, with winged horses prancing on the rooftops.

On the following day, they spotted something they were unable to ignore. There was a flotilla of rafts up ahead, manned by strange little creatures that they guessed must be sea goblins. They had webbed fingers and toes, large fish-like eyes and pale green skin. The explorers all groaned at the sight of them. Ursula had never come across a sea goblin herself, but their reputation was well known in the Ocean Squid Explorers' Club, and Jai and Max had both encountered them on previous expeditions.

'Troublesome little things,' Max said, frowning through his telescope.

'We'll just go round them,' Rosa suggested with a shrug. 'We're in a first-class galleon and they're in rafts. It's not as if they can catch us up.'

But Jai shook his head. 'We can't,' he said with a sigh. 'Sea goblins have protected status because there are so few of them left in the world. If one of them is flying a rescue flag, then any passing explorer from the Ocean Squid Explorers' Club has to stop to assist.'

'And they're *always* flying rescue flags,' Max said, lowering his telescope.

This was the problem with sea goblins. Unusually for aquatic creatures, they could not swim at all. In fact, the salt in the ocean irritated their skin so much that they broke into hives if they were submerged in it for any great length of time. Not only that, but sea goblins appeared to have no sense of self-preservation.

Scientists had often speculated as to why they did not simply go and live elsewhere. A nice tropical island, perhaps, or the mountains, or the countryside. But it seemed that sea goblins were drawn back to the water irresistibly, and it didn't matter how often you tried to settle them down somewhere else, after five minutes, they'd be making little rafts once again and setting off for sea with no provisions whatsoever. So it was not uncommon to find them stranded and in need of assistance like this.

'We'll have to stop and help them out,' Jai said morosely. 'Hopefully it won't take up too much time.'

'I have to say, I'm surprised that any of your clubs give such a thing as protected status to anything,' Rosa remarked. 'Your lot has always seemed more selfish than pirates to me. Barging into places to steal the "discoveries" you find there, stuffing animals for the sake of it and so on.'

Jai winced. 'The clubs haven't always conducted themselves well in the past,' he admitted. 'But they've all tried to help preserve the world in small ways too. The Polar Bear Explorers' Club, for example, has done much to safeguard the wild unicorn. And, well, not to brag, but I was awarded a medal by my own club for saving the yodelling turtle from extinction. The Desert

Jackal Explorers' Club always rescues any marble beetles that they—'

'Why would anyone save a yodelling turtle on purpose?' Rosa groaned.

'That's exactly what I said,' Max replied.

'Have you ever met one?' Rosa went on. 'They're a menace. If you think singing opera crabs are annoying, you haven't seen anything until you've seen a yodelling turtle. One of them made several members of my crew sick once. It was a nightmare.'

But they didn't have time to debate whether Jai should or should not have saved the yodelling turtles because at that moment the *Jolly Rosa* drew up alongside the flotilla of goblin rafts.

'Ahoy there!' Jai called. 'How can we help?'

A host of frightened goblin faces peered back up at them. There were ten rafts and at least thirty goblins.

'Please don't make us walk the plank!' one of them squeaked.

Jai sighed. 'We're not going to make you walk the plank. We're explorers. Do you need food? Provisions? A lift to the nearest island?'

'The mermaids will have to pay extra for goblin passengers,' Rosa warned, while the goblins below all cheered and applauded.

'Oh, yes!' they cried. 'We need all of those things!'

The explorers threw down ropes for the goblins to climb and helped them up on to the deck one by one.

'We'll drop you off at the nearest island,' said Jai.

Rosa shook her head in disbelief and strode off across the deck to see to the sails. Meanwhile, the explorers soon found that trying to care for thirty sea goblins was a full-time job. One or other of them was always getting tangled up in the rigging, or balancing precariously on the railings, or unwittingly antagonising the pirate duck, or trying to get into the hold with the space moles.

They'd been on the ship for less than an hour when Ursula saw several goblins lined up on the ship's rails, all taking up a diving pose as they prepared to leap into the water. Since they couldn't swim, they'd sink like stones.

'Don't!' she yelled. Or at least she meant to yell. Instead, she sang the word, and some of her mermaid magic must have been bound up in it because all the goblins threw themselves back down on to the deck at the same time.

'Oh, I'm sorry,' Ursula said, hurrying over to them. 'I didn't mean to use my magic on you. It's just that you mustn't dive overboard. The ship is going full speed ahead so you'd get left behind and, besides, none of you can swim and the saltwater irritates your skin, remember?'

The goblins nodded solemnly and promised they wouldn't think of jumping overboard. Barely five minutes later though, several of them were perched on the railings preparing to dive in again and Ursula had to sing another warning across the deck to stop them in time.

To make matters worse, the sea goblins couldn't eat the pirate food any more than the humans could, so the explorers had to share the contents of the sugar troll's hamper with them. Because there were so many goblins, there was hardly anything left for the explorers and they were all starving after two days.

They tried to take it in turns babysitting them, but the reality was that Ursula got hardly any sleep. She was the only one who could stop several goblins at once from whatever dangerous thing they were trying to do, and if it hadn't been for her, they probably would have lost half of them by then.

'At least it's giving you some real-life practice at magical singing,' Genie pointed out. 'And shows that all your work with the puppets has been paying off.'

Ursula supposed this was true. There was hardly any black left in her hair now, and she didn't even need to feel guilty about using her powers on the goblins when she was actually saving their lives over and over again. Still, she was relieved when land finally came into sight on the third day. They arrived late in the afternoon, disembarking to find a very pleasant island with golden sandy beaches and crystal-blue waters. Not only that, but there were extraordinarily beautiful birds too, singing a lovely song from the treetops.

'Isn't this nice?' Jai said, as they ushered the goblins ashore. 'There's lots of fruit and vegetables growing right here on the shoreline, look, and fresh water in that lake over there. There's even shade for the sand so your feet won't get burnt.'

'The singing birds might get a bit annoying after a while,' one of the goblins said, squinting up at the trees.

'Are you related to the crying shrimp, by any chance?' Max asked.

The goblins frowned. 'What are they?'

Ursula wondered whether Max might be on to something. The crying shrimp were peculiar little creatures who seemed determined to be unhappy, no matter what the circumstances. It was simply their natural state.

'Never mind that now,' Jai said hastily, frowning at Max. 'I'm sure you'll get used to the birds.'

'Thank you,' one of the goblins said. 'It was very kind of you to bring us here.'

The explorers wished them well and then returned to the *Jolly Rosa*, relieved to finally be free of the burden of the goblins, to say nothing of the fact that they'd be able to eat a full meal again that night.

They set sail and had gone some distance from the island when Max lowered his telescope, shook his head and said, 'It's a bit difficult to tell from this distance, but I'm almost certain those little twits are building new rafts on the beach. I thought they were tree houses at first, but they're definitely crafting masts.'

Jai grimaced. 'Well, we can't stick with them forever,' he said.

'And at least they're making masts this time,' Genie said. 'So perhaps their new rafts might have sails.'

The explorers all said a silent prayer for the sea goblins before taking out the sugar troll's hamper and sitting down to a much-anticipated dinner.

CHAPTER ELEVEN

Two days after leaving the sea goblins behind, the *Jolly Rosa* reached the spot where, according to the *Phantom Atlas*, Stardust City had been. It was a large, open expanse of sea, with no land in sight. The explorers were pleased about this because at least they knew there'd be room for the island when they released it from the snow globe.

It was a sunny morning and they had all gathered on the ship's deck. Despite the warmth, they were wearing their explorers' cloaks so they could be at their smartest when they greeted the fairies. Genie had also made herself some special headgear in honour of the occasion – a silver top hat with a selection of model rockets glued on top. Genie had asked Bess to stay out of sight so as not to frighten the fairies. And after much persuasion, the explorers had managed to convince Rosa to temporarily swap the pirate's Jolly Roger flag for the Ocean Squid Explorers' Club one they'd brought from the *Blowfish*. The last thing they wanted was to frighten the galaxy fairies with the sight of a pirate galleon the moment they were released from captivity, especially as most of the ghost pirate crew were present on deck too. None of them had ever seen a fairy city before and they were all very curious about it.

'I wouldn't have thought fairies would go in for cities much,' Rosa remarked, peering over Jai's shoulder at the snow globe. 'I thought country gardens were more their thing?'

'There are all kinds of fairies,' Ursula told her. 'Some live in country gardens, but others live under the sea, or in the jungle, or the desert. According to the Sky Phoenix Explorers' Club, there are even fire fairies that live inside volcanoes and ride miniature fire dragons and wear dresses made from molten lava. We think fairy cities are a bit different from human ones, though.'

Places had to be shrunk down a huge amount to fit inside a snow globe, so it was difficult to see them in any detail, but the fairy city was even trickier because it almost always seemed to be shrouded in a cloud of glittering fog. Every now and then the fog would part to reveal the edge of a building, or the corner of a garden, or the wing of a parked rocket, but most of the time it was impossible to see much inside the globe at all. The only reason they even knew that it was Stardust City was because of the plaque attached to the base.

'Well, here we are,' Jai said. 'Time to finally set them free.'

Ursula wished that the moment felt more exciting, but she couldn't help remembering the last time they'd released a stolen place and the disastrous consequences that had followed. They could only hope that this time would be different. Still, the explorers all felt a little niggle of worry as they assembled at the railings and held their breath while Jai carefully unscrewed the base of the globe.

As he did so, there was a bright white flash of light and then the snow globe was empty. Suddenly an island was sprawled in the ocean before them. At first, it was covered by the same glittering fog they'd seen inside the snow globe, but this quickly dispersed in the sea breeze and the fairy city towered above them in all its glory.

Ursula was amazed. Because this was a city, she'd expected something similar to Pacifica, but there were no futuristic glass buildings or metal towers here. Instead, there was a single gigantic tree that rose straight up out of the sea, and the fairy city seemed to sprawl along its various branches. It was like no tree

Ursula had ever seen before, though. For a start, it was much, much bigger, reaching so high into the sky that it was more like a mountain.

It didn't have the usual brown trunk and green leaves either. Instead, its trunk was sparkling silver and the leaves twinkled a bright, beautiful white. There was an abundance of rockets of all shapes and sizes, colours and designs. Some were zipping about in the air above their heads, flown by fairy pilots, while others were lined up on launch pads or perched upon branches.

Ursula realised it was the rockets that had been responsible for the glittering fog they'd seen inside the snow globe. The scent of rocket fuel filled the air, mixed with something icy cold and otherworldly that Ursula had never smelled before, but it made her think of faraway realms and distant galaxies, and she wondered if it could be stardust. Certainly, everything on the tree seemed to sparkle. The explorers didn't have the best view from the water because life on the tree started part way up the trunk, so Jai asked Rosa if she could fly the ghost ship up to give them a better vantage point.

'Slowly is fine,' he said quickly. 'We'd rather the parrots weren't shouting curses the whole way.'

The sails were duly changed and the *Jolly Rosa* ascended gracefully until it came to the first layer of branches. They saw little fairy homes lined up along these, mostly thatched cottages, some of which had their own gardens. And, at last, they caught a proper glimpse of the fairies themselves. Like most of their kind, they were small, dainty and very pretty, with a range of different skin and eye colours, but the thing they all had in common was their magnificent, glittering silver wings, which sparkled in the sun and threw out flashing diamond light as the fairies flittered to and fro in a flurry of excitement.

As soon as the fairies caught sight of the ghost ship, a group of them flew over to greet the explorers. Ursula saw that their wings weren't the only thing that sparkled – their hair did as well. And their clothes were stitched with stars and planets and glowing suns. When they drew closer, the fairies looked a little nervous at the sight of so many pirates gathered on deck, so Jai hurried to reassure them.

'Hello,' he said. 'We're from the Ocean Squid Explorers' Club. Your city was stolen away by the Phantom Atlas Society, but we've set you free. At least . . . that's what we hope we've done. You didn't ask to be put into a snow globe, did you?'

'Indeed, no,' one of the fairies said. Their fluttering wings showered the deck of the *Jolly Rosa* in silver sparkles. 'Thank you, young explorer.'

The fairy who'd spoken flew forward. Her silver hair was tied back in a ponytail and she wore a white dress with golden comets stitched all over it. 'I'm Esmerelda. We've waited many years for this day. It feels so good to have the sea air on our wings once again. You must come to the Space Fairy Explorers' Club. Our president will be most keen to meet you. It's near the top of the tree. Follow me and I'll show you the way.'

So there *was* a Space Fairy Explorers' Club! The explorers felt a rush of excitement. For a long time the world had thought that there were only four explorers' clubs in existence, but Stella and her friends had recently discovered a Sky Phoenix Explorers' Club, and it seemed that now the Ocean Squid team had learned about a new club too. The pirate fairy, Zara, had told them that the Space Fairy Club was supposed to be the oldest one in the world, and they were all eager to see it for themselves.

They followed their fairy guide higher and higher up the extraordinary silver tree. As they went, they saw a little more of the fairy city. One branch contained a row of shops selling a range of fairy items, from miniature space boots and rocket fuel to loaves of fairy bread and dainty iced cakes. The branch above held a library and an ice rink, while another contained a fleet of observatories with miniature telescopes all trained towards the sky. They rose up past schools, cafes, laboratories, rocket docking bays and gardens, before they reached the top of the tree and saw the explorers' club.

Ursula knew at once it was the clubhouse because it was the grandest building they'd seen so far, shaped like a sleek silver space rocket perched on a launch pad fixed to the very top branch, as if it was about to blast off into space. The words *Space Fairy Explorers' Club* glittered along the side and, when they got closer, Ursula saw there were also engravings of planets, aliens, moons and suns. A silver flag fluttered from the very top of the rocket, with the club's crest depicting none other than a space mole. The explorers could tell from the rows of circular windows that the building was several storeys high and must have seemed like a gigantic structure to a fairy, but to the explorers it was still only about the size of an adult human, and there was no way any of them would be able to fit inside.

They were therefore a little surprised when Esmerelda said, 'How many of you are coming in?'

'Er ... well, all four of us would love to,' Jai said, looking at the rocket wistfully. 'But we're too big.'

The fairy grinned. 'Not for long,' she said. 'Wait here a moment.'

She disappeared into the building and returned a moment later with a bundle of silver cloth draped over one arm and four fairy wands in her other hand. The wands were all silver too and each was topped with a single twinkling star.

'These are visitor passes,' Esmerelda told them. 'They'll enable you to come inside our clubhouse.'

She held them out and the explorers took them gently. They were so tiny and delicate in their hands that they had to hold them between finger and thumb.

'Just say your name and you'll activate the wand,' Esmerelda told them.

Jai went first and immediately vanished. At least, that's what the explorers thought had happened to begin with. But then they heard his voice – sounding small and very far away – exclaim, 'Great Scott!' and they looked down to see that Jai had actually shrunk to fairy size. He now stood on the deck staring up at them from a height of only a few centimetres, a shocked expression on his face. Jewel padded over to peer down at him in concern.

'Extraordinary!' Max exclaimed. 'You know, I think I prefer him this way. He can't bully us into scrubbing the deck if he's only a few centimetres tall.'

'Don't be so sure.' Genie hastily scooped up her brother and set him on the railings beside Esmerelda. 'It doesn't seem safe you being on the floor,' she said. 'Someone might step on you by accident.'

Many of the pirates were still lingering on deck, watching the proceedings curiously, and Ursula was suddenly painfully aware of their large boots and clumsy feet.

'These will help with that,' Esmerelda said, peeling off a layer of cloth and holding it out to Jai.

Ursula realised it wasn't just any old cloth, but a silky pair of silver wings that sparkled as much as the fairy's real ones did.

'They have loops for you to slip your arms through,' the fairy explained. 'As soon as you put them on, you'll be able to fly. We found it was safer for visitors that way and, besides, you'll need them to be able to move around inside the club. We don't bother with stairs and elevators. Not much point when we can all fly.'

Jai took the wings and slipped his arms through the loops as the fairy had instructed. Immediately, the cloth ceased to hang limply and spread out from Jai's shoulders as if they were real wings.

'They'll respond to your thoughts just like real wings would,' Esmerelda said. 'It might take a little while to get used to though, so be careful.'

Jai spread his wings and fluttered them experimentally. There was a definite wobbliness to his movements, but his feet left the rails and he rose up into the air a few centimetres, beaming in delight. The others were very keen to take their wands and wings and follow his example.

Ursula went last and the moment her hand closed around the wand, she shrank down to fairy size just as Jai and the others had done. It happened so quickly that her head spun for a moment, especially when she looked up at the nearby pirates staring down at her, who now all seemed like giants. Jewel seemed gigantic as well, and Ursula felt very exposed on the open deck where anyone might step on her, or some passing bird might mistake her for a mouse and dive in to snap her up in its beak. It was a relief when Esmerelda swooped down to hand over the wings. They felt delicate and slippery as silk in Ursula's hands, but she quickly put her arms through the loops and the limp material came to life on her shoulders. Ursula saw the wings appear on her shadow and then looked around to see the real thing glittering behind her.

Still keeping a tight grip on the wand, she concentrated on flying up to join the others. It was strange seeing them all as fairy versions of themselves, but they were grinning at her in excitement. No one could wait to enter the Space Fairy Explorers' Club.

The top of the tree was extremely high now they were fairy size, so they all felt a flicker of trepidation as they spread their new wings and launched themselves into the air, but they made it safely across the gap to land on the tree's branch. The rocket building in front of them looked as big as a spaceship, and the explorers felt anticipation prickle along their skin as they walked towards it.

CHAPTER TWELVE

Esmerelda led them along the branch towards the rocket. It was perched a little way off the ground on three tapered legs, so they had to fly up to reach the front doors, which glided open automatically at their approach. The explorers fluttered inside and into a grand lobby area. Everything gleamed in grey and silver, and there were various exhibits on display in glass cases around the edge of the room. Ursula saw hunks of space rock, peculiar moon-coloured flowers and what looked like alien claws behind the glass.

Paintings hung on the walls and it looked as if these depicted various discoveries the explorer fairies had made. Ursula saw strange landscapes with purple grass, flying trees and orange rivers, many-tentacled space monsters, gleaming galactic cities and extraordinary space rainbows. It was a lot to take in and she wished she had more time to look at everything properly.

Some sort of giant mobile consisting of a solar

system with icy-blue planets and ruby-red moons hung from the ceiling suspended on wires. There were lots of fairies flitting about too, all wearing the outfit that must be this explorers' club's uniform – a silver spacesuit with the club's insignia stamped on the chest, a pair of chunky lace-up boots and a bracelet that glowed and flashed at intervals. There was a lot of activity and excitement inside the club, but the fairies all paused what they were doing to look at the explorers curiously. Several fluttered down to meet them and the four children found themselves bombarded with questions as to who they were and whether they had any idea how Stardust City had finally come to be free.

'They're from the Ocean Squid Explorers' Club,' Esmerelda told them. 'They rescued us. I'm sure you'll all hear more about it later, but for now I think they should be taken straight to the president.'

'Of course. I'll take them.' A male explorer fairy came forward and introduced himself as Beau.

Ursula realised that the bracelets the fairies wore must also be communication devices when Beau raised his to his mouth, pressed one of the flashing lights and told some unknown fairy on the other end that he was bringing human explorers up to meet the president.

Esmerelda bid them goodbye and Ursula felt her

excitement grow even greater as Beau indicated the ceiling and said, 'This way.'

The other explorer fairies dutifully drew back to give them room, but a couple started clapping and then all of the fairies were suddenly applauding. Ursula was sure her face must have turned bright red, but it felt good to have helped the fairies and put their beautiful city back where it belonged. The explorers were still a little clumsy with their wings, but they managed to follow Beau as he swooped effortlessly past the mobile of planets and up to a circular hole in the ceiling, which led to the next floor. The building's levels were piled one on top of the other and the explorers flew up through the middle, passing libraries and dormitories and a canteen before they reached an observatory with lots of telescopes pointing to the windows and star charts hung on the walls. Beau told them that this was the level where the president's office was located, and they followed him out of the room and into a corridor.

Like the rest of the building, it gleamed a shining silver and the scent of rocket fuel lingered in the air. They walked to the end of the corridor to a door marked with the name *Luna Livinia Foxglove*. Beau knocked and a voice called for them to come in. The fairy opened the door and ushered the explorers inside but didn't go in himself. The door closed softly behind him and the explorers found themselves in a study – only it was nothing like the one used by the president of the Ocean Squid Explorers' Club. Ursula had only ever caught glimpses of that room, but it had seemed like a stuffy place, with a sea monster tentacle hung above the mantelpiece and sneering painted explorers gazing down from their portraits.

This room, on the other hand, was bursting with life. Strange green flowers grew up the walls, humming softly to themselves, and there were several small trees standing in pots, their purple branches swaying back and forth as if they were dancing to the flowers' music. There were animals in the room too, except none of them were stuffed but very much alive. They were creatures Ursula had never seen before and they all had something of an alien look about them, from the three-eared bunny hopping around on the floor to the large butterflies pulsing with golden light. There was even a funny little chipmunk perched on the edge of the desk and grazing from a bowl of nuts, but instead of the usual brown fur, this one was purple with orange stripes.

A fairy stood behind the desk, but quickly walked around to greet them. She wore the same uniform as

everyone else and had very long silver hair. It reached all the way down to her elbows and was plaited with tiny blue flowers the same colour as her eyes. Her wings sparkled just like the other fairies. It was strange seeing a fairy up so close, especially when she was as tall as they were.

'Hello,' she said in a soft voice. 'And welcome to Stardust City. I understand that we owe you a debt of gratitude? Thank you for freeing us. We've been held captive in the snow globe for years. And as you're explorers yourselves, I'm sure you'll understand how difficult it's been for us to be cooped up like that. I'm Luna, the president of the Space Fairy Explorers' Club.'

The children introduced themselves and Ursula felt a glow of delighted surprise that the fairy club had a female president.

'Please take a seat.' Luna indicated some comfy-looking beanbags – one of which had a little space cat curled up inside it – arranged in a semicircle around the window. They looked straight out on to the sparkling sea and the *Jolly Rosa*, which had descended back to the water. 'And tell me everything.'

The explorers took their seats and told the fairy all about the Phantom Atlas Society and how they had travelled through the Nebula Sea to free them. Luna was astonished when they got to the bit about being sucked into the portal.

'You're lucky you were on a ghost ship designed to withstand the coldness of the afterworld. If you'd been in a regular pirate galleon, the cold would have frozen you solid. To say nothing of the fact that there would have been no air for you to breathe. You'd have died instantly. You really shouldn't venture into space unless it's in a rocket or a spaceship.'

'We completely agree with you,' Jai said. 'We didn't know we were going to be sucked into space. That's never been a concern while travelling under the sea before.'

Luna frowned. 'You mean you didn't know about the space portals? There are several of them here. How did you think the Nebula Sea got its name?'

'Sometimes sea names are totally random,' Max protested. 'We recently spent some time in the Jelly Blue Sea, but it's not actually *made* of jelly and we never came across any jelly islands or jelly sharks or anything like that.'

'Well, that's only because you didn't go deep enough into it,' Luna said. 'There are definitely jelly sharks there.'

'Really?' Max looked suddenly interested.

'Oh yes, I've seen them myself. They're very small – you might mistake them for piranha at first – but they're sharks, all right. And made of jelly from nose to tail. Oceans get their names for a reason. Why do you think we've never ventured into the Ocean of Bones? Or the Ocean of Cursed Pirate Gold? Not that we go in for ocean exploring too much – although there is a great deal of overlap between ocean and space exploration, we generally prefer to travel among the stars. It's safe enough in a rocket. Or at least as safe as exploring can ever be. But when we discovered the space portals, we decided to put a magical barrier around the Nebula Sea to avoid any passing sailors or marine life from getting sent out into the galaxy by mistake.'

Ursula was confused. 'But ... we saw loads of marine life on the way here. Turtles and crabs and seahorses and—'

'They're all galaxy fish,' Luna cut in. 'They can move between the sea and space no problem. In fact, they often come to the Nebula Sea to get warm. Space is freezing, you see, so the ocean is like a huge bath to them.'

'And are all these animals – and plants – from outer space too?' Genie asked, looking around the office.

The cat they'd noticed earlier was now settled in Jai's lap, purring contentedly. Ursula was sure it must be a space cat because it had a row of orange spines along its back.

'That's right,' Luna replied. 'We only ever take back living specimens, and always with their permission.'

'How do you ask a tree for permission?' Max asked, looking at the purple trees. They'd stopped dancing but one of them had climbed right out of its pot and made itself comfortable on Luna's chair, with its roots propped up on the desk.

'We learn their language, of course,' the fairy replied. She looked surprised by the question. 'Don't you learn the language of whatever place you venture to?'

The explorers all fidgeted uncomfortably.

'Not historically, no,' Jai admitted. 'But I hope that one day it can change.'

'Maybe,' Max said doubtfully. 'It's a little hard to learn a screeching red devil squid's language while it's trying to consume you and your entire ship, though.'

'You have to be careful with exploration,' Luna replied. 'We've learned a lot over the many hundreds of years since the club started. Not all places welcome visitors and that's their right. We always leave immediately if we realise we're not wanted.'

'We scoot pretty quickly if we're being attacked by a squid too,' Max replied.

'It sounds like our club could learn a lot from yours,' Jai said. 'There are many of us who want to change the way things have always been done.'

'Well, learning different languages is the best place to start,' Luna said. 'As soon as we realised that, it revolutionised our club. That's why the space mole is our emblem. They can speak any known language in the universe, you see, and they're one of the most intelligent species alive in space, so they make for the absolute best companions on an expedition.'

'Intelligent!' Max exclaimed. 'They didn't seem very bright to me. They almost murdered my robot duck, and the two we accidentally brought back on the ship with us practically gouged out my eyes before we got them in the hold.'

Luna looked appalled. 'You don't mean you're keeping a couple of space moles captive? I thought you said you were only in space a few minutes before an octopus pulled you back?'

'We were, but before we saw the octopus we tried to get some moon dust to increase the ship's power,' Jai explained. 'The space moles attacked us then.'

'I'm not surprised,' Luna replied. 'Moon dust is food to space moles. Why didn't you just ask them if you could take some?'

'We didn't know they were there until it was too late,' Ursula said.

'Besides, it was a bit tricky to ask them anything, what with all the eye-gouging,' Max said. 'If they could speak our language, why didn't they? We didn't understand a word of that chittering noise they were making.'

'Oh dear.' Luna looked troubled. 'Space moles are very proud creatures. They wouldn't speak to you in your own language if you'd made no effort to communicate with them first. You'd better bring them into the city so I can apologise and explain the situation.'

'Of course—' Jai began.

At the same time, Max said, 'If it's all the same to you, can we not spend too much time messing about with the moles? It's just we need your help to stop the Collector before she can steal any more places, the way she did to you. Now that she has Stella at her bidding she can create endless snow globes, you see, and we've already been travelling for three weeks, so—'

'Yes, I understand the urgency,' Luna replied calmly. 'And certainly we will assist in any way that we can. But I absolutely must speak to the space moles first. They're our most precious space friends and I need to ensure they're all right.'

'We haven't hurt them,' Genie hurried to say. 'And I've been taking them food every day. But of course we'll bring them to you.'

'Or perhaps you would be willing to come to them on board the *Jolly Rosa*?' Jai asked. 'It's only that … Max wasn't wrong about them being quite, er, scratchy, and their claws are really very sharp.'

And so it was agreed that Luna would return to the ghost ship with them. The fairy suggested the explorers keep hold of their wands and wings so that they could fly back to the pirate ship, and Ursula loved every moment of their journey down the tree. Even though her wings were made from cloth, they must have merged with her in some way because she could feel the air brushing past them and the warmth of the sun on them as well. She longed to stop at every branch and explore the fairy city but forced herself to follow the others to the ship.

The pirates stood well back when they alighted on deck, perhaps wary of treading on them by accident.

Max turned to Luna and said, 'How do we return to our usual size? If we're going to visit the moles then I'd rather be back to normal, thanks very much. I don't fancy being towered over by a furious giant mole.'

'Maybe it would be an enlightening experience for

you,' Luna suggested. 'It might help you understand things from the mole's point of view. But all you need to do is remove the wings and tap the star of the wand to your forehead and you'll be returned to your usual size.'

The explorers did so, although Ursula felt a little burst of reluctance to be losing her wings so soon. Luna asked them to put the wands and wings in their pockets for safekeeping, and then they went down to the hold and stepped inside.

'I think they've made a nest in that treasure chest over there.' Genie pointed it out. 'That's where they often come from when I bring their food anyway.'

Sure enough, two little mole heads suddenly popped over the edge. The moment they saw Luna, they scrambled over the side and raced towards her, chittering in a rapid, indignant sort of way. The fairy flew down to the floor and spoke calmly to them in their own language, and after a few minutes the moles seemed to calm down a little.

'Please tell them that we're dreadfully sorry,' Jai said. 'We didn't mean to frighten or upset them.'

'You can tell them yourself,' Luna replied. 'They understand every word you say. I've explained why you did what you did and that there was no intention to harm. They've told me that Genie always spoke kindly to them when she brought their food.'

'That's no excuse for kidnapping us, though,' one of the moles piped up.

Even though Luna had told them the moles could speak every language, it was still a shock to hear one of them suddenly speak human words in a high-pitched little voice.

'*Kidnapping* you?' Max exclaimed. 'Now hold on a minute! You two are stowaways if anything. We were trying to flee your planet when you forced your way on board and started scratching everybody.'

'We had to see you off to protect our families!' the other mole exclaimed. 'Who knows how much of our space dust you might have stolen otherwise?'

'Fat chance of that,' Max replied. 'You almost killed my robot duck.'

'Perhaps we might agree that mistakes were made on both sides?' Luna suggested. 'And leave it at that.'

'We acted hastily – I can see that now,' Jai said, crouching down to the moles' level. 'Please know that it was a life-or-death situation for us. We didn't mean any harm and we're truly sorry for any that we caused.'

This seemed to pacify the moles a little. 'We're certainly relieved to hear that the galaxy fairies are all right,' one of the moles said, turning to Luna. 'We'd not heard anything from you in so many years.'

Luna quickly filled them in about the Phantom Atlas Society, and the moles were appalled and promised they'd do anything they could to help.

'Any foe of the galaxy fairies is a foe of ours.'

'That's most kind of you,' Luna said. Then she looked at the explorers. 'We're at your service,' she said. 'How can we assist?'

'Well,' Jai replied. 'We were hoping that you and your rockets might be able to help us find the Collector. And Stella. Would you be willing to take on a dangerous new mission?'

CHAPTER THIRTEEN

A short while later, Ursula and the others found themselves shrunk back down to fairy size and standing in one of Stardust City's many space centres. It contained a rich hive of information about the surrounding solar system, and the explorers were all mesmerised by framed drawings of faraway planets, and catalogues of space dust, and various designs of spacesuit.

'What's an astronaut's log?' Ursula asked as they flew through a room filled with them, lined up on bookshelves.

'An account of the expedition,' Luna replied. 'An astronaut is another name for a space explorer.'

'And how is space food different from regular food?' Jai asked as they went past a door marked *Space Food Larder.*

'Oh, well, eating in space isn't like eating on a planet,' Luna replied. 'The food needs to be light and easy to store and it needs to last for a long time too. There are no fridges in space, you see, and there's also the lack of gravity to contend with. It's quite tricky to eat food while it's trying to float away. Also, an astronaut's sense of taste is affected in space. It's all a bit complicated, but it's to do with how fluids work differently up there. Anyway, most of the space food our explorers take with them comes in packets, or in stick or cube form. My personal favourites are the bacon cubes, followed by chocolate sauce straight from the tube.'

But of course the most fascinating things in the space centre were the rockets themselves. Luna led the way to a large metal hangar where they saw rows and rows of gleaming spacecraft, all different sizes and designs. Some looked like they'd only accommodate one fairy, while others appeared large enough to carry an entire crew. The area was so huge it would easily have been able to accommodate Bess if it had been human-sized, but as it was a fairy hangar, when Bess appeared outside, she could barely get her giant eye to the window.

Although she'd done as Genie asked and stayed out of sight to begin with, it was only a matter of time before she became too curious about what the explorers were doing and tried to join in. There were several teams of fairy engineers working on the rockets, but fortunately the whole city had already been notified about the explorers' presence, including the fact that they had a shadow kraken with them, so no one started screaming when Bess peered curiously through the glass.

Ursula longed to talk to the fairy engineers and find out all about how the rockets worked. As she already had some engineering knowledge from submarines, perhaps she might be able to understand a little bit about the inner workings of rockets too? Something about their long, pointed shape told her that these vessels were even faster than the *Blowfish*.

When she asked Luna, the fairy nodded and said, 'They're the fastest known way of travelling we have invented so far. On our last manned mission – just before the Collector stole our city – we were able to travel all the way to Andromma in just two weeks!'

She beamed, clearly expecting them to be impressed, but of course the explorers had no idea what she was talking about.

'Is Andromma a planet?' Genie hazarded.

Luna looked surprised by their ignorance. 'Yes. Do you really not know anything at all about our solar system?'

The explorers shook their heads and felt embarrassed.

'We'd love to learn, though,' Jai said. 'Once we've stopped the Collector.'

'Yes, she definitely needs to be dealt with first,' Luna agreed. 'And I'm sure we can help you find her. As I said, our rockets are extremely fast. We could travel all the way around our own world in a day if we wanted to. Of course, we'll have to go a little slower if we're looking for signs of Scarlett, but we can still cover the planet much faster than you'd be able to in sleighs, dirigibles and even submarines. And all our rockets are fitted with magic detectors, so if there's an ice princess with Scarlett then we can set our equipment to look for ice magic. There aren't too many snow queens left in the world, so far as we're aware, so that should certainly speed up the process of finding them.'

'That's great!' Jai said, looking delighted. 'When can you start?'

Luna smiled. 'Right away.'

After the engineers had performed their maintenance checks, the fairy pilots arrived to take command of their rockets. Ursula and the others told the assembled group all they knew about the Collector and the Phantom Atlas Society, and described both Scarlett and Stella. Even without the rockets' magic detectors, they hoped there would be some physical signs of Scarlett's activity. After all, she had hosts of pirates and sea gremlins working with her as well as the Pacificans, and she'd escaped with Stella on a large dirigible that wouldn't be easy to disguise. Ursula felt a little surge of hope and excitement when a hole opened up in the ceiling and a launch pad rose up from the floor in preparation for blast-off.

'Come on,' Luna said. 'We'll go to the gallery to watch them take off.'

The explorers followed her to the top floor of the space centre, where they had an excellent view of the first rocket perched on the launch pad. Bess floated in the air nearby, eager to see the show as well. A clock on the wall of the observation deck counted down in time with the one on the launch pad, and the explorers all held their breath until, finally, a big zero flashed red and the rocket blasted into the sky in a burst of smoke.

Ursula could barely believe how quickly it shot up into the air. She'd never seen any vehicle go so fast. In a matter of seconds, it had disappeared from their sight entirely, leaving only a thin trail of rocket fuel behind to mark the way it had gone. A second rocket took off soon after that, then another and another, until almost a hundred had departed from the city's various hangars.

Ursula found herself grinning and saw that her friends all wore the same expression. They felt a sense of triumph at having made it this far. There were still a lot of unknowns up ahead, and a great deal to fear from the Phantom Atlas Society, but at least they had made a meaningful contribution by releasing the fairies of Stardust City and enlisting their help. The explorers all felt much better knowing that there was a huge fleet of rockets out there, searching the world for Scarlett.

'I only wish we could have gone with them,' Max said wistfully. 'It would have been quite something to travel on board a fairy rocket.'

For now though, there was nothing to do but wait. Luna estimated that it would take about three days for the rockets to search the world and was confident that they'd return with news of Scarlett then. In the meantime, the explorers were permitted to keep their guest wands and wings in order to explore the city. Not only was this fascinating and thrilling, but it gave them something to do while impatiently waiting for news. Plus the fairy city was a much nicer place to hang out in than the ghost ship.

Ursula desperately wanted to transform into her mermaid form and go for a swim in the sea, but the fairies told her there were several known space portals nearby, so she didn't dare risk it. Instead, she spent a lot of time with the fairy engineers, learning about how the rockets flew. She found herself missing Old Joe more than ever, knowing he would be equally fascinated.

Aside from the rockets, Ursula also liked discovering the many delights of the fairy city with her friends. They were treated like royalty everywhere they went and showered with gifts and food. Genie enjoyed visiting the fairy aquarium, while Max was fascinated by the exhibits in the space centre, and Jai couldn't get enough of the books in the fairy library.

They all especially loved it when the sun set for the day and the tree lit up with dozens of twinkling fairy lights. The galaxy fairies enjoyed spending their evenings outdoors, and the explorers were invited to join them for their al fresco space teas, with cake planets, rocket brownies and astronaut lollipops. The exploding candy and marzipan space moles were pretty good too.

Although sometimes Ursula found she forgot they'd been shrunk to fit into the fairies' world, at night there were plenty of reminders because of the other life on the tree. Various creatures were attracted by the lights, and a couple of times they saw sea snails creeping along the branches, or crabs scuttling up the trunk. The first time the explorers saw a giant snail looming over them, they worried they might be snapped up as dinner, but the fairies assured them there was nothing to fear and the only creatures they had to watch out for were the seagulls.

On the afternoon of the third day, the explorers were passing the time at the theme park at the top of the tree when a message came asking them to meet Luna back at the club. The explorers were all on the big Ferris wheel at the time but they had become a lot more used to their wings over the past few days, so they hastily handed their sticks of candy floss over to the fairies in the seat below them and flew straight to Luna, desperately hoping there would be news of Scarlett.

But when they entered the president's study, the fairy shook her head and said, 'It's not good, I'm afraid.' She tapped her bracelet and went on. 'I've had a message back from one of our pilots. She says they've searched everywhere and found no sign of them.'

'But that's not possible,' said Max. 'Scarlett has to be somewhere.'

'They've been everywhere,' Luna insisted. 'Well ... everywhere except the Terrible Valleys. That place is uninhabitable by all accounts, so there seemed little point. It's impossible that she's there.'

'Scarlett is very resourceful,' Jai said. 'It doesn't pay to underestimate her. If that's the only place you haven't looked, then that's where she must be.'

'My pilots are worried about the vultures,' Luna said. 'They've been known to bring aircraft down – but I'll ask them to fly over, just in case. I'd be amazed if they found anything, though.'

The explorers had to impatiently wait another full day before Luna called them back. They knew it was bad news at once by the grave expression on her face.

'We've found Scarlett,' she said. 'Or at least we've found Stella, so I assume the Collector must be close by. She's in the Valley of Volcanoes.'

The explorers had all heard of the place but of course none of them had ever been. Indeed, no Ocean Squid explorer would ever go near there. Aside from the fact that it had no sea, the Terrible Valleys was far too dangerous a place for exploration. It contained more than twenty peril-filled low areas between mountains, all joined up with one another, so there was very little in the way of safe havens or shelters to be found along the way. Furthermore, the landscape around the Terrible Valleys was mostly inhospitable desert and even the Desert Jackal Explorers' Club, who usually loved hot, barren, forsaken places with lots of scorpions, had only gone as far as the Valley of Carnivorous Plants before giving up and turning back.

'There's nothing for it,' Jai said, glancing at the others. 'If that's where Stella is, then that's where we have to go too.'

'We should notify Stella's father and the other Polar Bear explorers,' Ursula said. 'Then we can all make our way there together.'

'How are we going to send the Polar Bear explorers a message, though?' Ursula asked. 'The *Jolly Rosa* doesn't have a radio on board.'

'We can assist with that,' Luna said. 'I can send a fairy messenger to locate them, although it might take a little while if you don't know where they are?'

'They're using the compass charm on Stella's bracelet to follow her,' Ursula said. 'So they'll be heading towards the Valley of Volcanoes, even if they don't know that's where she is yet.'

'I'll despatch a messenger today,' Luna said. She raised her arm to indicate the bracelet they'd seen her use to communicate. 'They'll give the explorers one of these and you can have a matching one. That way you can speak to each other directly, as if you were using a radio. In the meantime, can we give you a lift to the Terrible Valleys in one of our rockets?'

The explorers were thrilled. Not only would this be much faster than travelling by ghost ship, but they'd have the exciting experience of travelling by fairy rocket too.

'We'd love to!' they all exclaimed.

And it seemed they had discovered Scarlett's hideout only just in time since their parrot charm only had one single silver feather left. Its magic wouldn't hide them from her for much longer.

CHAPTER FOURTEEN

The explorers returned to the *Jolly Rosa* to explain what was happening to the crew, who were relieved to be able to vanish back into the ghost pearl finally. As Rosa had already said, no living thing could remain on board when that happened, so they would have to take Jewel with them to the Terrible Valleys too. Luna was a little unsure when they explained the situation to her.

'A dizard is one thing,' she said. 'They just sleep most of the time from what I can gather. But a sabre-tooth tiger? How do we know she won't run wild and devour half the crew?'

'She's not a sabre-tooth, she's a *sugar*-tooth,' Jai said. 'She's very friendly and well-behaved. And she only eats sugar mice. She would never hurt the crew.'

'You'll have to discuss it with the pilot,' Luna finally said. 'It's her rocket, so it's her rules.'

The explorers were escorted to the hangar where the fairy in question was doing the final checks on her spacecraft. She had long silver hair and wore the same spacesuit as the rest of them, only hers had a lot of brightly coloured badges sewn on to it, depicting various aliens. A pair of little green Martian earrings dangled from her tiny ears and space mole bracelets jangled at her wrists. She fluttered down from the rocket when she saw them and stuck out her hand to introduce herself.

'I'm Bertie,' she said, with a grin. 'Short for Roberta, but no one calls me that except my mum. Hey, we match!' She pointed at Genie who was wearing a space mole hat. 'I like your cowgirl boots too. Very sparkly!'

'Thanks,' Genie said. 'I love your Martian earrings! And thank you for agreeing to transport us.'

'My pleasure. It's going to be quite a ride going to the Terrible Valleys. I hope you lot are ready to hang on to your hats! Or cloaks, or whatever it is that explorers have.'

'It's very kind of you to take us,' Jai said. 'And we're hoping you might agree to having another couple of passengers too. You see, we have a dizard and a sugar-tooth tiger travelling with us. I know the tiger might seem alarming, but I promise she's very friendly and—'

'Of course, of course, the more the merrier,' Bertie said, waving her hand. 'Your tiger is welcome to come as long as she doesn't trouble my aliens. They'll all have to stay on the ground floor to begin with since we don't have guest fairy wings designed for anything other than humans. But you can get another couple of wands from the club that will let you shrink your animals down to fairy size, along with anything else you want to bring with you.'

'Thank you,' Jai said, relieved.

'I have a shadow kraken too.' Genie indicated Bess, who was drifting around the hangar, peering at the rockets in an interested sort of way. 'She'll probably disappear back into the shadow world most of the time we're travelling, but she might try to stick her tentacle into the rocket from time to time.'

'That's fine too,' Bertie replied. 'But perhaps you could ask her to try to avoid blocking my view from the cockpit? I like to see what kind of trouble we're flying into.'

'I'll tell her,' Genie promised.

'What kind of aliens have you got on board?' Max asked, looking up at the rocket a little warily. 'Nothing of the brain-eating variety, I hope?'

'Oh no, nothing like that. Just a couple of orphaned jelly-legs at the moment.' Bertie pointed at one of the patches on her spacesuit, depicting a bizarre-looking creature that seemed to be made up almost entirely of legs. 'These badges are all the aliens I've met so far,' she explained. 'The jelly-legs and space-rabbits are my favourite, but I really hope one day I'll meet a toffee-nut-billy-bong-space-tortoise to add to my collection. They're meant to be the fastest animal in the universe, you know. Anyway, the jelly-legs are spending some time with me until I can get back into space to reunite them with their own kind. They're a bit odd to look at and love being tickled, so watch out for that, but they're harmless otherwise.'

Relieved, the explorers collected the wands from the club before shrinking their animals, the sugar troll's hamper, Ursula's trident, the ghost pearl and their various other possessions. Then they retreated to the nearest branch of the tree and returned the ghost ship to the pearl by speaking its name three times once again. The great ship vanished instantly but they could just about see it inside the pearl when the mist parted slightly. Ursula tucked the pearl carefully away in her pocket and then the explorers returned to the hangar to climb aboard Bertie's rocket.

'Here.' The fairy held out one of the bracelets they'd seen the others wear. 'Luna said to give you this. Keep an eye on the little blue light; when it starts flashing and beeping it means that the other explorers have the second bracelet and are trying to contact you. You can use it to communicate with Stardust City if you need to as well.'

'Excellent.' Jai slipped the bracelet on to his wrist. 'Thank you.'

'No, thank *you*,' Bertie replied. 'For releasing us from the snow-globe prison. Now, do you have all your bits and bobs? Your tiger is very beautiful, by the way. I've never met a sugar-tooth before.'

'Thanks. Her name is Jewel,' Jai told her. 'And, yes, I think we have everything.'

Without any further ado, the explorers followed Bertie on board the rocket. Poor Bess looked like she wanted to follow too but there wasn't room for her massive form, so she did her best to peer in through the tiny windows instead. The metallic interior of the rocket gleamed shiny and silver, and was set out in a similar way to the clubhouse itself, with holes in the floor for them to fly from one level to the next.

'We'll get the animals settled first and then you can come up to the control room with me for blast-off,' Bertie said.

Their entrance to the rocket had been into a kind of storage area, which Bertie said contained space food and other supplies for the journey, but which she'd also used to make a comfortable bed for her aliens.

'These are the jelly-legs,' she said. 'Herman and Penelope.'

The explorers all leaned forward to peer into a basket. Two strange creatures were so coiled up around each other inside that it was hard to tell where one ended and the other began. They were both a bright fluorescent green and their legs were long and thin, rather like a jellyfish's tentacles, except they had little feet at the end of each one – actual feet that looked unnervingly human with five small toes that squirmed and wiggled in pleasure when Bertie reached in to pet them.

Her greeting seemed to wake them up and the aliens tumbled out of their basket in an ungainly sort of way. Ursula saw they each had a fluffy little body perched on top of their legs, with three eyes peering out from behind the fur. When they saw the explorers, they both immediately flopped over on to the floor and stuck their legs in the air, waving their small jelly feet at them.

'What are they doing?' Genie asked.

'They want you to tickle their feet,' Bertie said. 'Tickling is their absolute favourite thing, you see.'

'Cool.' Max reached down and obligingly tickled the jelly-legs.

The aliens must have had a little mouth hidden inside all that fur because they let forth a volley of rather high-pitched giggles that finally ended in a burst of hiccups – only these were no ordinary hiccups. With each one, a tiny purple flower came out of their mouths and floated up towards the ceiling where it stuck and shone with a softly pulsing light.

'The flowers will disappear after an hour or two,' Bertie told them. 'It's quite fun to tickle them, but I've found it's best to stop after five minutes or so. Otherwise they start hiccuping other things, and some of them aren't so pleasant.'

'Like what?' Genie asked curiously.

'Oh, it could be anything,' Bertie said. 'I've had cactuses and lemmings a couple of times. And a whole bunch of grapes once, which was quite handy because I was just in the mood for grapes. But this one time Herman did a particularly big hiccup and out popped a bear.'

The explorers all stared at her.

'I beg your pardon?' Max finally said.

'A big grizzly bear it was,' Bertie replied. 'It ate everything in the hold before it finally vanished. Gave me quite a shock. I thought it was best to stick to a five-minutes-maximum tickling policy after that.'

'Very sensible,' Jai said. He looked horrified at the idea of having such an unpredictable creature on board. 'How did they even manage to hiccup out a creature that was bigger than they are?'

Bertie shrugged. 'Not sure, really. Jelly-legs are a mysterious breed. For a moment when the bear first came out it was tiny. I actually thought it was a nut to begin with. But the moment it landed on the floor it transformed into an enormous beast. I flew out of here pretty fast, I can tell you. Still, it could have been worse. At least the jelly-legs were in their shrunken state, or else who knows how big the bear might have been.'

'Is this not their natural size then?' Ursula asked.

'Oh no,' Bertie replied. 'They were probably about the size of a cat before, but I had to shrink them to fit them on to my rocket. Speaking of which, shall I give you the tour?'

The explorers were very keen to see the rocket properly, so they said goodbye to the jelly-legs and Jewel. The dizard was still asleep inside the sock, so they hung it up carefully from a peg on the door, then followed Bertie into the rocket.

It was nowhere near as large or luxurious as the *Blowfish*, but it was an extraordinary vessel just the same. There were five floors altogether: the storage hold they'd already been in, an engine room, sleeping quarters, a little kitchen and the control deck right at the top of the rocket. They ended the tour there and Bertie fiddled with a few knobs on the controls before turning back to them with a grin.

'This is one of my favourite bits,' she said. 'Everyone sit down and buckle yourselves in.'

'What about Jewel and Pog?' Jai asked.

'Don't worry, the jelly-legs know the drill. They'll wrap their legs around your animals to hold them secure for blast-off.'

The explorers took their seats and Ursula was pleased to find that each chair was positioned next to a little circular window, similar to the portholes they had back on the *Blowfish*, so they could still see what was going on.

Bertie strapped herself into a chair behind the controls and there were some clanks and whirs as a launch pad manoeuvred them up on to the roof of the hangar.

'I'm sorry, but would you mind asking your kraken to shift out of the way?' Bertie asked apologetically. 'It's just that she's blocking our exit.'

Genie obligingly called out to Bess inside her head and the kraken moved to one side. Then the countdown clock began, as they'd seen in previous launches. The explorers all felt a surge of excitement as they got closer to one, and then *lift-off* was announced and the entire rocket trembled as its engines geared up to their full power with a deafening rumble. Ursula could feel the vibration through the back of the chair and the soles of her feet, and found herself gripping the safety straps tightly as the rocket left the ground and accelerated up into the sky.

It travelled so fast to begin with that Ursula felt as if a giant, unseen hand was pressing her firmly down into the chair, and the pressure was so great that she doubted she'd have been able to stand up even if she'd wanted to. The now-familiar scent of rocket fuel filled the room as Ursula peered out of the window and saw Bess keeping pace with them just outside. The branches and leaves of Stardust City were spread below, with the vast ocean sparkling all around. Seconds later, they were in the clouds and the world beneath was lost from view.

CHAPTER FIFTEEN

Bertie made some further adjustments on the controls and the rocket slowed down a little. To Ursula's relief, the pressure on her shoulders lifted.

'Everyone OK back there?' the fairy pilot asked, glancing round at them with a grin.

She seemed impressed when they all replied that they were. 'No one's feeling space sick yet then?'

'We're not in space,' Max pointed out.

'That's true enough, but take-off can upset people if they're not used to it,' Bertie replied. 'We don't need to sustain full power once we're in the air, so the rocket can turn horizontal now. I'll just need you to stay strapped into your seats while the rooms reorganise themselves.'

'Reorganise?' Ursula asked, startled.

'We don't bother with seats in space,' Bertie explained, adjusting the controls once again. 'Because there's no gravity up there, you see, so you all float around and it doesn't much matter which way up you are. But if we're travelling within the atmosphere then we need the rocket to be arranged differently.'

She pressed another button and the rocket stopped going straight up and lowered its nose to go horizontal instead. This meant that rather than being seated on the floor, the explorers found themselves strapped to the walls and would have dropped out of their seats altogether if it hadn't been for their harnesses. It was very uncomfortable hanging from the straps in this way, but fortunately Bertie quickly pressed another couple of buttons and the room began to spin. At least, that's what it felt like to Ursula. The walls revolved slowly down so they were all on the floor once again.

The same thing happened in the other rooms. The walls and floors slid about and reorganised themselves to fit in with the new horizontal position of the rocket. It all happened very quickly and Ursula marvelled at the clever engineering and design involved. Now that the rocket was flying horizontally rather than vertically, the holes between the rooms appeared in the walls rather than the floor, allowing Jewel to come bounding in a few moments later, looking a little wild-eyed and startled by the whole experience. Even her fur was puffed up like an ordinary cat's. Perhaps she feared they were in some kind of danger because she'd brought the sock, which Pog was sleeping in, hanging out of her mouth. The little dizard was still just a sleepy lump at the bottom, so the blast-off experience didn't seem to have affected her in the least.

'It's all right, Jewel,' Jai said as the tiger rushed straight over and headbutted him anxiously. 'You're safe. Everything's OK.'

'You can unbuckle yourselves now,' Bertie informed them.

The explorers hurried to do so. Ursula peered out of the nearest window and saw that they were surrounded by clouds, just as they had been in the ghost ship.

'How long will it take to reach the Terrible Valleys?' she asked.

'Oh, not long at all,' Bertie replied. 'We should be there in about five hours.'

The explorers were cheered to hear this. Even if they'd been able to go part of the way on board the *Blowfish*, the journey would have taken them many weeks. And the Terrible Valleys were nowhere near a sea so they would have had to use the ghost ship to fly over land too.

Ursula, in particular, was already longing for cold, blue waves against her skin and scales. It was like a thirst she couldn't satisfy and she felt a flicker of worry about how long she could be away from the ocean before she became ill like her mother. Her skin already felt drier than usual and she'd noticed a few flaky patches on her legs. But there was nothing much she could do about that now, so she pushed the thought from her mind and joined in with the others as they continued to explore the rocket.

They'd missed lunch in all the preparations for departure, so Bertie invited them to share some of her supplies, and the explorers offered the contents of the sugar troll's hamper in return. Ursula was excited about trying space food, but in fact it wasn't nice to eat at all. The space ice cream in particular was a big let-down since it was nothing like real ice cream, but rather a dry, crumbly block of rather tasteless powdery stuff. Still, at least the cubes of roast chicken dinner were something savoury. The one disadvantage of the sugar troll's picnic basket was that almost everything inside it seemed to be sweet. It contained endless cakes, puddings, sweets and jellies, with just the occasional cheese straw or ham sandwich if they were lucky. This had seemed like fun at first, but the explorers were now a bit tired of sticky desserts.

As they finished the meal, Ursula felt a flash of homesickness for the Ocean Squid Explorers' Club. Yately, the chef, was kind to her and often gave her little treats whenever she snuck into the kitchen. And she suddenly longed to see Old Joe and his dog Mutt, and to work alongside him on the submarines once more ... But a shudder of unease passed through her as she realised this was unlikely to happen again. If the club had been restored to its rightful place then the other members would now know that Ursula was half mermaid, and it might make her an enemy in their eyes.

Ursula's hope all along was that her role in saving the club might go some way towards redeeming her, but of all the clubs, Ocean Squid seemed the most set in its ways and she felt a sharp flare of worry at the thought that it might not be enough. Not only would being a girl make her unwelcome as an explorer, but being a mermaid might mean she couldn't be an engineer either, and then what would she do? The club was her home. Her human side meant that she couldn't remain underwater long-term, so Mercadia wouldn't be an option and nor was a mermaid school.

Besides which, Ursula loved the Ocean Squid Explorers' Club, and the thought of never again seeing the floodlit fountains or the turtle lanterns, or the sea-salt roses, to say nothing of her dolphin friend Minty who lived in the ocean nearby and the sea fairies below the surface, made her feel cold all over. She shivered as they finished clearing up their lunch.

Jai noticed and said, 'Are you OK?'

Ursula hurriedly said she was but as the afternoon wore on she found that a bit of a cloud had descended over her and she was finding it difficult to enjoy the experience of the galaxy fairy rocket because she kept thinking that this might very well be her last ever expedition, and the final time she travelled with her explorer friends.

'Hey.' Genie nudged her. 'I know you told Jai you were OK but are you really? You don't seem quite yourself.'

Ursula looked at her friend. Genie was wearing galaxy fairy head boppers she'd made back at Stardust City, and her eyes were kind as always.

'I guess I'm just ... feeling a bit worried about the club,' she replied. 'Sometimes it feels like I don't fit in anywhere.'

'That's not true,' Genie said.

'You fit with us,' Jai agreed, looking up from where he'd been tickling a jelly-legs.

The four explorers were sitting in the storage hold, playing with the aliens while they watched the clouds drift by outside the window.

'Jai's right,' Genie said. 'You might be half mermaid and half human but all of you is an explorer.'

'I'm not sure the club will see it that way,' Ursula

replied a little glumly. 'I wouldn't even mind so much if I could carry on living there as an engineer, but I'm worried they won't allow that either now they know the truth about me.'

'But you played such a large part in rescuing the club,' Genie protested. 'Surely they have to take that into account?'

'I wouldn't be so sure,' Max said with a grim expression. 'You know how stuck in the mud they can be. It takes them about a hundred years to change their minds on anything, especially with that stuffy old coot Jacob as president.'

'And if girls can't be explorers, then you and I won't be able to go on any more expeditions,' Ursula said to Genie.

'I'll probably still be excluded too,' Max said. 'Jai will be the only one to hang on to his explorer's cloak.'

'But we're a team,' Jai protested. 'I don't want to go on expeditions without you three.'

'It doesn't matter what you want.' Max shrugged. 'They'll assign you to another group.'

The explorers fell into a troubled silence. Ursula guessed this was something her friends probably hadn't thought much about either, but now they were closing in on Scarlett, the end of their expedition loomed one way or another, and they knew the four of them couldn't continue to travel like this forever. Her friends looked so downcast that Ursula felt bad for dampening the mood.

'I guess there's no point worrying about it now,' she said, attempting to change the subject. She tried to keep her tone bright, but a lump still came into her throat as she went on, 'I've still got my engineering experience. I might be able to retrain somewhere else. There's got to be a way of finding a job and a place to live ...'

'No,' Jai said, quietly but firmly. 'Whether we succeed in our mission against Scarlett or not, the service you've done the Ocean Squid Explorers' Club, at great personal risk, is too much. If they don't see that, and acknowledge and reward it – for both you and Genie – then it's not a club I want to be a part of any more.'

Ursula gasped. 'You don't mean that,' she said. 'The club is ... well, it's everything to you.'

'It has been,' Jai agreed. 'In the past. But some of their policies should have changed a long time ago and if they can't see that after all that's happened then I will leave.'

'Me too,' Max agreed. He tickled the jelly-legs sprawled happily in his lap, producing a flurry of hiccups and more flowers that floated up to the ceiling. There was an entire garden up there now. 'I mean, technically

I'm still expelled, but if they do let me back in, I won't accept it unless Ursula and Genie can come with us.'

'We could always apply to join one of the other clubs,' Jai suggested. 'The four of us, together.'

'But it's submarines and ships and the sea that you love,' Ursula replied. 'It's what we all love.'

She couldn't imagine them trekking through mosquito-infested jungles with the Jungle Cat Explorers' Club, or shivering in snowdrifts with the Polar Bear Explorers' Club, or sweating in scorpion-filled deserts with Desert Jackal explorers. Her friends might not have any mermaid blood in them, but the sea called to them just as strongly as it did to her.

'Well, we'll think of something,' Jai insisted. 'Perhaps we'll start our own club?'

'Can we do that?' Genie asked.

'Why not?' Jai replied. 'There's no law against it. For years we all thought there had only ever been four clubs, but we know now there're at least six with the discovery of the Sky Phoenix Explorers' Club and the Space Fairy Explorers' Club. If we started our own ocean exploring club, I bet we'd receive applications from some of the people our club hasn't accepted in the past. Girls, of course, and maybe even mermaids too? Anything is possible. We'll find a way to make it work.'

He squeezed Ursula's arm briefly. 'But no matter what, don't think for a moment that after all this the two of us will be returning to the Ocean Squid Explorers' Club if they don't welcome you and Genie too. That's never going to happen.'

'Hear, hear,' Max said.

Genie took Ursula's hand and held it tightly. The lump in Ursula's throat had grown so large she could hardly speak and she suddenly felt tears filling her eyes. She *did* fit in somewhere after all. She fitted in right here with her explorer friends, and that wasn't going to change, no matter what lay ahead.

The jelly-legs in Max's lap gave a very loud hiccup just then and Jai said, 'How long have we been in here? Perhaps you'd best stop tickling that jelly-legs. I'm sure it must have been more than five minutes—'

But then the little alien let out another hiccup and, instead of a purple flower, an entire troupe of tap-dancing frogs appeared. Or at least they resembled frogs, but Ursula guessed they were another kind of alien because they had red skin rather than green. The explorers were perfectly content to watch them performing their energetic dance until Bertie noticed what was going on and ordered them all to come through to the other room quickly.

'Those are brain-eating alien frogs!' she exclaimed. 'They'll try to have you for dinner as soon as they finish their dance!'

The explorers didn't need telling twice. They all raced to exit the room, scooping up the jelly-legs along the way. There was a hairy moment when they realised they'd forgotten poor Pog, who was still sound asleep inside her sock, and Jai had to risk life and limb to run back in to fetch her. But then the door was safely fastened and Bertie seemed cheerful enough about the mishap.

'No harm done,' she said. 'They'll have disappeared in an hour or two, and at least they won't gobble up all my space food like the bear did.'

Just then, the bracelet on Jai's wrist started to flash and all the explorers held their breath in excitement. Could this mean that the galaxy fairy had caught up with the Polar Bear explorers and delivered their message? Genie leaned over to press the flashing button and a kindly male voice immediately came through to them.

'Hello? This is Felix Evelyn Pearl, Stella's father. Do I have the honour of addressing the Ocean Squid explorers?'

CHAPTER SIXTEEN

The conversation that followed was full of excitement. Ursula and her friends learned that the Polar Bear team had been getting closer and closer to the Terrible Valleys and were now only a day's journey away. Travelling with Stella's dad were Shay, Ethan and Beanie.

'We're likely to arrive a little after you do,' Shay told them. 'Some time tomorrow, hopefully.'

'If we don't all get gobbled up by something first,' Ethan's exasperated voice came through the bracelet. 'We've had several close shaves already, so it's not looking good so far.'

'How are you travelling?' Ursula asked.

There was no snow in or around the Terrible Valleys so she guessed they must have abandoned their usual sleighs and sleds.

'Flying carpet,' Shay replied. 'It's a long story, but we came across a Weenus's Trading Post, and by a stroke of luck he happened to have four working carpets to trade.'

'I don't know about a stroke of luck,' Ethan said. 'Mine seems to go haywire whenever I try to ride it.'

'Perhaps if you treated it a little more courteously,' Felix suggested mildly, 'then it might behave better for you.'

'It's a carpet!' Ethan scoffed. 'I don't know what the world has come to if I have to be courteous to a carpet. Next thing you know we've all got to be polite to door handles and considerate to dustpans—'

'The point is, we'll see you there,' Shay said.

The explorers discussed their next steps and agreed that it might be a bit conspicuous if a bunch of flying carpets and a fairy space rocket went sailing straight into the Valley of Volcanoes, so they decided to meet in the neighbouring valley instead, which unfortunately was the Valley of Carnivorous Plants. No one was particularly happy about going near such a place – Ethan least of all since he was convinced he was going to be gulped down by an enraged sunflower of some kind, and didn't seem much cheered when Beanie, who was an expert on the various ways explorers had met their demise, told him that this had never happened before.

'I'll be the first then,' Ethan grumbled. 'Lucky me.'

'Oh no, if you *were* to be consumed by a sunflower it would be extremely *un*lucky for you,' Beanie said.

'Carnivorous sunflowers have over a thousand teeth, you see, so it would be terribly painful.'

'We'll meet you there,' Jai said. 'If we convene on the outskirts and don't poke into the Valley of Carnivorous Plants any further then we have to, then hopefully no one will be attacked by flowers of any kind.'

They ended the call with a renewed sense of optimism. It would be good to meet up with their Polar Bear colleagues, especially when venturing into such unknown territory.

Bertie's estimate had been accurate, and by that evening they were flying over the Terrible Valleys. 'Terrible' was certainly the right word for them. And it didn't help that because they were all shrunk down to fairy size inside the rocket, everything looked as if it belonged to the land of the giants as well. First they flew over the Valley of Poisonous Puddings, then there was the Valley of Fiendish Frogs and what appeared to be the Valley of Angry Gnomes.

'What a terrible place,' Genie said as they all stared out of the window in dismay. They'd gathered together to have their dinner in the kitchen and the view down below mesmerised them as they ate.

'That one doesn't look so bad.' Max pointed. 'It looks like the Valley of Rainbows or something.'

Jai frowned. 'That can't be right. There must be something more to it or else it wouldn't be here in the Terrible Valleys.'

The place certainly *looked* like a valley of rainbows though, arcing through the air in a fantastic kaleidoscope, crossing and criss-crossing each other from every angle, sending shimmering bright lights up to the clouds. It was especially pretty now that the sun was setting and the warm golden glow of the sky made the rainbow colours even more vibrant. Not only that, but the valley appeared to be green and lush with little babbling brooks dotted here and there – very different to the inhospitable, barren, acrid valleys surrounding it.

'Perhaps it's an anomaly?' Jai suggested. 'And there's nothing terrible about it at all.'

'Well, fortunately we won't need to find out,' Max replied. 'Since we won't be in the Terrible Valleys for long.'

Bertie had assured them there was more than enough fuel for the rocket to fly around in circles all night. And they all agreed it would be safer to remain in the safety of the sky rather than land and try to make camp in such dangerous surroundings. It seemed like a foolproof plan and the explorers were just enjoying some delicious sugar-troll ice cream from the picnic hamper when something hit the side of the rocket with a thud, making them all jump.

'What was that?' Ursula exclaimed.

'I don't know.' Bertie stood up, looking worried, and they all pressed their faces against the windows.

'Perhaps a bird took a swipe at us?' Genie said. 'I'm pretty sure we just flew over the Valley of Vultures.'

'Maybe,' Bertie replied. 'I hoped I was flying high enough to avoid them—'

Before she could finish speaking, there was another thud as something knocked against the rocket.

'It *was* a vulture!' Max exclaimed. 'I saw it! There are more of them coming too – look!'

He pointed and the explorers saw that he was right. Dozens of vultures were shooting up from the valley below like arrows, their beaks razor sharp and their eyes coldly determined. Every bird was even bigger than the fairy rocket itself.

'Drat!' Bertie exclaimed. 'I'd best go and make some defensive manoeuvres before one of those birds tries to gobble us up.'

She flew to the control room and the explorers followed. The fairy took her seat and switched from automatic pilot to manual control. Through the windows, the explorers could see more vultures soaring towards them and heard the dismaying thump and thud as they lashed out with their huge claws. Bertie performed some pretty nimble flying, zigging and zagging the rocket across the sky so skilfully that the vultures couldn't keep up and soon dropped back, returning to their own valley in defeat. The explorers gave a cheer, thinking that the danger was passed, but then a red light started flashing on the dashboard and an alarm sounded too.

'Drat!' Bertie exclaimed again. 'One of them has punctured the fuel tank.'

'*Punctured* it?' Jai was aghast. 'Surely the walls are too thick for a beak to do that, even if it does belong to a giant bird?'

'Afraid not,' Bertie replied grimly. 'Travelling in space isn't like being underwater. There isn't the same amount of pressure to contend with so the rockets don't need armour-plated walls like your submarines. A thinner structure helps us take off more easily, but it also leaves us more vulnerable to problems like this. We're going to have to find somewhere to land.'

The explorers groaned.

'Can't you fix the problem from the air?' Max asked.

'Nope, not a chance. We're leaking fuel so we've got to land, and quickly.'

'Why don't I call the *Jolly Rosa* again?' Ursula said, already reaching for the ghost pearl. 'The rocket could land on the deck and then we wouldn't have to go into the Terrible Valleys just yet?'

Everyone thought this was an excellent idea, but when Ursula retrieved the pearl and said the magic words, they got a shock. Instead of the ghost ship appearing around them, a rolled-up piece of parchment dropped into Ursula's lap instead.

'What's that?' Max asked, peering at it. 'Has Rosa sent you a treasure map?'

Ursula unrolled the parchment and found that it was indeed a treasure map, but printed on the other side was a letter from the ship's captain. She apologised in a half-hearted sort of way, but explained the crew had decided that having the explorers on board wasn't worth the extra aggravation.

Nobody here wants a repeat of the space moles or otherworldly vortexes of any kind, she wrote. *Sorry, kids, but you're on your own . . .*

'Drat!' Max exclaimed.

'I guess there's nothing else for it,' Jai said. 'We're going to have to land the rocket after all.'

'We should head back towards the Valley of Rainbows,' Genie said. 'It's the only place here I want to stay.'

'It's not too far,' Bertie replied, checking out of the window. 'We should be able to get there.'

'I don't like the look of it,' Max said. 'It just seems too good to be true.'

'Well, it's either that or poisonous puddings and fiendish frogs,' Ursula pointed out.

'At least you know where you are with a fiendish frog,' Max muttered.

'Whatever you decide, can you do it quickly?' Bertie said. 'Every second we delay is losing us fuel.'

'I agree with the girls,' Jai said. 'Let's head for the rainbows. At least there's a chance that it's a perfectly nice valley, whereas we know for a fact that the others are perilous.'

Max shook his head and didn't look at all happy but he was outvoted, so Bertie turned the rocket around and pointed it towards the Valley of Rainbows. It came into sight again quickly enough and Ursula was reassured by the scenic rolling green hills and sparkling blue brooks, to say nothing of the stunning rainbows themselves. Surely a place as lovely as this couldn't possibly be dangerous? Why, they might even come across some unicorns or Pegasi there. She'd heard that the magical horses were drawn to rainbows.

They were just starting their descent when Bertie exclaimed, 'Shoot!'

'What is it?' Ursula asked.

'Those dratted vultures have damaged one of our landing wheels,' the fairy replied. She glanced over her shoulder at them. 'You'd all better strap yourselves in and brace for a bumpy landing. Don't worry about your pets – the jelly-legs will take care of them again.'

The explorers hurried to buckle themselves into their seats. But unlike take-off, this felt more frightening than exciting, especially as they were landing in an unknown place and knew that the landing was going to be rough. Ursula couldn't help wondering how well the rocket's exterior would be able to protect them if it was so thin that vultures could peck through it with their beaks, and she found it hard not to envision crumpled metal and fiery explosions – much as she tried to push this mental image away.

Very soon, the rocket was descending through the rainbows, and the inside of the cabin flashed green and red and indigo as they passed all the way through. The steep mountains rising up on either side of the valley would have made it very difficult for a human-sized rocket to land, but luckily the fairy craft was small enough to aim for the flat land in the middle.

'I'm going to point it at that field down there, with all the blue flowers,' Bertie said, gesturing out of the window at a large green space.

The explorers held their breaths and Ursula realised she was gripping her safety straps so tightly that her knuckles had gone white as the ground rushed up to meet them.

CHAPTER SEVENTEEN

'This is it,' Bertie said. 'Hold on to your hats.'

They still had two of their landing wheels, but they all felt the absence of the third as the rocket crashed down to the ground, groaning as it bounced and skidded through the field, flattening the flowers and rattling the explorers around in their seats before finally skidding to a stop. Ursula could smell engine fuel and see smoke outside the window, but at least they all appeared to be in one piece.

'Everyone OK?' Bertie asked, glancing back.

They assured her that they were and then Jai congratulated the fairy on her excellent piloting. 'That could have been much worse,' he said.

'Thanks,' Bertie replied. 'I'd always prefer not to crash-land but it just can't be helped sometimes. We should go and check on the animals and then we'd better look at what kind of damage has been done.'

They all hurried to the hold where they found

their various creatures none the worse for wear. Bertie pressed a button to release the exit ladder and then they all clambered down to take stock of the situation. Jewel padded out alongside Jai, and the jelly-legs tumbled out with them too. The rocket lay smoking in a field that looked absolutely gigantic to the explorers. Each blade of grass was as tall as they were, and the blue flowers towered above them.

'You might want to restore yourselves to full size,' Bertie suggested. 'You'll be less vulnerable that way, and I might need you to pick up the rocket in a bit. Could you make the jelly-legs big too? I'd hate for them to be mistaken for snails or something and get carried off by a bird.'

The explorers took out the fairy wands and did as she suggested. Ursula, for one, was most relieved to be back to her usual height, with the grass and flowers small and underfoot once again. Bess had appeared beside Genie, waving her tentacles sadly at the damaged rocket. Jai transformed Jewel back to full size too, and it was a comfort to them all to have a big tiger there, even if she was a sugar-tooth. Max increased the size of the jelly-legs and the aliens frolicked happily at their feet, rolling around in the grass.

The valley itself was vast, even in their human size,

with the mountains towering over them and myriad rainbows criss-crossing the sky above. They could see some fluffy white rabbits grazing in a nearby field and also a couple of pretty deer. There was no sign of any vultures and the only sound was the rushing water from a nearby brook, along with some rather pleasant birdsong. It all seemed safe enough so far, but the fairy rocket was in a sorry state.

'This is bad,' Bertie said in a glum voice. 'Really bad. The hull is severely damaged and the third landing wheel has been completely ripped away.'

'Can we repair it?' Max asked.

'It would be simple enough if we were back at Stardust City, but I haven't got the tools or materials here,' Bertie said.

It was a severe blow, but there was nothing to be done about it. It looked as if they'd be travelling on foot the rest of the way.

'At least we managed to get here quickly,' Genie said, trying to find a positive in their situation. 'And we landed in one piece.'

'I'm really sorry about your rocket,' Jai said to Bertie. 'We'll make sure you get back home after this is over.'

For now, all they could do was fetch their possessions from the spacecraft and restore them to full size. Then

Jai carefully scooped up the rocket and put it in his bag for safekeeping.

'The sun will go down soon,' Jai said, 'so I guess we should find somewhere to camp for the night.'

It didn't appear they would have too much trouble with this, since everywhere they looked seemed perfect. It was even a fairly pleasant temperature in the Valley of Rainbows – unlike the roasting heat they expected to find in the surrounding area.

'We really did get very lucky with this place,' Genie said as they set out their things beside a little brook.

When Jai cautiously tasted the water he found it was clean and fresh and ideal for drinking. Max found firewood in a nearby copse of trees and the explorers soon made themselves a very comfortable little camp, with a fire crackling merrily. The sun blazed through the rainbows as it sank, causing great shimmers of brilliant, multicoloured lights to wash over them in waves. It was a spectacular sight.

The only thing that marred the experience for Ursula was that she was beginning to feel a real craving for the ocean and the dryness she'd noticed on her legs earlier was spreading, so it was an effort not to fidget and scratch. She really hoped this would be over quickly so she could be back in the water soon.

'Who would have thought we'd find something so lovely in the middle of such a horrible place?' Genie said. 'It just goes to show that good things can happen out of something bad.'

'I still don't trust it,' Max said.

Unlike the others, he hadn't lain back on the grass to watch the rainbow sunset but was sitting bolt upright, Ducky poised in his arms as if he expected to have to shoot stink-berries at something at any moment. The robot terrapin he'd made on board the ghost ship was perched on his shoulder too, in case laser-beam eyes were called for.

'I would have preferred not to crash my rocket,' Bertie admitted. The little fairy was perched on a spare piece of firewood, making a daisy chain. She'd removed her spacesuit and now wore a purple dress with a space-mole print. 'But this is a beautiful sight and I'm very glad to see it.'

After a short while, some of the wildlife they'd noticed earlier came over to the explorers and, to their delight, seemed remarkably tame. Before long, Ursula, Max and Jai all had rabbits snuggled contentedly in their laps, while Genie had befriended a beautiful long-legged fawn who curled up beside her. And the little deer wasn't an ordinary brown, but rainbow patterned.

The explorers noticed that a couple of the rabbits had the same colouring, and so did one or two trees in the distance.

'All right, this bunny is pretty cool,' Max admitted, finally putting his robots aside to pet the rabbit curled up in his lap. 'Maybe this place isn't so bad after all.'

The only problem they had was the jelly-legs. Bertie told them they came from a desert planet and had probably never seen grass before, which perhaps explained why they were so taken with the stuff. Either way, they spent so much time rolling around in it that their bare feet were tickled by the long blades, and soon they began hiccuping.

'Oh dear, we're going to have to stop them,' Bertie said. 'We don't want any more of those tap-dancing, brain-eating frogs to pop out.'

The explorers all agreed this was something they most certainly did not want, so Jai and Genie shifted the bunny rabbits from their laps and persuaded the jelly-legs to come for a cuddle instead.

In the next few minutes, the sun vanished beneath the horizon but the fire crackled cheerfully, providing them with plenty of light. And now they could see that the rainbows themselves had changed. The explorers had expected them to disappear from view as they were

swallowed up by the night sky, but instead their colours transformed into metallic silver and white and bronze and gold. They became shining night rainbows, which glowed with a shimmering light of their own, and the sight was every bit as lovely as the more colourful day-time version.

Bess materialised beside them and gazed up at the sky in wonder, her long tentacles sprawled out on the grass. The other animals didn't seem to care for the sight, though. The moment the sun set, the rabbits and the deer hurried away into the trees so quickly that the explorers were a little startled.

'It's like they know something we don't,' Max said, looking around suspiciously.

The valley seemed quite peaceful, however, with only a few bats swooping to and fro in the sky above them.

'We should get some sleep,' Jai finally said. 'We don't know when we might next be able to find shelter.'

The others agreed this was a good idea. Besides, what with all the drama and tension of the vulture attack and subsequent crash-landing of the rocket, Ursula suddenly felt as if she could hardly keep her eyes open. The grass looked soft and inviting, and she longed to curl up in it and get some rest.

'It all seems safe enough, but do you think someone should keep watch?' she asked. 'Just in case?'

No one seemed very enthusiastic about this idea and Ursula guessed they were all equally tired.

'Bess will keep an eye out for us,' Genie finally said. 'She'll wake me up if she sees anything suspicious.'

'Jewel will be on the lookout too,' Jai said, patting the tiger. 'I've noticed she's more active at night and she's got better hearing than any of us. If something doesn't sound right, I'm sure she'll let us know.'

Everyone was happy with this idea and Ursula was especially glad they'd gone to the Island of Sugar Trolls because it certainly made her feel safer in a strange place having a big sugar-tooth tiger stretched out alongside them. Bess looked fearsome enough but there wasn't much she'd be able to do against an actual threat.

So Jai threw another couple of logs on the fire to keep it burning and then they all settled down around it, using their cloaks as pillows. There was no sound except for the rushing water from the brook and the crackle and spit of the fire and it wasn't long before they all fell asleep. A short while later, however, they were woken by the ominous sound of Jewel growling. It wasn't a noise any of them had heard her make before, and it was enough to make the hairs on their arms stand on end.

'What has she seen?' Ursula asked, propping herself up groggily.

The other explorers were doing the same around her. The fire was still burning, so it couldn't have been very long since they'd fallen asleep.

'I don't know,' Jai replied.

The jelly-legs were both sleeping soundly, but the tiger was staring straight up into the night sky, and Bess was waving her tentacles in an agitated sort of way and looking up too.

'Bess says they can hear something,' Genie said.

'Probably just bats,' Bertie yawned.

But Ursula could sense that it was something more. 'The bats were there earlier and they didn't bother either of them then,' she pointed out.

'Did you hear that?' Max asked sharply. 'It sounds like ... buzzing.'

The others were suddenly aware of it too – a loud buzzing sound that seemed to be coming from directly above them.

'Have the bats started buzzing?' Genie asked, puzzled.

'I think the rainbows are doing it,' Bertie said, looking worried.

Ursula thought she was right. The noise was too loud for a couple of bats and it was getting louder all the time. Soon the ground itself began to tremble beneath them.

'I don't like this,' Jai said. 'Rainbows shouldn't buzz. Let's pack up our things.'

They hurriedly stuffed their possessions back into their bags and woke up the jelly-legs, who immediately rolled happily over in the grass and stuck their feet up in the air, expecting a tickle.

'Perhaps we should head into the forest?' Genie suggested, glancing towards the nearby copse.

'But we don't know what's in there either,' Max pointed out.

Ursula had to admit that in the silvery light of the night rainbows, the trees looked more sinister than they had before – tall and thin and brooding. Her grip tightened around her trident.

'The rabbits and deer ran in there,' Jai said. 'So perhaps they know it represents shelter at night. I think we ought to—'

But that was as far as he got before the rainbows above them exploded. Or at least that's what it seemed like. All of a sudden there were dozens and dozens of bugs bursting out from the glowing arches and buzzing angrily down towards the ground.

Chapter Eighteen

Ursula was dismayed to realise that the bugs were wasps – only they didn't have yellow and black stripes, but rainbow ones instead. They were still unmistakably wasps though, and no one wanted to find out what one of their stings was like. Jai and Max scooped up an alien each and then the explorers all ran for the safety of the treeline.

It was darker within the forest because the branches and leaves cut out some of the light from the rainbows, but the explorers could still just about see where they were going as they followed the winding path. They'd hoped to leave the rainbow wasps behind, but to their dismay a few of them flew down in pursuit and buzzed angrily along behind them, swooping towards their heads in a horribly determined sort of way.

Max pulled his robot terrapin from his pocket and pointed it over his shoulder towards the wasps. The robot's laser-beam eyes took out a few of them and the rest were soon confused by the low-hanging branches and left behind in the foliage. All except for one wasp who seemed completely fixated on Genie for some reason.

Perhaps it was attracted to her bright clothing, or the galaxy fairies waving around on her head boppers, but either way it seemed determined to reach her. Bess flew through the forest after them but of course was powerless to do anything about the wasp, which finally managed to catch up with Genie and land on her hair.

'Genie, watch out—' Max called.

He lifted his robot terrapin but then hesitated in case the laser beam should hit Genie instead. The next moment, the wasp had crawled to the back of Genie's neck and she gave a yelp of pain as it stung her. Max knocked it off with the robot terrapin and the impact seemed to daze the insect because it flew about in wonky circles, allowing the explorers enough time to escape. When they were finally a safe distance away and no more wasps seemed to be following, they all stopped to catch their breath and to gather round Genie in concern.

'I'm OK,' she said, rubbing her neck. 'It hurt, but only about the same as a normal wasp sting.'

'We'd better take a look anyway,' Ursula said.

Genie lifted up her hair and everyone gasped. For a horrible moment they thought there was another wasp there, but then they realised it was actually just the mark it had left. Ursula had been expecting inflamed red skin, but instead there was a small, neat print of a rainbow wasp on Genie's neck.

'What is it?' Genie asked, craning round as if she might be able to see for herself.

'It's left a really strange mark,' Bertie said.

'It's actually kind of cool,' Max said, peering at it. 'Like you've got a little rainbow wasp tattoo.'

'Are you sure you're OK, Genie?' Jai asked. 'The mark doesn't hurt?'

Genie passed her hand over it. 'No, it doesn't hurt. It itches a bit, though. Do you think it will come off?'

'Hopefully,' Jai replied. 'Our parents will be very cross if they think you've got a tattoo.'

He rubbed at it with his thumb but it remained firmly in place.

'I've always wanted a tattoo,' Max said. 'I'd get a robot shark, obviously. Or maybe a robot penguin.' He looked at Jai. 'I suppose you'd choose a blob of plankton?'

'I would never have a tattoo in the first place,' Jai said, looking horrified. 'They're not regulation. And besides, they're—'

'Never mind,' Max said, already losing interest and turning to Genie. 'Do you want to see the mark for yourself? We can use Ducky's reflective wing and a pocket mirror to show it to you.'

A moment later, Genie peered into the mirror. 'It's actually quite pretty,' she said. 'What a shame the rainbow wasps were so unpleasant. You would have thought something much nicer would have come out of a rainbow. Like rainbow hummingbirds or something.'

'Maybe if we were in another part of the world,' Max said. 'I told you there was something wrong with this place! The Valley of Rainbow Wasps doesn't have quite such a pleasant ring to it, does it? If only you'd all had the sense to listen to me.'

'Well, the Valleys of Fiendish Frogs and Poisonous Puddings don't exactly sound like a picnic either,' Jai snapped. 'These are the Terrible Valleys, so everything here is likely to be unfriendly. This isn't a part of the world that any of us would ever choose to explore. That's probably why Scarlett decided to hide here in the first place.'

'Well, it wasn't too bad in the end,' Genie pointed out. 'We've all faced worse than a wasp sting and lived to tell the tale. We can just spend the rest of the night here in the forest and then move on in the morning.'

For the first time, the explorers took a closer look at their surroundings. The trees were dark and still around them, the branches hung with some kind of plum-like fruit. A carpet of leaves and twigs rustled beneath their feet. It seemed like an ordinary forest, but they were experienced enough travellers to know that appearances could be deceiving.

'We shouldn't take it for granted that we're safe here,' Max insisted. 'The rainbows looked perfectly ordinary too, until angry wasps shot out of them. For all we know, these trees are about to start biting people, or the leaves on the ground might be hiding a bunch of fire ants, or the twigs might get up and try to—'

'Yes, yes, we get the idea,' Jai replied. 'We should all exercise great caution. I think we should be as quiet as possible and touch nothing, not even the fruit.'

He indicated the purple fruit hanging from the tree branches.

'Agreed,' Max said. 'Remember what happened to the Polar Bear explorers when they picked fruit on the Black Ice Bridge? It turned out not to be fruit at all, but screeching red devil squid babies.'

'That's definitely fruit,' Bertie said. 'I can smell it.'

'Even so,' Jai replied, 'best leave it alone. And we'll take watch in pairs for the rest of the night.'

Where they were seemed as good a place as any to stay, so the explorers made themselves comfortable once again, although they didn't unpack much this time. Everyone wanted to be able to move on quickly if necessary. Jai and Ursula took the first watch, accompanied by Jewel, while Max, Genie and Bertie lay down to try to sleep. Bess found the trees too crowded, so she'd faded away to wherever shadow animals went when they weren't with their whisperer, but the two jelly-legs snuggled down to sleep too.

Ursula and Jai sat back to back, keeping watch in opposite directions with Jewel stretched alongside them. Jai laid his harpoon gun beside his knee and Ursula was glad of her trident across her lap. Time passed and gradually they started to relax a little. The forest seemed quiet and peaceful enough. A bunny hopped by a couple of times but that was about it. Ursula found it difficult to keep from fidgeting, though. Her skin felt so dry and tight, like she'd spent too long in the sun, and her thoughts turned with longing to the cool blue of the ocean. She scratched at her arms a couple of times, causing flakes of skin to come off.

'Are you OK?' Jai finally asked.

'Yes, sorry.' Ursula put her hands in her lap and tried

to stop scratching. 'It's just ... this is the longest I've ever been out of the sea. The mermaid part of me is getting a bit desperate for the ocean.'

'How long can you be away from the sea before it makes you ill?' Jai asked, sounding concerned.

'I don't know,' Ursula admitted. 'Not long, though. I think it's already starting to affect me.'

She'd always had the ocean on her doorstep when she'd been living at the explorers' club, and they'd travelled by submarine on all their previous expeditions, so she'd been surrounded by the sea at all times and able to take frequent swims. It felt strange and horrible now to be so far away from it, and Ursula felt a flutter of panic in her stomach. She swallowed it down with an effort. There was nothing she could do about it right now.

Jai reached back to squeeze her shoulder. 'All this will be over soon,' he said. 'We'll rescue Stella and stop Scarlett, and then we can go back home.'

Ursula nodded. She hoped he was right, but the truth was that a difficult and uncertain path lay ahead and none of them could know how it would finish, or whether they would all be OK at the end of it.

A few hours later, Ursula and Jai swapped watch duty with Max, Genie and Bertie for the remainder of the night. While they'd been there, a few more rabbits had emerged from the forest and were hopping contentedly about nearby, which reassured the explorers. It had been safe when the rabbits and deer were with them before so they hoped their presence meant the same thing now.

Ursula's eyes itched with tiredness and she was grateful to lay her head down on her cloak, close her eyes and finally fall asleep. Her dreams were filled with the deep, endless blue of the ocean and the delicious cold feel of the waves on her tail as she played with her dolphin friend Minty. They were just making their way to visit the sea fairies when Ursula was ripped painfully from her dream by someone tugging her earlobe. She sat up, blinking in confusion as she rubbed the sleep from her eyes.

'Come quick!' Bertie said, still pulling at Ursula's ear. 'Something's wrong with Genie.'

Suddenly Ursula was wide awake. The forest was no longer as dark as it had been – the sky above was lightening to dawn and she guessed the sun would be up very soon. They had made it through the night. But when she looked over at Genie, she saw that Bertie was right. Her friend was hunched on the ground and Max was leaning over her in concern. Ursula shook Jai awake beside her and they both hurried over.

'What is it?' Jai asked, dropping to his sister's side. 'What's wrong?'

'I'm not sure,' Genie replied. 'I just feel a bit . . . strange.'

Bess hovered over her but the kraken didn't appear quite herself either. Her tentacles drooped sadly and she seemed more listless than usual.

'My neck is burning,' Genie said.

'Let's have a look.' Ursula moved Genie's hair aside and they saw that the little rainbow wasp was still there, but it was moving – rippling and shifting until it was no longer a wasp at all, but a girl made of rainbow colours.

The next moment Jai gave a cry of alarm. Beneath her fairy head boppers, Genie's hair rapidly started to change colour before their eyes. In a matter of moments it was as multicoloured as the wasp had been – and so was Bess. The great kraken looked astonishing with her tentacles all painted a different colour.

'Oh, it's stopped hurting,' Genie said, removing her hand from her neck. Then she saw the expressions on her friends' faces. 'What? Why are you all looking at me like that?'

'You've gone rainbow-coloured,' Ursula said. 'Like Bess.'

She pointed up at the kraken and Genie gasped at the strange sight. Bess seemed rather confused too because she kept raising her tentacles to wave them slowly in front of her eyes.

'Here, look.' Max held up Ducky so that Genie could see herself in his reflective wing.

'Do you feel all right?' Jai asked.

'Yes, fine,' Genie replied. 'You know, it's actually kind of pretty.'

She pressed her hand against the nearby tree to stand up, but to their astonishment, as soon as she touched the tree, it changed colour too. The brown bark and green leaves were replaced with shimmering rainbow colours. She gave a yelp of surprise and stumbled back into Max. When her hand brushed against him, the same thing happened again. Max's clothes, hair and skin all turned rainbow-coloured.

'Genie, stop moving!' Jai said. 'Just stay exactly where you are.'

She did as he said, looking horrified. 'Sorry, Max! It doesn't hurt or anything, does it?'

'What do you mean?' Max asked. Then he caught sight of himself in the robot duck and groaned. 'I really hope this isn't permanent. My sisters will think it's hilarious.'

'It must be a side effect of the rainbow wasp's sting,' Jai said. 'I guess that's why some of the trees we saw were rainbow-coloured. The rabbits and deer probably get stung sometimes and spread the colours too.'

'You look like one of the rainbow people,' Bertie remarked, peering up at Max.

'One of the what?' he asked, frowning.

'Oh, haven't you heard of them? They live in the rainbows, you know. We've come across them once or twice while flying our rockets. They're ever so lovely. Very serene and benevolent, and extraordinarily wise. Say, perhaps Genie's touch has turned you into an actual rainbow person? Can you spit out any pearls of wisdom? That's something the rainbow people often do. They open their mouths and an actual pearl drops out with a deep and meaningful truth written on it.'

'I don't think so,' Max said. He opened his mouth experimentally and they saw that even his tongue was now rainbow-coloured. 'I don't feel any wiser than normal – I just look ridiculous.'

'I'm so sorry,' Genie said again, looking downcast.

'It's not your fault,' Max replied. 'And it could have been a lot worse. To be honest, I would have expected a wasp to kill you dead with one sting in the Terrible

Valleys, so I guess we got off pretty lightly— Oh, for goodness' sake, now what?'

The sun had begun to rise as Max spoke and – to the explorers' dismay – this had an immediate effect on the nearby rabbits. They had been hopping around the forest floor quite contentedly up until then, but suddenly they all scarpered, running out of the forest with the same urgency that they'd run into it the night before.

'We'd better follow,' Ursula said. 'The rabbits warned us of the danger last time.'

The explorers hurried to gather up their things. At the same time the sun finally came all the way over the horizon and sunlight filtered in through the branches. Almost immediately, birds woke up above them and began to sing. They were pretty little creatures with fluffy blue feathers and bright, beady eyes. Nothing changed apart from that, and the explorers hoped they would be able to leave the forest without any problems.

'After all, it took a while for the rainbow wasps to appear after the sun went down,' Max pointed out. 'So even if there is anything unpleasant in the forest during the day, hopefully it won't appear straight away.'

The explorers were comforted by this possibility but they walked quickly even so. Nobody wanted to take any chances after the rainbow wasps. Max and Ursula carried a jelly-legs each and Jewel padded along beside them, while Bess drifted overhead, occasionally inspecting her rainbow tentacles in mild confusion.

They'd run deeper into the forest than they'd realised last night, and it took an uncomfortably long time to journey back through it, but finally the trees started to thin around them and they knew they were almost at the outskirts. Before they could reach the perimeter though, the birdsong around them began to change. It had been pretty and warbling, but all of a sudden it became staccato and angry instead.

'I've never heard birdsong like that before,' Genie said, looking worried.

'I wouldn't even call it singing,' Max replied. 'More like bird shouting.'

Realising this couldn't signal anything good, the explorers sped up. The edge of the forest was in sight when a little bird landed on a branch just ahead of them. It looked ordinary at first, with its fluffy blue plumage. But then it changed colour – its feathers turned an inky black with yellowy-white tips. And when it opened its mouth to sing, the same raucous squawk they'd just heard burst out. But that wasn't all.

A tiny lightning bolt shot from its beak too. It hit the ground at their feet, sizzling the dry leaves.

The next second, another bird landed on the branch, followed by another and another, until the trees around them were full of the creatures, all shrieking out that strange song and all shooting lightning bolts. They showered down around the explorers, so it was like being caught up in the middle of a giant storm cloud. Max fumbled to retrieve his robot terrapin, but a nearby bird must have thought it was food because it swooped down to snatch the tiny robot from his hand.

'Hey!' Max yelled at the bird. 'Bring that back! It's—'

He broke off with a yell as a lightning bolt landed at his feet, forcing him to jump back.

'Forget the terrapin,' Jai gasped. 'We need to get out of here.'

The explorers sprinted the remaining few paces to the edge of the trees, hoping that the birds wouldn't follow them. They very nearly made it. They'd just burst out of the treeline and could see the rolling green fields, beautiful rainbows and babbling brooks from yesterday, along with the smoking remnants of their campfire. They were running straight towards the campfire when the birds behind them gave a burst of their storm singing once again and a couple of lightning bolts shot beyond the treeline – one of which struck Jai squarely between the shoulder blades, sending him flying to the ground.

He landed with a grunt, but Max soon dragged him up again and then they all ran as fast as they could. When they reached the brook and no birds had followed them from the forest, they threw themselves down by the water's edge, gasping for breath.

'Are you OK?' Genie asked, gripping Jai's arm.

'I think so.'

His hair stood on end from the lightning strike, and he said that his skin tingled where it had struck him, but other than that he seemed fine.

'Perhaps we should take a look at your back,' Max said, clearly thinking of Genie's rainbow-wasp mark.

Jai removed his cloak and pulled up his shirt and, sure enough, there was a little bird mark printed right between his shoulders.

'You'd better not touch anyone,' Max said. 'I don't much fancy being turned into a rainbow-coloured lightning bolt. This day is bad enough as it is, what with losing my robot terrapin. I finally manage to create a robot with laser-beam eyes only for some stupid little bird to snatch it up.'

'Well, I don't think I can turn you into a lightning

bolt,' Jai said. 'Because you already touched me, remember? When you helped me up. So I guess it doesn't work like that. Maybe I won't be affected by the birds in any way?'

They all hoped that this was the case.

'We have to rename this place the Valley of Rainbow Wasps and Lightning Birds,' Max said. 'What next?' He looked around suspiciously. 'Do you think the rabbits are about to start spitting hailstones at us? I suppose the deer probably fart out blizzards and this babbling brook will stop babbling any second now and start screaming instead. Or, even worse, yodelling.'

'Hopefully not,' Jai replied. 'But we should move on as fast as we can.'

Pretty as it was, everyone had had more than enough of the Valley of Rainbows by then, so they decided to skip breakfast and head off straight away.

'What's the best way of travelling through this area going to be?' Ursula asked. 'From the sky it looked like there were two more valleys between this one and the Valley of Volcanoes. Are we going to have to climb up and down the mountains each time?'

'It'll take ages,' Max groaned. 'But I guess there's no alternative.'

Each of the valleys was surrounded by its own

mountain range, so in order to get from one place to the next, it looked like they would have no choice but to scale them.

'It's such a pain we can't use the ghost pearl. It would have been ideal,' Max said.

'Could we use the wands to turn back into fairies and fly up?' Genie asked.

'Perhaps, but you'd be at risk from the vultures then,' Bertie pointed out. 'I've seen several of them circling overhead and fairies are food to birds.'

'We'd have to leave the rocket behind too,' Jai said. 'As well as the animals since they don't have any wings. I wouldn't want to have them exposed like that, and anyway, we've got to take the dizard with us for when we find Stella.'

It seemed there was nothing for it but to climb the mountains.

The explorers set off and it took them a couple of hours to travel through the Valley of Rainbow Wasps and Lightning Birds. The mountains between the valleys were steep and forbidding with no obvious footpaths. Climbing them was going to be long, hard work, and Ursula was dismayed by how much time they would lose, to say nothing of how treacherous and difficult it was likely to be. They would certainly miss their rendezvous with the Polar Bear team and would just have to hope the other explorers would wait for them.

Suddenly, Jai began rubbing at his nose.

'What's up?' Genie asked.

'Nothing,' he said. 'I just really need to— ACHOO!'

He let out a sudden, ferocious sneeze. And to their astonishment a lightning bolt came out with it. It was just like the ones they'd seen shoot from the birds, only this one was much bigger and human-sized. It flew straight into the side of the mountain, cutting a jagged hole right through the rock.

'Hey, that almost took my hair off!' Max exclaimed. 'That's all we need – one of us shooting lightning bolts left, right and centre.'

'Sorry,' Jai said, sniffing. He reached for a handkerchief, but then thought better of it in case blowing his nose should have some other unforeseen and unfortunate consequence.

'Just watch where you point your sneezes,' Max grumbled.

'Actually, it might be a good thing,' Ursula said, peering at the mountain. 'That lightning bolt has made a tunnel in the rock. It's narrow, but I bet we'd be able to squeeze through.'

'What a stroke of luck!' Genie exclaimed. 'Walking through the mountain will be much faster and safer than trying to climb or fly over it.'

'I don't know,' Jai replied dubiously. 'The mountain range is big. I don't think the lightning bolt will have shot all the way to the other side.'

'Well, even if the lightning didn't blast all the way through, you can always sneeze again, can't you?' Max asked.

'Not on demand,' Jai protested.

'That's all right, we'll just tickle your nose with a feather or something,' Max said. 'Did anyone bring a feather?'

'We don't need a feather,' Ursula said. 'We have the trident.'

'Might it not be a bit unsafe shooting out lightning bolts in such a confined space?' Jai asked.

'Probably,' Ursula replied. 'But so is trying to climb a mountain with no equipment or turning into a fairy when there are vultures around.'

The explorers and Bertie talked it over a little longer before, finally, they decided that time was of the essence if they wanted to meet up with the Polar Bear explorers that afternoon. So they set off into the tunnel.

CHAPTER NINETEEN

It was strange walking through the inside of a mountain. The cold air smelled damp and they were all very aware of the vast amount of rock above them. Before too long, they reached a dead end where the lightning bolt tunnel had run out, and then it was necessary for Ursula to use the trident to carve out the next part. Fortunately, the trident was much more precise than a lightning sneeze – the bolt it fired cut straight into the mountain without too much shrapnel, although it suddenly seemed a less good idea now that they were actually inside the mountain.

Ursula couldn't help worrying that if they blasted too many holes through the mountain, they might destabilise it altogether and bring the whole thing crashing down on top of them. Polar Bear explorers lived with the constant threat of avalanches in the Icelands, but it wasn't a concern the Ocean Squid group were familiar with.

To make matters worse, Ursula could feel that deep thirst for the sea once again. It seemed to burn beneath her skin more intensely than ever inside the mountain – perhaps because it wasn't natural for a mermaid to be encased within so much stone and rock. The jelly-legs didn't particularly seem to care for the mountain either. After a little while, they startled the explorers by starting to glow in the dark.

'They do that when they're nervous,' Bertie explained. 'I don't think their home planet has any mountains on it.'

Max and Jai were currently carrying an alien each and they did their best to soothe them, but the jelly-legs continued to glow a luminous green. It had got very dark inside the tunnel once they left the entrance behind, so at least this helped the explorers to see where they were going. It was quite a soft light though, so Ursula spoke the magic words to make her trident glow as well. Jewel, too, was unhappy about the mountain and kept herself pressed close to Jai's side, the fur on the back of her neck standing slightly on end and her ears very straight and alert.

'I wonder if anyone's ever walked through the inside of a mountain before or whether we're the first?' Genie wondered as they continued along the dark tunnel.

'We're probably the first,' Max said. 'No one else would be so foolhardy.'

'It will make a fine addition to our flag report,' Jai said.

'Well, the inside of a mountain is exactly what I would have expected so far,' Max said. 'Rock, rock and more rock.'

He was right, of course. There was nothing above, below or around them except for the same slate-grey rock. It wasn't the most inspiring or interesting landscape, but Ursula considered it was probably for the best in the Terrible Valleys. Sometimes, boring was better. She was about to say as much to her friends when they reached another dead end and Ursula had to use the trident again.

As before, the lightning bolt shot straight into the wall of rock ahead of them, cutting a way through the stone, which smoked slightly in the aftermath. On the previous occasions there hadn't been any noise except for the initial blast, but now the mountain made a strange, rumbling sound.

It wasn't the most reassuring noise and to make things worse, the rock around them seemed to tremble slightly as well. Everyone froze. It was difficult not to picture the calamitous avalanches so often described in the flag reports of the Polar Bear Explorers' Club. Thankfully, the shuddering stopped after a minute or so, but the jelly-legs glowed brighter than ever.

'I knew this was a bad idea,' Jai said. 'I told you we should have climbed over the top.'

'Well, we must be almost through now,' Max said. 'So we might as well keep going.'

Part of Ursula thought they should turn back too, but then they would have wasted even more time as they'd still have to climb the mountain. Besides which, it was probably getting dark, and no one wanted to be in the valley when night fell and the rainbow wasps came out. So they continued on through the rocky tunnel. They walked quite a long way before they came to another dead end. Suddenly, the mountain seemed to shudder once again. The explorers could feel the vibrations of it coming up through their boots. But it only lasted a few seconds before it stopped.

'Must be an aftershock,' Max said. He looked at Ursula. 'I don't think we ought to linger here. You should hurry up and do your thing.'

Ursula felt nervous about using the trident again, but as they had no other option, she pointed it at the wall and concentrated her thoughts. A jagged lightning bolt cut its way through the rock once more, but this time the mountain didn't just shudder – it actually shook. It was so bad that the explorers lost their footing and tumbled to the ground. Not only that, but this time there was also a weird sound – a sort of groaning noise from deep underground. For a moment, Ursula was convinced the entire mountain was about to collapse on top of them. But finally it stopped and the explorers scrambled back to their feet.

'It's probably just the rock settling,' Max suggested, although he looked unsure.

Ursula shook her head. 'It came from below us,' she said. 'Not above.'

'Well, perhaps that's a good thing?' Genie suggested. 'It means the mountain isn't about to collapse.'

'Who knows what it means?' Jai replied. 'Let's just get out of here as fast as we can.'

They all followed him, quickening their pace down the tunnel. The jelly-legs weren't just glowing any more, but humming softly to themselves as well. They all hurried along in a tense, anxious group.

Twice more they reached dead ends, and Ursula's trident made the mountain shudder and rumble around them. The shaking seemed to get worse and the noise was louder each time. On the third occasion, something very strange happened. The mountain didn't just shake – it tipped. The explorers found themselves sprawled on the wall rather than the floor.

'What the heck?' Max gasped. 'Did we just knock the mountain over?'

Before anyone could reply, the stone shook about them and then the mountain seemed to right itself, so they found themselves on the floor again.

'This doesn't make any sense,' Jai gasped. 'Mountains don't fall over and then stand back up.'

Whatever was happening, they all felt it couldn't be good, so they hastily carried on until at last they reached the final wall in the rock. They could tell they'd reached the edge of the mountain because there were a couple of small holes which let in chinks of cold air and light and the smell of swamps. The explorers pushed against the wall, hoping that their weight might topple the final stones, but they were fixed firmly in place.

'There's nothing for it,' Max said.

Ursula took aim and set loose one final bolt. It blasted apart the last of the rocks and they were finally out the other side with a valley full of swamps and bogs stretching before them in the moonlight.

'We made it!' Max exclaimed.

He spoke a little too soon, however, because this

time the mountain didn't just give a rumbling noise – it actually roared. The explorers and the tiger ran from the tunnel, all fearing it was about to collapse on top of them. But the mountain didn't fall down, it went *up*. Before their eyes the mountain rose higher and higher into the sky, the moonlight shining through the perfect hole they had made. Not only that, but the mountain next to it started to rise as well and so did the next one and the next one. Sprawled on the ground, the explorers stared open-mouthed.

'That's not a mountain!' Max exclaimed. 'It's a—'

'Dinosaur!' Ursula gasped.

What they had taken for a ring of mountains was, in fact, a row of spikes on the back of a great, colossal creature. Its movement knocked some of the dust and gravel from its back in a shower of tiny stones and they realised it wasn't rock at all, but tough, leather-like scales. This was a beast of unimaginable size, with stubby legs, a rounded back, a flat head and a long, spiked tail. The explorers gaped in terrified awe as it stood up and shook itself, dust and stones raining down around them.

'Quick, let's find shelter!' Jai gasped. 'Before it can gobble us up.'

Ursula was about to point out that the dinosaur

looked like a type of stegosaurus, which was a vegetarian – but then its tail crashed down mere metres away, reminding them that even if it wasn't going to have them for dinner, it could still squash them flat. The impact felled a tree nearby, so the explorers snatched up their things and ran across to it. Once they'd scrambled over the other side of its trunk they peered back over the top.

'I can't believe we were shooting a hole through a dinosaur!' Genie groaned. 'No wonder it was shuddering. I hope we didn't hurt it too much.'

'The size that thing is, it probably just felt a bit like a fly tickling its nose,' Max said.

Ursula was worried the dinosaur might be pretty miffed about the whole thing even so, and that it would come charging straight towards them, but then the creature gave a big yawn – blasting out some stale-smelling dinosaur breath – before settling itself back down. The ground trembled around them as the mountains – or dinosaur spikes – slotted back into their old places where the creature had worn a groove deep beneath the earth. The explorers held their breath as the dinosaur huffed and snuffled a bit before it fell back to sleep, and everything was still and quiet once again.

'Right,' Jai finally said. 'I don't care what anyone says. The next time we come up against a mountain, we're climbing over it the old-fashioned way.'

They all felt that they'd had a lucky near miss, so everyone was in agreement about this. For now though, they had arrived in the next valley. It was time to see what the swamps and bogs held in store for them. And in this part of the world, it surely couldn't be anything good.

CHAPTER TWENTY

The sun shone brightly over the landscape, revealing a great stretch of swampland that reached all the way to what the explorers hoped was just a simple mountain range – and not another sleeping dinosaur – on the other side of the valley. Swamp trees grew up around the edges of the water, and sometimes out of the swamp itself, making it hard to see what lay ahead, but it looked as if most of the valley floor was flooded. The whole place smelled terrible, like rotting eggs. Glugs and bubbles came from the surface of the green water at regular intervals.

'I really hope those *are* swamps,' Max said. 'And not – I don't know – the snotty nostrils of giants who just happen to be lying down for a nap or something.'

The others shuddered.

'It's best not to speculate,' Jai said quickly. 'In fact, it's rule seventy-four in the captain's rule book.'

Ursula hoped Max was wrong, but their experience with the dinosaur mountain made her wary too.

'I don't suppose anyone thought to pack a blow-up boat?' Max said glumly. 'Or a collapsible canoe?'

'Afraid not,' Ursula replied.

'We'll have to find some other way of crossing the swamps,' Genie said. 'There's lots of trees here, which means there's fallen wood. We can make a raft. After all, we are Ocean Squid explorers, aren't we!'

Learning how to build a raft was part of all Ocean Squid Explorers' Club members' training. You never knew when you might find yourself shipwrecked on a desert island somewhere with no other way back home. Ursula and Genie might not have been official members of the club, but Jai and Max had both passed their raft-making tests with flying colours.

'It's doable,' Jai said with a sigh. 'It'll just take time, that's all.'

'Then we'd better make a start,' Ursula said.

She used her trident to carve pieces of wood from the fallen tree, and the explorers tied them together with vines. By lunchtime they had two rafts that would be able to carry their party, as well as sticks of wood they could use for oars. They all helped make them and it seemed that Genie's rainbow power was still very much in operation because her touch immediately turned both rafts multicoloured. Jai insisted on adding a flagpole to one of the rafts and attaching the Ocean Squid Explorers' Club flag, but was then a little worried that the second raft didn't have one too.

'What does it matter?' Max said. 'No one will know the difference but us.'

'It's regulation,' Jai replied. 'All expedition vessels, including rafts, are supposed to display an Ocean Squid Explorers' Club flag at all times.'

'We could cut the flag in half if that makes you feel any better?' Max suggested. 'One half for each raft.'

Jai looked faintly ill at the suggestion. 'Absolutely out of the question,' he said.

'Well, we could tie one of the jelly-legs to a flagpole instead?' Max suggested. 'They look a bit like jellyfish, don't they? Which is similar to a squid.'

Jai sighed. 'If you're not going to make any serious suggestions, would you please just stop talking?'

Max shrugged. 'I thought the jelly-legs idea was pretty good. I'll keep my pearls of wisdom to myself in future.'

'You don't have any pearls of wisdom,' Jai said in a tired voice, 'since you're not actually a rainbow person. I still can't get used to you looking like that, by the way.'

Ursula had to admit it was pretty strange to have Max, Genie and Bess all dazzling with vibrant colours.

It almost hurt to look at them in the direct sunlight, but soon enough they'd be in the gloom of the swamps.

To appease Jai, Ursula and Genie emptied out their bags to see if they might be able to fashion a homemade flag out of something, but it was no use. They'd only brought the essentials with them and there was nothing that could be turned into a flag.

'It just goes to show that you should always bring a spare flag with you on an expedition,' Jai said.

After the dangerous events of yesterday, they briefly discussed leaving the jelly-legs in the rocket in their shrunken form for their own safekeeping, but the little aliens were most put out about this idea and pressed themselves up against the windows in a beseeching sort of way until they were allowed back out.

Ursula was a little nervous when they pushed the first raft out on to the water, half fearing that it would sink as soon as one of them stepped on to it, but although it bobbed around a bit, it remained floating on the surface and soon they were all aboard. Ursula, Jai, Jewel and the dizard took the first raft, while Genie, Max, Bertie and the jelly-legs took the second. Bess seemed glad to be around water again and floated down into the swamp.

They quickly left the bright sunshine behind as

they sailed into the swamp itself. There were so many trees growing there that the branches cut out much of the sunlight, only allowing small amounts to shine through the foliage. The water around them was dark green, making it impossible to tell how deep it was or what might be lurking beneath. Max was convinced he saw an alligator at one point, but it turned out just to be a floating log.

'I bet there *are* alligators here, though,' he said. 'There must be all kinds of dreadful things lurking in these waters. Absolutely crawling with swamp monsters and swamp trolls, probably.'

'What did I say about speculating?' Jai sighed. 'Look, let's just try to get to the other side of the swamps, OK? In fact, we should probably try to proceed as quietly as possible. That way if there are any swamp monsters lurking about then they might not realise we're here.'

And so they glided silently along, leaving only faint ripples of water in their wake. Now that they'd stopped talking, they became more aware of the noises around them. It was teeming with life, and they could hear various birds, rats, frogs, insects and other creatures chirping and squeaking and croaking from the banks and branches of the trees. There seemed to be a lot of very noisy swamp owls who kept up a constant hooting and twit-twooing, as well as swamp crickets and even a rather moth-eaten-looking swamp duck that honked indignantly at the explorers as they glided past on their rafts. There were dozens of fireflies too, winking and blinking their bright golden lights in the shadowy gloom.

And there were clearly creatures in the water as well. The swamp was too murky to see much, but every now and then there would be a splash nearby, or they would catch a glimpse of a fin or a flipper before the creature vanished back beneath the surface. It was disconcerting to have no idea what they might be floating over, especially as they only had a flimsy raft between them and the swamp. Ursula suddenly very much missed the *Blowfish* with its armoured hull and harpoon cannons.

Still, the afternoon passed by as they moved peacefully through the swamps. It seemed that if they didn't disturb the swamp creatures, then the creatures didn't disturb them. Bess soon became bored with the journey and faded away back into the shadow world. Ursula wished she could skip this part too. She hoped they might get through the valley without incident when Bertie suddenly said, 'What's that noise?'

'What noise?' Ursula replied.

The galaxy fairy frowned. Her silver wings sparkled

in the greenish light that flickered through the trees. 'It sounded like . . . well, like a party whistle.'

'In the middle of a swamp?' Max looked incredulous. 'Seems a strange place to be having a party.'

'Swamp creatures will have birthdays too though, won't they?' Genie said.

'It was probably an owl,' Jai replied.

'Shall I take a look ahead?' Bertie offered.

'Probably best not,' Jai said. 'There's an awful lot of bird activity in the trees up there and I'd hate for you to get snapped up by something.'

And so the rafts proceeded slowly together for a few more minutes before Max suddenly said, 'I think I heard it too! A party whistle, I mean.'

The explorers paused their rowing to listen. And there it was – the *toot, toot* of a party whistle.

'Maybe it's just a funny kind of swamp frog?' Genie suggested. 'And its croak sounds a bit like a party whistle?' They all agreed that this was the most likely explanation.

Since much of the swamp was choked with plant life or else blocked by floating logs, the explorers didn't really have much choice about the route they took. It was simply a matter of navigating their way through the obstacles as best they could, so there wasn't much they could do to avoid the whistling sound. They got closer and closer to it as they went on, and it wasn't just one whistle any more either, but several, all happening in a little chorus.

'It sounds like the frogs – or whatever they are – might be just up ahead,' Jai said, glancing back at the other raft. 'So, everyone, keep your wits about you.'

The rafts glided around the corner . . . but it wasn't frogs that awaited them after all, it was a party. The branches of the swamp trees were tied with dozens and dozens of balloons, as well as streamers and bunting, all in the same swampy-green shade. A homemade sign read: *Happy Birthday, Milton!* And sitting on the banks, or perched on stones and logs in the water, were a whole load of swamp monsters.

Some were fat and some were thin but they were all about the size of an adult human – and they all had green skin, lots of fins, webbed fingers and bulging, fish-like eyes. And they all wore party hats and held party whistles the same shade of green as the balloons and bunting. They'd been hooting and tooting on their whistles enthusiastically, but one by one they fell silent as they noticed the explorers on their rafts.

There was an uncertain moment when everyone simply stared at each other, and Ursula really wasn't sure if she and her friends ought to feel afraid or not. After

all, swamp monsters were exactly the type of creature they'd dreaded meeting in the swamp, but it was hard to be too unnerved when the monsters in question seemed to be in the middle of having a birthday party.

Then one of the swamp monsters spoke. 'Rainbow people! Mum, are you kidding? All they can do is spit pearls of wisdom and who wants that for their birthday? This is the most rubbish entertainment ever. I *told* you I wanted a puppeteer.'

Ursula saw that this monster wore a sash that said *Birthday Boy* on it, along with a big badge that said *101 Years Young*. He also wore an extremely grumpy, almost mutinous expression.

'But there must be some mistake,' one of the other swamp monsters – presumably Milton's mother – said. 'I ordered a puppeteer. I know I did.' She frowned at Max. 'You there! Rainbow Person. What's the meaning of this? I booked the puppeteer weeks in advance. What does your agency mean by sending you instead? Everyone knows a rainbow person is the most boring kind of entertainer for a child's birthday party.'

'Child?' Max repeated. 'His badge says he's a hundred and one!'

'Look, son, I know you're disappointed, but if they haven't got any puppeteers then they haven't got any puppeteers,' another monster said, giving the monster mum a supportive pat on the shoulder. 'Besides, I think it might be rather fun.' He glanced up at Max and his tone abruptly changed from coaxing to commanding. 'Well, come on then, rainbow person, let's have a pearl of wisdom for the birthday boy.'

'How many times do I have to say it? I'm not a rainbow person,' Max snapped. 'I'm an explorer and a robot inventor, and entirely human.'

'You *look* just like a rainbow person,' the monster mum said suspiciously, to murmurs of agreement from the others.

'A rainbow person wouldn't be so bad-tempered though, surely?' suggested another. Their eyes turned on Genie. 'And I don't think a rainbow person would wear such a peculiar hat either. Is that a *mole*?'

'They really aren't rainbow people,' Jai said. 'It's ... well, actually, it's rather a long story involving rainbow wasps and—'

'I don't care!' the monster called Milton wailed. 'I don't *want* a rainbow person! I *hate* rainbow people and I hate wisdom. I want puppets!'

'Darling, I know!' The monster mum wrung her hands. 'And I really did try, but—'

'A-CHOO!'

Something must have irritated Jai's nose because suddenly he let out a sneeze – and it seemed that his lightning powers were still going strong, because a lightning bolt shot from his mouth, lighting up the clearing for a moment before it vanished into the water, causing the surface to smoke.

'Oh, and a lightning man too! How marvellous!' The monster dad seemed to be keeping his voice unnaturally bright as he turned his attention to Ursula. 'And what are you? A sleet maiden, perhaps? Or a hailstone damsel?'

'None of us are weather people,' Ursula said. 'But I—'

'I hate them!' Milton practically screeched. 'I *hate* them!'

The monster mum sighed. 'I really am sorry, darling. Look, we can always add them to the snack table. I'm sure they're all very tasty. Especially the rainbow people.'

To the explorers' dismay, Milton looked a little cheered by this. They weren't happy when they saw the snack table in question either, which seemed to have all kinds of horrible slimy things on it, as well as one or two whole dead rats and a squashed turtle that looked as if it had been left out in the sun for way too long.

'I was about to say that *I'm* a puppeteer!' Ursula said hastily as she dragged her puppets out from her bag. 'And these puppets are magical. Made by mermaids. You'll never have seen anything like them before.'

Milton looked as if he was teetering on the edge of whether or not this was acceptable, so Genie said, 'And I'm a party planner and decorator! How would you like your swamp and all your decorations and hats and things, to be rainbow-coloured?'

'I didn't know that a rainbow person could do that!' the monster mum said. 'But if you can then, yes, that would be lovely. Wouldn't it, Milton?'

'I suppose.'

The birthday monster was watching Genie with an air that was half interested anticipation and half doubt that she'd actually be able to do as she'd said. Praying that she still had the ability, Genie reached her hand out towards the nearest tree. It immediately transformed from a dull green and brown thing into a kaleidoscope of vibrant colours that extended to the balloons and bunting hanging from it too. The swamp monsters were absolutely delighted by this and gave loud cheers. Even Milton managed a small smile. A short while later, Genie had transformed every tree in this part of the swamp, as well as the water, the balloons and – to their great excitement – the monsters themselves.

Then they all gathered around Ursula's raft expectantly and she hastily put on an improvised puppet show with her mermaid, water horse and dolphin puppets. These puppets, of course, weren't controlled by their strings but by Ursula's singing. She was glad she'd put in so many hours of practice as she was now able to get the mermaid puppet to create flowers from the moss, while the dolphin performed a series of impressive water tricks and the water horse galloped across the surface of the swamp in a circle so fast that a great fountain of rainbow-coloured water erupted in an arc. When it came to the end, the swamp monsters applauded enthusiastically and even Milton seemed pleased.

'Thank you.' Ursula gathered up her puppets and gave a bow. 'Thank you. I'm really glad you enjoyed yourself, Milton, but now it's time for us to be going.'

'Going?' the monster mum looked startled.

'Afraid so,' Max said. 'We've got lots more parties to get to and plenty more birthday boys and girls to—'

'No, no, there must be some mistake,' the monster mum said. 'I paid for the platinum package.'

'And, er . . . what does that involve?' Jai asked with a hopeless look at Ursula.

They were all rather worried that they might be stuck performing puppet shows for half the night.

But then the swamp mum said, 'It means we eat the entertainer after the performance, of course.'

CHAPTER TWENTY-ONE

The explorers stared at the swamp mum. The other monsters were nodding enthusiastically and licking their lips in anticipation. One of them was even tying a napkin around his neck.

'We expected only one puppeteer, of course,' the monster mum went on. 'So the fact that there's four of you is a bonus.'

'No wonder the original puppeteer didn't turn up!' Max exclaimed. 'Look, none of us agreed to be eaten, so you can forget about that straight away.'

'Sorry,' the monster dad said, and weirdly he *did* sound almost apologetic. 'But you haven't much choice, I'm afraid. It's what Milton wants, you see.'

The monsters who'd been sitting on the banks slipped into the water, and they all began to advance towards them. Soon the explorers' rafts would be surrounded. Jai reached for his harpoon gun, Max already had Ducky in his arms, poised to shoot out stink-berries, and Jewel was baring her teeth at the monsters, but Ursula could see it was no use. Even if she joined in with her trident, they still had only three weapons and a sugar-tooth tiger to wield against more than twenty swamp monsters. It would just be a matter of time before one of them managed to reach the rafts and tip them all into the water. It seemed like they had only one potential way out of this, so she opened her mouth and started to sing.

There was an icy coldness in the melody that made the hairs on Ursula's arms stand on end and a chilly strangeness that made her head ache. She'd spent hours practising her persuasive singing on the puppets, of course, but the swamp monsters were alive with wills of their own, and there were loads of them. They were a lot more resistant than the sea goblins, and she had to concentrate all her attention on bending them to her will. It felt odd and wrong, and she didn't like the way the song felt inside her throat – like a bad taste in her mouth – but it was important that she kept going.

When her song first filled the air, the monsters looked confused, and then an unfocused, glazed look came over their faces and suddenly they weren't swimming towards the explorers any more, but changing direction. Golden, glittering musical notes filled the air as Ursula used her song to direct them back towards the bank, gently guiding them to curl up underneath the snack table and fall asleep. Milton himself was the last monster to go. It seemed his willpower must be the strongest out of the lot of them because he kept turning back around towards the explorers with a hungry look in his eye. But when the others were asleep, Ursula could focus all her energy on him and, at last, he gave a big yawn and swam to join the others. He crawled up on to the bank, climbed on top of the pile of snoozing swamp monsters, curled up into a ball and promptly fell asleep.

Ursula let the song trail away into nothing and an eerie silence filled the air around them as the last few golden notes shimmered away. She felt suddenly tired and was sure that more blue and purple must have appeared in her hair. The others were all looking at her, and Ursula worried she might see fear or disgust in their gazes, but they were only proud of her and pleased.

'It looks like all your hard work paid off,' Jai whispered, briefly gripping her shoulder. 'Well done.'

'I don't know how long it will last,' Ursula replied under her breath. 'We shouldn't linger here.'

She knew from the textbooks Mrs Parnacle had given her that mermaid magic could be powerful but was often fleeting. The sooner the explorers got away from the swamp, the better. So they picked up their oars and began to row past the monsters as silently as they could.

Jai started rubbing at his nose just then and the other explorers all shook their heads frantically at him. If he sneezed out a lightning bolt now, they'd really be done for. Fortunately, with a superhuman effort, he managed to keep the sneeze from erupting and soon they were out of the monsters' swamp and on to the next one.

They rowed as quickly as they could after that, as no one wanted to be pursued by irate – not to mention hungry – swamp monsters. The explorers heard them wake up just ten minutes after they'd left and there was a lot of angry bellowing, but to their relief they didn't attempt to pursue them. Perhaps they felt it was too much effort, especially as they couldn't be sure which direction the explorers had gone and they were better off cutting their losses and enjoying the dead rats and squashed turtle instead. Besides which, it seemed to Ursula that Milton was the kind of birthday boy who'd be determined to find something to ruin his birthday party anyway.

Shortly after leaving the monsters, Genie's hair returned to its normal colour, and the same happened to Bess and Max. The tattoo-like marks disappeared from both Jai and Genie's necks too. To their relief, it seemed that the changes wrought by the rainbow wasps and lightning birds weren't permanent after all.

They were just coming to the end of the swamps when the bracelet on Jai's wrist began to flash and beep. When he pressed the button, Shay Silverton Kipling's voice came over the other end, telling them that the Polar Bear team had reached the Terrible Valleys and were camping on the mountain range that ran between the Valley of Carnivorous Plants and the Valley of Volcanoes.

'We're almost there,' Jai said. 'But we've been a little waylaid.'

Briefly, he explained what had happened with the vultures and the crash-landing of the rocket.

'What kind of imbeciles would fly any kind of vehicle directly over a valley full of enraged vultures?' Ethan's voice came to them clearly through the bracelet.

'We didn't know they were enraged at the time,' Ursula replied defensively. 'And we didn't know they'd be able to fly up that high, or attack the rocket, or—'

'Sounds like there's an awful lot you didn't know,' Ethan sniffed.

'Sorry about him,' Shay said, coming back on the

line. 'Ignore him if you can. That's what we all do when he gets this way. Where are you now?'

'In a valley full of swamps and bogs,' Jai said. 'We're just coming to the end of it now, I think. The mountain is up ahead. It'll probably take us all night to climb it, but then I think the Valley of Carnivorous Plants is on the other side.'

'That's right,' Shay replied. 'You really don't want to be making your way through that place on foot, though. It's nasty, with all kinds of greedy, gobbling plants. We came up against a carnivorous cabbage in the Icelands once and barely lived to tell the tale.'

'Well, I don't think we have much choice,' Jai replied. 'It's the only way to reach the Valley of Volcanoes.'

'No, it isn't!' Shay said cheerfully. 'We'll send the magic carpets to give you a lift now. One of them might have to make two trips if you have a sugar-tooth tiger and a couple of jelly-legs with you, but it'll be safer than trying to walk through the valley and you won't have to climb the mountain either.'

'What kind of idiots bring a couple of aliens with them on an expedition?' Ethan whined in the background.

'Would you cut it out?' Shay said. 'You're being really rude and unhelpful right now.'

'It's only what we're all thinking,' Ethan insisted.

'I'm looking forward to meeting the tiger *and* the aliens,' Shay replied with a sigh. 'Are you guys still there? Or has Ethan's complaining driven you to end the call? I wouldn't judge you one bit if you've already hung up.'

'We're still here,' Jai replied. 'And a lift on your magic carpets would be amazing – thank you.'

Soon after that, the explorers piled off the rafts at the edge of the bank and made the rest of their way to the mountain on foot. Once there, they'd barely put their bags down before the four promised magic carpets arrived. Ursula had never seen a magic carpet up close before and she was entranced by their beautiful rich colours, along with the woven patterns depicting camels and genie lamps and jewelled scarabs. They all had tassels at the four corners too and the carpets waved these at the explorers in a friendly manner.

One by one, they climbed on to the carpets. Max and Ursula took a jelly-legs each, Bertie went with Genie, and Jai's carpet must have been extra strong because it was able to carry both him and Jewel. They rose up into the sky so fast that Ursula's hair lifted off her shoulders and she had to grab on to the front of the carpet to steady herself.

The swamps dropped away and then the carpets were sailing right over the mountain range, with Bess trailing along happily in their wake. Ursula looked across to her friends on their own carpets and grinned. This was exactly the kind of thing she'd dreamed about when she'd hoped to become an explorer one day. As soon as she saw the next valley, she was especially glad they weren't hiking through it on foot. It looked even more deadly than the swamp monsters and the rainbow wasps.

She could see a wide range of carnivorous plants down there, many of which were crawling about on their roots hunting for rabbits and other small prey. There were the carnivorous cabbages that Stella and her friends had come across, but there were also gigantic, greedy grapes, scoffing sweetcorn, peckish peas and what looked horribly like munching mangetout. Ursula shuddered. In that moment she was glad that the sugar troll's hamper consisted mainly of sweet things. She felt like she never wanted to look at another vegetable again.

The flying carpets made swift progress over the valley as the setting sun painted the sky orange around them. There was an unpleasant moment when a flock of vultures decided to take an interest in the flying carpets, but Max pointed Ducky at them and the stink-berries repelled them effectively enough. Finally, they reached the mountains on the other side of the valley. They looked exactly the same as the ones they'd travelled through before and Ursula very much hoped this really was a mountain range and not another slumbering dinosaur.

They flew right over the peaks and immediately had an excellent view of the valley beyond, the one they had travelled all this way to find – the Valley of Volcanoes. It sprawled in a red spectacle of fire and fumes. Some of the volcanoes were almost as tall as the mountain range itself, while others were no bigger than a tree. But they all bubbled and spat with molten lava, which sprayed out at intervals, smoking on the already scorched earth.

Ursula had worried it might be hard to locate where exactly Scarlett was hiding out with Stella. After all, there were dozens of volcanoes there. But in fact it was immediately obvious because there was only one volcano that was frozen solid. It stood in the centre of the valley – a pinnacle of ice that sparkled in the sunset. It looked strangely beautiful, as if it was made from glass. Certainly that must be where Stella was, which meant it was where Scarlett was too.

Genie asked Bess to go back into the shadow world for now in case her presence gave them away. Then the magic carpets swooped down into a little mountain cave. It was so well camouflaged in the rock that Ursula didn't think she would have seen it at all, but it looked like it stretched back a long way as there was plenty of room inside for everyone.

The Polar Bear team were already there, gathered around a campfire. They all got to their feet when the Ocean Squid explorers arrived and Ursula recognised Shay, Beanie and Ethan at once. With them was Shay's shadow wolf Koa, as well as a man with chestnut hair and kindly eyes who she guessed must be Felix, Stella's father.

'Just in time,' Shay said with a smile. 'We were about to have dinner. And, man, are we glad to see you guys. If you're anything like us, you must be bone tired. Come in and sit down. We've got lots to catch up on.'

The explorers were very glad to gather around the campfire. After the previous night, it felt most welcome to be tucked away inside a proper shelter alongside friends and, best of all, with a goose that laid magical eggs. Felix had brought Dora, the bird they'd discovered in the Icelands.

'You just think of the food you would most like to

eat,' Shay said, as he pressed a golden egg into Ursula's hands, 'and you'll find it inside the egg.'

'And after the main course, the egg does the same thing for dessert,' Beanie told them. 'The jellybeans inside the egg are really, really good. I've found a couple of entirely new flavours that I've never had anywhere else.'

'And Beanie eats a *lot* of jellybeans,' Ethan said.

After so many meals from the sugar troll's hamper, the Ocean Squid explorers were especially glad to have their own egg each and to be able to request their personal favourite dinner. Ursula thought of the pizza that Yately made whenever he was in a good mood. To her delight, it appeared in the egg and tasted and looked just as it did at the club, even coming out starfish-shaped. Afterwards, she held her egg and concentrated on Yately's fudge octopuses and was thrilled to find that these came out exactly the same too. As they ate their meals, the explorers caught up on each other's expeditions.

'It sounds like you've been out of the loop for a while,' Shay said. 'What with travelling by ghost ship and all. So I'm guessing you haven't heard the bad news?'

The Ocean Squid explorers all went tense.

'We haven't had any radio communication with

anyone since we spoke to President Fogg at the Polar Bear Explorers' Club,' Jai said. 'And that was several weeks ago now. What's happened?'

'Scarlett's been busy,' Shay said grimly. 'The explorers' clubs have gone.'

Ursula was horrified. '*All* of them?' she exclaimed.

'Well, last we heard, the Sky Phoenix Club was managing to hold out because they were attacking any flying machines or sea gremlins that came by, but Scarlett might have found a way to trap them too by now. We've been out of touch with the outside world for a while as well.'

'She probably started with the clubs because she thought that they were the greatest threat to her,' Felix said. 'After what happened to the Ocean Squid Explorers' Club, the others finally realised the danger and agreed to send out teams of their own to try to find Scarlett.'

'They haven't come anywhere close, though,' Ethan said, curling his lip. 'They wouldn't listen to us about using Stella's bracelet to track her down. They said they didn't trust anything belonging to an ice princess. So they went charging off in all the wrong directions.'

'They spent too long with their preparations too,' Beanie said. 'Scarlett captured the Desert Jackal and the Polar Bear clubs before a single team had left.'

'A few Ocean Squid teams managed to set out before Scarlett captured the club again but they refused to travel overland and, last we heard, they're just circling round and round the ocean in their ships and submarines,' Shay said, 'looking in all the wrong places.'

'So far as we know,' Felix said quietly, 'we're the only explorers that are anywhere close to Scarlett and Stella.'

'And it's even worse than that,' Ethan said. 'Since capturing Stella, Scarlett hasn't wasted any time. She must have got her to make snow globes practically non-stop because she's already snatched up dozens of places from around the world, starting with the most beautiful. The Floating Island of Diamond Waterfalls, the Sapphire Desert, the Marzipan Islands, the Pinecone Mountains, Crystal Cove . . . The list goes on and on. And it'll be even bigger now too.'

'At this rate there'll be nothing left!' Jai exclaimed.

'Nothing except the inhospitable or dangerous places no one wants to go to anyway,' Shay replied grimly. 'Places like the Terrible Valleys and the Scorpion Desert and the Poison Tentacle Sea.'

'The world will become one big, dry gulch,' Ethan said mournfully. 'Full of zombie vultures and bogey-flicking trolls and not much else.'

Ursula was appalled. Of course she'd known that Scarlett's aim was to capture the places she deemed worthy of protection, but she'd never imagined the scale of her ambition, or just how ruthless she would be in stealing away so many places. Many times during this mission Ursula had looked forward to returning home and it was a shocking and frightening thing to realise that the world as she knew it was already gone.

'What about Mercadia?' she asked, thinking of her mother and the other mermaids there. 'Has Scarlett captured that?'

'We don't know for sure,' Felix said. 'But we've heard that Scarlett has a particular appreciation for mermaids, so it's certainly possible. I'm sorry.'

Ursula felt a cold chill of dread run through her. It was a deeply disturbing thing not knowing whether her mother was safe or not, and she hated that she had no way to contact her to find out. It was all the more reason to stop Scarlett once and for all. In a subdued mood, the explorers proceeded to fill each other in on their expeditions. Like the Ocean Squid team, the Polar Bear explorers had faced some perilous situations and dangerous moments, although Ethan maintained that nothing they'd done had been as foolhardy as blasting their way through a dinosaur spike.

'We could be sitting inside a dinosaur spike right now, for all we know,' Ursula pointed out. She looked at the fire and said, 'Perhaps we should put it out? The heat might annoy it?'

'I think it will be all right,' Felix said. 'In fact, the dinosaur might even quite like it. They're partial to heat. That's why we keep our pygmy dinosaurs in the orangery back at home. It's the warmest room in the house, you see, and they love to bask.'

Once they'd finished their meal, the explorers discussed their next plans.

'I guess you saw the frozen volcano when you flew over?' Shay said. 'It seems a safe bet to think that Stella must be in there somewhere.' A look of worry passed over his face. 'I only hope Scarlett is treating her well.'

'The kidnapped children of the inventors seemed OK,' Jai said. 'I mean, they were locked in a cell, but Scarlett wasn't deliberately cruel to them.'

'And my sister Jada said they were allowed out for exercise and to use the bathroom,' Max added.

'It's different this time,' Felix said quietly. 'Scarlett probably viewed those children as innocent bystanders. She was only using them to get the inventors to do what she wanted, after all. But she seems to feel personally let down by Stella. As an ice princess, she expected

Stella to be on her side and I think it irked her that she wasn't. We can't know what life has been like for Stella this past month. I hope we find her not too changed, but captivity can be a heavy weight to bear.'

Ursula could hear the concern in his voice. There was also, for a moment, such an expression of torment in his eyes that it was almost painful to look at him. Like most fairies, Bertie had taken an immediate shine to Felix, and she patted him on the knee sympathetically.

'We have a dizard,' Ursula said, eager to try to cheer him up. She reached into her bag and dug out the sock where the little reptile still snored softly in the toe. 'He should come in handy for rescuing Stella.'

Felix looked faintly puzzled. 'Dizards make for very placid pets from what I hear. Much less trouble than a polar bear, I'm sure. They're possibly a bit too lazy to involve themselves much in a rescue mission, though. They sleep almost all the time, from what I understand.'

'A sleeping lizard inside a yucky old sock,' Ethan said with a curl of his lip. 'What an excellent plan. How fortunate for us that you came along.'

'I'm not sure I'd call it an *excellent* plan,' Beanie said. He glanced at the Ocean Squid explorers and hastily added, 'Not that it wasn't very kind of you to try to come up with a plan, of course.'

Ursula quickly explained about the fire wizard they'd met at the mermaid academy and how he'd stolen a mermaid's voice to create the magic cuffs that currently bound Stella.

'We need to break the handcuffs to free her from their influence,' she said. 'And the fire wizard said that they're practically indestructible. The only thing in the world that will damage them is a bite from a dizard. So he lent us his own pet to do it – her name is Pog, by the way.'

'This is excellent,' Felix said. 'And it's most welcome to get some encouraging news at last. Well done, indeed.'

'That's all very fine,' Ethan said, 'but how exactly are we going to get to Stella? We're assuming she's inside that frozen volcano and the compass charm points in that direction, but does anyone have any idea what a frozen volcano actually *is*? I mean, could they really be living inside it, or are they in the ground underneath, or what?'

'There's no way to know for sure,' Shay said. 'I guess we'll just have to find out ourselves. Which means getting to the volcano, and in as stealthy a manner as possible. We can't know whether Scarlett has posted any lookouts and we don't want to be spotted before we arrive.'

'That might happen soon anyway,' Jai said, pulling out the pickled parrot charm.

'Oh yuck, don't tell me this is some other bizarre pet you've brought along!' Ethan exclaimed.

Ursula rolled her eyes. 'Hardly,' she said. 'It's clearly been dead a long time. It's the charm that's been protecting us from the Pacificans' psychic gaze. It's worked up until now, but there's only one silver feather left. Once it turns green, there'll be nothing to prevent the Pacificans from seeing where we are and telling Scarlett.'

'You mentioned that you'd performed a cloaking spell to prevent her from finding your team,' Jai said, looking at Ethan. 'Could you include us in that?'

Ethan looked irritated. 'That's the trouble with being a magician,' he said. 'Everyone always expects you to solve all their problems for them.'

'That's a bit of an exaggeration, Prawn,' Shay said with a sigh. 'Can you do it or not?'

'No,' Ethan snapped. 'I can't always simply summon up magical solutions out of my hat, you know.'

Beanie frowned. 'You're not wearing a hat,' he said.

'It's a figure of speech,' Ethan replied. 'The point is that this particular spell required rather a lot of meticulous preparation and careful execution, to say nothing of the fact that I require a magician's kitchen which, in case you haven't noticed, is back at home.'

The Ocean Squid explorers all felt rather despondent at this. The parrot could lose its final charmed feather at any moment, and if that happened then they might have endangered the entire rescue mission by coming – a fact that Ethan was keen to point out.

'As soon as Scarlett knows you're here, we've lost the element of surprise,' he said. 'You ought to have stayed away.'

'We haven't lost the last feather yet—' Genie began, but even as she spoke the final feather turned green and everyone fell into dismayed silence.

CHAPTER TWENTY-TWO

'Well, that's torn it,' Ethan said bitterly, scowling at the pickled parrot.

'What's done is done,' Felix said in a mild tone. 'Scarlett would soon have discovered our presence here, one way or another. And the addition of the dizard could be invaluable.'

'For all we know, Scarlett isn't even actively looking for us any more,' Genie pointed out. 'If she expects it not to work then it would be wasted time and effort to have the Pacificans concentrating on us.'

There wasn't much they could do about it either way. But all the same, though it was getting late, Jai wondered whether they should set off towards the volcano straight away, rather than wait for morning as they had first planned.

Shay shook his head and indicated the magic carpets, which had rolled themselves up tightly in the corner. 'The carpets won't fly at night,' he said. 'We've tried to persuade them to before, but it's a no-go. They won't take us anywhere until the sun comes up, and it's too dangerous trying to pick our way down the mountain in the dark. We're all tired too. I say we stick to the plan – try to get a good night's sleep and then set off first thing in the morning.'

It seemed they had little choice in the matter. So, reluctantly, they used their cloaks as pillows and settled themselves down around the fire. Shay had been right about them all being tired and silence fell in the cave.

Yet though Ursula's eyes itched with fatigue, she couldn't manage to nod off. Her longing for the sea was almost like a physical thirst now, except that it affected her entire body. She kept thinking she could hear waves crashing around the inside of the cave, like the ghostly echo inside a seashell. Her skin itched and flaked horribly as well. Plus, she was worried about what lay ahead for them all. While they'd been travelling here, it had been easier to put it out of her mind, to box it up as something to be concerned about later. But now they were here, the Collector was a threat that could no longer be avoided and finally needed to be faced.

Snuggled up beside Jai, Jewel must have been having a nice dream because she was purring loudly in her sleep. Ursula could tell by the deep breathing and occasional snoring that the rest of her companions had fallen asleep too. All except for one – it seemed that Felix was still awake. He'd taken himself over to the cave mouth and was settled in the entrance with the two jelly-legs sprawled on his lap, absent-mindedly tickling them as he gazed out at the Valley of Volcanoes spread below.

Ursula could see a burst of the glowing purple flowers floating up towards the cave ceiling, like a shower of confetti, and it occurred to her then that in all the excitement of reuniting and discussing the Collector and Stella's rescue, it was possible that no one had warned the Polar Bear team about the jelly-legs and what could happen if you tickled them too much. No one was likely to want a bear on the rampage inside the cave – Ethan would never let them hear the end of it – and Ursula couldn't sleep anyway, so she went over to tell Felix how it worked.

'A bear? Really?' he exclaimed when she'd finished. 'Good lord. What extraordinary creatures. Well, I've been tickling them for about five minutes already, I think, so I suppose I'd best stop. Sorry, old fellows.'

The jelly-legs were still squirming happily in his lap with their feet stuck hopefully up in the air. Felix couldn't resist one last tickle, but it seemed that Ursula had warned him only just in time because the hiccups had changed already. One of the aliens produced the usual purple flowers, but the other one hiccuped out a bag of striped humbugs.

'Ah, my favourite!' Felix picked up the bag. 'Are they safe to eat, do you suppose?'

'I think so.' Ursula glanced back at the sleeping galaxy fairy. 'Bertie said something about eating some grapes that they hiccuped up once. I guess they disappear from your stomach after a while, but there's nothing to stop you enjoying the taste of them.'

'In that case, would you care for one?' Felix held the bag out to her and Ursula accepted a sweet before sitting down on the other side of the cave entrance.

The view from there was nothing short of spectacular, with the valley glowing blood-red below them, the air filled with the scent of lava and ash. The ice volcano looked even more beautiful in the dark too.

'I take it you can't sleep either?' Felix said, helping himself to a humbug.

Ursula shook her head. 'I've been trying,' she said. 'But there's too much going on inside my head.'

'I understand,' Felix replied. 'There is much to be concerned about right now.'

'If only there was no such thing as the Phantom Atlas Society,' Ursula said with sudden feeling. 'Then

Stella would be safe and we could be on an exploring expedition rather than a rescue mission.'

As she spoke, she heard Genie's voice inside her head pointing out that if it weren't for Scarlett, the two girls wouldn't be part of the Ocean Squid team at all. It was a strange and uncomfortable thought for Ursula to realise that all the adventures she'd been on since leaving the club, and the wonderful friendships she'd made, would never have happened if it hadn't been for the Collector.

Perhaps Felix's mind was going in a similar direction because he said, 'The problem is, Scarlett is not entirely wrong. In fact, much of what she says is correct. People *have* done untold damage to the world, and explorers must take their share of the responsibility for that. For too many years we have gone blundering into places with no respect for the land, or people, or creatures that we found there. We've taken whatever we liked with no thought for the consequences. Our clubs are all lined with slaughtered, stuffed animals, stolen plant specimens and pilfered artefacts. There is not much that can be done about the animals now, but the remainder ought to be returned to their rightful places.'

He sighed. 'I have been thinking as much for years, but thinking something and actually taking action are two very different things. It is hard, sometimes, to know where to draw the line. To know when it's best to attempt to change something from the inside, or else abandon it altogether and start anew elsewhere. The Polar Bear Explorers' Club has been my entire life, to the detriment of anything else a lot of the time, but there is much that is wrong with it. Sometimes it requires someone determined enough and committed enough, like Scarlett, to come along and shake things up.'

Ursula was shocked to hear Felix talk about the Collector like this. 'You almost sound as if you admire her,' she said, a faintly accusing tone in her voice.

'I suppose I do in some ways,' Felix replied. 'I admire her a little, and I am scared of what she might do, and furious about what she has already done, all at the same time. She had a very strange upbringing, by all accounts, with only a cruel father for companionship and nobody else's ideas or opinions to counteract his. It is very easy for us to sit in judgement on her, but who knows what any of us may have turned out like in such circumstances. Humans are nurtured by love and attention, just as plants are nurtured by sunlight and soil. Everything that is in any way good about me comes from the love and care and many kindnesses bestowed upon me by those I hold dear.'

Ursula thought he must be right in this. Her own life

had been full of love and happiness for the brief time she'd lived with her parents on Peekaboo Island. And at the club she had been lucky to have Old Joe, with his affection for her, as well as Yately and the other staff who had shown her plenty of kindness. If she'd had no one but cold Mrs Soames, the years might have killed something inside Ursula as well. And Stella herself was testimony to this idea too, of course. Ice princesses were supposed to grow up into cruel snow queens, but Stella's heart had not frozen as normally happened because it had been too full of the warmth of her love for Felix.

'Don't get me wrong, though,' he went on now. 'I'm not saying that I agree with Scarlett. Far from it. She has crossed many lines of her own. Taking Stella by force, of course, as well as kidnapping those children, and stealing away people and places that had no wish to be taken. She has caused untold suffering and hardship.'

He glanced over at the sleeping explorers and his eyes lingered on Beanie. Ursula knew that the boy's father had been snatched away in one of Scarlett's snow globes while his team was exploring the Black Ice Bridge. Beanie and his friends had found and rescued him when they'd discovered the Collector, but of course many years had been lost – time that could not be returned – and it must have been an agony for Beanie and his mother all those years when his father had been missing and presumed dead.

'And this is where it becomes difficult,' Felix went on. 'In seeking to avoid one evil, we inadvertently commit another. I have been fortunate enough to go on expeditions since I was a small boy and I have almost lost count of the many spectacular and wonderful things I have been privileged to see and experience. The song of the blue-crested dodo on Jellyfoot Island, the incredible waterfalls in the water forests of Ollo, the purple and blue sunsets in the mountains of Thesp . . .' He counted them off on his fingers. 'The list goes on and on. Yet by far the greatest adventure I've ever had has been that of being a father to Stella.'

'You took her from the snow when she was a baby, didn't you?' Ursula said. Everyone was familiar with Stella's story by now, and there was something about it that had always seemed rather wonderful to Ursula. 'She's lucky you came along when you did.'

'Perhaps,' Felix replied, but he looked strangely troubled. 'My sister Agatha was most put out about it at the time. She told me in no uncertain terms that I wasn't qualified in any way to be a father, that I wouldn't have a clue what I was doing, and she was quite correct, of course. Many times I wondered whether I had done

Stella a disservice by bringing her home with me – and whether she might not have been better off placed into the care of an orphanage as Agatha insisted. Certainly I could see the sense in what she said. I even visited an orphanage once with the idea of perhaps taking Stella there, but it seemed such a soulless, unhappy place, and I simply couldn't bear to do it.'

'I'm sure Stella preferred to stay with you,' Ursula said. 'I'm not an orphan but I felt a bit like one sometimes growing up at the club. It can be very lonely. A home and a family is better.'

'I always thought so,' Felix replied. 'In fact, I always insisted upon it whenever Agatha broached the subject. But since Stella's been gone, I can't help but wonder if I acted badly after all. Maybe the true reason I didn't take her to that orphanage was because I already loved her and I wanted her for myself. Perhaps I was thinking of me rather than her. Exploring is a dangerous profession, as you well know yourself, Ursula. Had Stella gone to a normal family, she would probably never have ventured into the exploring world. She would not have been in danger untold times. She would not now be the prisoner of the Phantom Atlas Society. It never does to be too certain that you are the one in the right, and these days I find myself troubled more and more by the idea that

I have made all the wrong choices and travelled down all the wrong paths. If anyone is responsible for where Stella is now, it is me. Loving someone is the biggest adventure you can ever go on and so, of course, it carries with it the highest stakes. The biggest potential for both joy and heartache. My choices and actions are partially responsible for bringing us here to this moment, and I can't help feeling I've let Stella down, at least a little. Whatever it takes I must get her to safety, and I would gladly lay down my life in order to do that.'

Ursula suddenly gave a little shiver, although she wasn't actually cold. 'Don't talk like that,' she said. 'We'll get Stella back. And we'll stop Scarlett somehow. And we'll go back home – all of us.'

Felix gave her a small smile but there was a melancholy look in his expression that Ursula didn't like the look of. 'I hope you're right,' he said. 'Now we really ought to follow the others' example and try to get some sleep.'

Although she felt as wide awake as ever, Ursula knew they should at least attempt to rest, so they returned to the glowing remains of the fire and settled themselves down beside the others. This time, it turned out that even the hard floor couldn't keep her awake for long. Minutes after lying down she was sound asleep.

Chapter Twenty-Three

The sun woke the explorers bright and early the next morning as it streamed in through the entrance to their cave. There had been no sign of Scarlett during the night, so if she knew where they were since the pickled parrot charm had worn off, she'd taken no action towards them yet. Ursula felt stiff and dusty and dirty, and longed for the soft beds and warm baths of the *Blowfish*. The explorers shared a quick breakfast before gathering up their things and preparing to leave the cave. The magic carpets wouldn't be able to take all of them at once, so they would have to make several trips to get everyone down the mountain.

'Do you think we should split up?' Shay asked. 'Someone is more likely to spot us if all eight of us go together.'

'Not to mention a galaxy fairy, a pair of jelly-legs aliens, a sugar-tooth tiger, and a shadow wolf and kraken,' Ethan said, counting them off on his fingers.

'And a dizard,' Genie said, holding up the sock in which Pog was snoozing. She'd swapped her fairy head boppers for ones bearing the squids of the Ocean Squid Club, and they jiggled about happily whenever she moved.

'Perhaps some of us should stay behind?' Jai suggested. 'The animals and aliens, at least.'

None of the explorers wanted to be left behind, of course. And as for the animals, Shay and Genie said that their shadow companions could be asked to stay out of sight, but they wouldn't stray too far because it might be useful to have them help keep a lookout for danger. Pog, of course, had to go with them to help with the cuffs when they found Stella.

Bertie was keen to help but the jelly-legs were still determined to follow her wherever she went, and the fairy was worried that if they left them behind, the little aliens would attempt to slip and slide their way down the mountain on foot. So she reluctantly agreed to stay with them in the cave instead and to keep Jewel with her too.

'I'll keep an eye out from up here,' she offered. 'And if I see anything untoward then I'll . . . I don't know . . . send a signal or something.'

It was blisteringly hot. All the heat from the

volcanoes made the air sticky and humid, and it wasn't long before everyone was extremely uncomfortable. They travelled down the mountain in two groups and then it was agreed that the teams would split up and approach the ice volcano from opposite directions. After all, no one knew which way would be best and they could still communicate with each other using their galaxy fairy bracelets.

So they parted ways at the base of the mountain. Everyone felt an element of trepidation about that, as it somewhat went against the unofficial expedition code. They'd all read enough flag reports to know that bad things often happened when explorers split up. People were washed over the edge of waterfalls or fell into bear pits, or were devoured by ravenous alligators and so on.

But this was different. This wasn't simply an expedition into the unknown. It was a rescue mission into what they all knew for a fact would be dangerous territory, containing a deadly enemy, with stakes that were higher than they'd ever been before. And so the normal rules no longer applied and splitting up was the lesser of two evils. The Polar Bear team went one way and the Ocean Squid group walked the other.

Ursula was a little jealous of the other team's flying carpets, and the Ocean Squids briefly discussed using the fairy wands and wings so that they could fly too. But in the end they decided there was too much spitting lava, not to mention the vultures that were still circling the sky above; overall, it was probably safer to be their usual large size rather than to be able to fly.

Even so, travelling through the Valley of Volcanoes on foot was an unpleasant slog. The heat, the lava and the vultures made it a truly inhospitable place, and something about the smoke and ash made Ursula long even more for the cold blue waves of the ocean. She was getting quite worried about her skin by now, which was itching and flaking terribly.

They spent much of the morning trudging through the valley, dodging the falling blobs of molten lava and using Ducky to shoot stink-berries at any circling vultures that took too much of an interest in them.

'If only I still had my terrapin!' Max moaned. 'His laser-beam eyes would definitely come in handy around now.'

The explorers reached the ice volcano just after lunchtime. Jai switched the galaxy fairy bracelet on to silent mode, as they'd agreed with the Polar Bear explorers. Bertie had told them the light would still flash if one of them wanted to communicate but it wouldn't make any noise, which seemed the safest thing while they were sneaking into Scarlett's territory. Nobody wanted a beeping bracelet to give them away at just the wrong moment.

The volcano loomed above them in all its icy splendour, sparkling and glittering in the sunlight. Ursula felt a rush of dread as she looked at it. Stella had explained previously that she was able to use frost magic without it affecting her too much, but ice magic was different. It was cold and hard and pitiless and threatened to freeze her heart solid. Even the small amounts she'd performed on her expeditions had made her temporarily unfeeling and uncaring towards her friends. And this volcano was huge, so Stella had used a *lot* of ice magic.

Ursula recalled Felix's words about how they might find Stella changed from the person they knew, and she suddenly feared he might be right. If she'd used too much magic then the change might even be permanent and she'd now be like all the other villainous snow queens. They might already be too late, and after coming so far, it was a terrifying thought. But the only way to find out was to press on. And first they had to get inside the volcano.

Although the sides sloped up fairly steeply, the explorers would probably still have been able to climb up if it hadn't been frozen. As it was, the surface was far too icy and slippery for them to hope to scale it by foot.

'There's nothing for it,' Jai said. 'We'll have to use the fairy wings to reach the top.'

'Perhaps that's not a bad idea anyway,' Genie said. 'Once inside we'll be protected from the lava and vultures, and there'll be less chance of Scarlett spotting us if we're shrunk down to fairy size. She won't be expecting that, will she?'

The explorers were glad to have *something* on their side when it came to an element of surprise, as it had always seemed that Scarlett was one step ahead of them in the past.

'What about Pog?' Ursula said doubtfully. 'He's small but still quite heavy for a fairy. Will we be able to carry him between us?'

'Ducky can take him,' Max said. 'Here, hand him over.'

Genie passed over the little dizard, still snoozing happily inside his sock. Max lifted a flap on Ducky's metal side and adjusted a few settings to program him.

'There we are,' he said, passing over the sock for Ducky to clamp firmly in his beak.

Then the explorers rummaged in their bags for their wands and wings. One by one they shrank themselves down to fairy size. It felt very strange standing next to Ducky now that he towered over them like a giant, and even though Ursula knew Max had designed and programmed him, it was still a bit unnerving to be so close to a giant robot duck.

'He won't decide to eat us, will he?' she worried.

'Not a chance,' Max said. 'Just stay well out of the way if he decides to start shooting stink-berries.'

They all shuddered. Stink-berries were powerful and potent enough at the best of times. Nobody much fancied finding out what they might be like if they were practically the same size as they were.

'Everyone, keep your wits about you,' Jai said. 'Scarlett's bound to have put safety measures in place.'

If Ducky seemed gigantic, the volcano was monstrously huge to them in their fairy form, and Ursula felt a chill of fear touch her blood. Suddenly, she didn't want to go inside it and face whatever horrible thing they found there – she wanted to go home to the club, or off on a fun adventure with her friends instead. But of course there was no club to return to, and from the sound of it, a distinct lack of places in which to have adventures. If the explorers failed in their mission now, they wouldn't only have lost Stella, they'd also have lost their homes and their clubs and their entire way of life.

Seeing the trepidation on all their faces, and feeling the same thing himself, Jai said in an encouraging tone, 'We made it this far. And we've derailed Scarlett's plans before. We can do it again.'

Ursula hoped and prayed he was right. Either way, there was nothing left to do but try. So the explorers spread their wings and started to ascend the volcano. As Jai had predicted, the frozen surface was lined with booby traps. The explorers saw various pits, spring-loaded traps and even a nasty-looking giant catapult that would probably have hurled them all the way back to the Valley of Rainbow Wasps and Lightning Birds. But Scarlett clearly hadn't anticipated anyone trying to fly up the side of the mountain, or perhaps she'd been unable to design any traps that would work in mid-air. Either way, the explorers managed to travel all the way to the top of the volcano without any incident.

At last they landed on the rim and peered cautiously over the edge, unsure what exactly would lie before them. But a strange sight met their eyes. Sunlight poured in through the open top of the volcano, clearly illuminating everything. There were giant curving pillars of lava that looked as though they had been about to erupt from the volcano but had been frozen solid before they could do so.

And it turned out that Scarlett hadn't merely got Stella to freeze the volcano, she had made her transform it into something resembling an ice palace. There were steps carved into the lava pillars, and these were joined together by glittering ice bridges too. Archways of ice leading off into unseen frozen rooms sparkled around the massive circumference of the volcano. About halfway down they could see a solid floor of ice that glowed faintly red – presumably from the trapped lava still bubbling in the volcano beneath it.

There were decorative touches too. Statues of the globe that formed the Phantom Atlas Society's crest adorned the lava pillars, and elaborate ice chandeliers hung from beneath the bridges. It was beautiful, but it was cold and hard as well, and Ursula felt a fresh wave of despair at the sight. It had been bad enough when she'd thought Stella had simply frozen the volcano, but transforming the inside into a palace of ice was even more magic than they had anticipated – far more ice magic than Stella had ever dared risk before. Surely her heart would be frozen solid by now?

'I wonder if the Polar Bear team are already inside?' Genie whispered.

'Probably,' Max replied. 'They might have had to abandon the magic carpets, though. It looks like it would be quite tricky trying to navigate them through all the pillars and bridges.'

'I guess we should just head in and explore,' Jai said. 'As quietly as possible since we've no way of knowing who or what is inside.'

It was eerily quiet. Everything seemed too still and silent. The explorers were glad their fairy wings meant they could travel silently as they swooped down into the volcano. The archways to the rooms started right at the top, and the explorers flew through the first one to find out what was inside. Stella's ice magic had carved right through the rock to make windows, allowing plenty of natural light to flow in. The explorers found a small room that was lined with bookshelves, except instead of books it held enchanted snow globes. They lined every shelf, each containing some stolen place or species.

It was exactly the same in the other rooms at the top of the volcano. They were all storage for snow globes. The explorers longed to snatch them up from their shelves and thrust them into their bags, but in their fairy form, the globes were as big as they were. Even if they used their wands to shrink them, there were far too many here for them to carry.

The rooms got larger as they descended and,

after a while, some of them started to fulfil other purposes. There was one that was full of maps of the world, another that held a host of leather-bound atlases, and yet another that looked like some kind of architect's station for flying machines and submarines. Ursula knew that Scarlett had an interest in these things and that she specialised in creating exploration vehicles.

'Perhaps we should linger here for a moment?' Max suggested. 'There doesn't seem to be anyone around and I might be able to use the equipment to fix the fairy rocket.'

They all agreed it would be useful to have a functioning rocket in case they needed to make a quick getaway, so Jai handed it over. It had been inside his bag so it had shrunk again, along with everything else. Max spent some time repairing it while the others kept watch from the doorway.

'I can't tell for sure without Bertie here to test it, but I'm pretty certain I've repaired the wheel and patched up the fuel tank,' Max said when he joined the others a little while later.

Jai slipped the rocket back into his bag and they continued with their exploration. There were living rooms too, and grander spaces such as a music room full of gleaming instruments including a harpsichord made from ice. There was an art room with the most beautiful paintings and sculptures. And of course a library filled to the brim with rare and precious books. Ursula knew that Scarlett had managed to snatch her old headquarters up in a snow globe when she'd been forced to flee the Black Ice Bridge, and she guessed that many of these things came from there. The explorers fluttered silently from room to room, but there was no sign of people anywhere.

'Did you notice that everything's designed for two?' Max whispered to the others as they flew into a dining room. He nodded towards the table. 'There are only ever two chairs. I noticed it in the music room and the library.'

Ursula saw that he was right. The dining room here was long and formal, easily big enough to seat twenty people. Yet there were only two chairs positioned facing each other at either end. She had thought that the Pacificans might be staying here too, or else some of the sea gremlins or pirates, but perhaps it was only Scarlett and Stella. Or maybe they weren't here at all? Maybe they were somewhere else altogether and were just using the volcano to store the snow globes. But Ursula didn't believe Scarlett would go off and leave her precious collection unguarded. If the snow globes were here, then Scarlett must be close by.

The dining table was laid out with cutlery and crockery stamped with the Phantom Atlas Society crest, and portraits of previous Collectors as well as Scarlett Sauvage herself lined the walls. There were also a couple of extremely large bones on the floor by one of the chairs.

Jai pointed these out and said, 'Remember the hyenas at Pirate Island?'

When they'd found Scarlett there, she'd had two great beasts with her, apparently as pets. They were large, formidable animals long thought extinct, and Ursula wasn't cheered by the sight of the bones.

'Well, at least if the hyenas are here then Scarlett probably is too,' Max pointed out. 'And that's a good thing. Right?'

The cowardly part of Ursula almost wished Scarlett *wasn't* here, but she knew Max was correct.

'Well, come on,' Jai said. 'Let's see what's in the next room.'

The explorers flew back out to the ice pillars and chandeliers. Ursula guessed they were about halfway down the volcano by this point, and several bridges criss-crossed the gap between the ice pillars in the centre. Here, at last, they found signs of life. There was a person walking over one of the bridges just below them. A girl wearing a pale blue gown with snowflakes stitched all over it. She had long white hair tied back in a plait and wore a sparkling tiara. Ursula's breath caught in her throat. It was Stella herself! And she wasn't bound in chains in some dungeon as they had feared, but walking free on the bridge. She still wore one of the fire cuffs though, and this glowed brightly around her wrist. Ursula was just about to call down to her when someone else beat her to it.

'Stella!' Felix's voice cried from below.

It was the first time they'd heard anyone speak in anything above a whisper inside the volcano, and his voice echoed around the large space. At once, Stella froze halfway along the bridge. The explorers peered down and saw that the Polar Bear team were standing outside a room they'd apparently just vacated on the other side of the bridge. They were facing Stella directly, whereas the Ocean Squid team were positioned above her and so couldn't see her face. But Ursula knew at once that something was wrong. Stella wasn't greeting them or running towards them or showing any signs of happiness at all. Instead, she was as still as a statue and there was a strange, stretched moment of silence in which reality seemed to shift around them.

Then Stella took a deep breath, but it wasn't to speak to Felix or her friends. Instead, she raised her voice and called, clearly and calmly, 'Scarlett! There are intruders in the volcano!'

CHAPTER TWENTY-FOUR

Although Ursula had worried about this exact scenario ever since laying eyes on the frozen volcano, she still felt sick with horror as she realised that her fears had come true and Stella was now a cold-hearted ice princess who no longer wanted to be rescued. Scarlett appeared within moments, accompanied by her two monstrous hyenas. She looked very much as they'd seen her before, dressed in a simple long-sleeved white shirt and dark trousers tucked into tall boots. Her black hair was pulled into an untidy ponytail and she wore a necklace with a little red fish pendant that Ursula didn't remember seeing before. Scarlett's mouth curved into a cruel smile at the sight of the Polar Bear team.

'Well, well, well,' she said. 'We were wondering how long it might take you to get here, weren't we, Stella? Tell me, how did you manage to avoid all my traps outside? You didn't come by hot-air balloon – I would have spotted that on the horizon way in advance.'

Genie leaned in close to Ursula's ear. 'Perhaps Stella is just pretending?' she whispered. 'Scarlett must have been close by because she appeared really quickly.'

Ursula very much hoped it was the case but the ice princess didn't *look* like she was acting.

'They probably roped the Desert Jackal Club into giving them some magic carpets,' Stella said. There was no warmth in her voice as she gazed at them, and Ursula could only imagine how difficult that must be for the Polar Bear team, and for Felix in particular.

'Well, it doesn't really matter how you got here,' Scarlett said. 'I knew you'd be along at some point, trying to spoil everything as usual. And now that you finally *are* here, it's one less thing to worry about.'

'If you were expecting us, I would have thought you'd have scores of pirate guards lining the staircases,' Ethan said.

Scarlett's lip curled. 'Pirates don't want to come to the Terrible Valleys any more than anyone else does,' she said. 'Besides, they're uncouth, foul-tongued and bad-smelling. I don't need or want them. Same goes for the Pacificans. Good riddance.' Her eyes flicked to Stella. 'I've got the only partner I want right here. Thanks to her, I don't need to worry about intruders because I've got multiple impenetrable prison cells to put them in.'

'Here,' Stella said, drawing an empty snow globe from her pocket. 'I just finished this one.'

She threw it over to Scarlett, who caught it deftly and was just in the process of unscrewing the base when Ethan muttered some magic words beneath his breath and threw a spell at her. Ursula knew that Ethan had often got his spells wrong in the past, but she also knew that he'd been much more committed to practising recently and that his magic had improved a great deal as a result. Today was a good example of that because it looked like his spell was a perfectly formed magical net. It was heading straight towards Scarlett and looked large enough to capture both her and her hyenas. But Stella spoiled it. With no hesitation at all, she threw out her hand and froze the net so that it became brittle and shattered upon hitting the floor.

'Stella!' Ethan cried. He sounded aghast, so perhaps he'd hoped she was just pretending to go along with Scarlett too. 'That net would have put them all to sleep!'

Stella ignored him and addressed the Collector. 'I told you he was a magician,' she said. 'And the wolf whisperer has a boomerang, so hurry up with that snow globe.'

Scarlett didn't need telling twice. With the snow globe still in her hands, she spoke in a clear, strong voice, 'The Polar Bear intruders.'

Ursula and her friends watched, horrified, as the Polar Bear team were immediately swept up inside the snow globe, which Scarlett screwed closed with a click.

'Thanks,' she said with a smile at Stella. 'I don't much fancy going to sleep in an enchanted net.'

Stella shrugged. 'Perhaps now you'll finally believe where my true loyalties lie. You've seen that I no longer care about any of those people. I'd be quite content never to see any of them again.'

'You probably won't,' Scarlett returned. 'This is one snow globe I don't plan to open any time soon. Come on. Let's go and add it to our collection.'

Scarlett turned and headed off down the stairs, followed by Stella and the two hyenas. A few moments later they were lost from sight and a hushed quiet fell upon the ice volcano once again. The Ocean Squid team were left gazing at one another in horror.

'It looks like we came to rescue someone who doesn't want to be rescued,' Max said. 'What do we do? If we cross her path she'll turn us over to Scarlett or blast us with her ice magic.'

It was a dismaying prospect. Ordinarily, they'd have been thrilled to find Scarlett here alone without hordes of pirates to do her bidding, as it would mean they could outnumber her. But thanks to Stella, they'd already lost one adult and three children from their group. Now there were only the four of them left. Besides which, as Max had pointed out, Stella had ice magic she could wield at them if she chose.

'We've got my voice,' Ursula said. 'People aren't swamp monsters, so I don't know if I'm strong enough to deal with both of them at the same time, but if we could get Stella and Scarlett on their own ... perhaps I could influence them temporarily. It won't last long though, so whatever we do, we'll need to act quickly.'

'Maybe we could find some empty snow globes from somewhere?' Genie suggested. 'It sounds like there are plenty of them around. That way, all Ursula would need to do is to get Stella and Scarlett to hold still for a few moments while we trap them in the globes.'

'It won't work on Stella,' Jai pointed out. 'Remember what she wrote in her flag report for the Black Ice Bridge expedition? Ice princess magic creates those snow globes in the first place and she can use it to break out too. But it's not a bad idea for Scarlett and those hyenas. At least then we'd only have Stella to worry about. And if we managed to free the Polar Bear team and get Stella on her own then maybe we could ... I don't know ... get through to her somehow. Her friends have done it before, haven't they?'

Ursula wasn't too sure about that. She knew that Stella's friends *had* managed to melt her heart before, but from what she understood, that had been achieved after Stella had performed only a very small amount of ice magic. This was different. Still, with the lack of any better plan, they would just have to try and hope for the best.

'Come on then,' she said. 'It's a shame we don't have invisibility cloaks too, but hopefully, if we remain in our fairy form and stay close to the ceiling, they won't notice us until it's too late.'

The explorers spread their wings and continued to make their way down the ice volcano, following in the direction that Stella and Scarlett had gone. Most of the rooms they flew by were full of snow globes, but although they kept an eye out for ones containing the Ocean Squid Explorers' Club and the other clubs too, there was no sign of them anywhere. There were also several rooms that had shelves lined with empty snow globes, presumably waiting for places that hadn't been stolen yet.

'This is what we want, right?' Max said, flying over to one eagerly. 'You just unscrew the base, say the name of the thing you want to trap and that's that?'

It sounded easy enough, but now that the explorers

were looking up at the snow globes, they realised they had a problem. In their fairy form, the globes were just too big. Not only were they as big as them, but they had heavy lead bases too. The explorers wouldn't be able to carry one, even between them, so they left them where they were for now.

Finally, they reached the bottom level of the volcano. It seemed that Stella hadn't actually frozen the entire thing because they could see molten lava through the ice floor beneath them, glowing a fiery red as it bubbled and spat. It looked like it might come bursting up through the floor at any moment, so Ursula and the others hoped that Stella's ice magic was strong enough to contain it.

There were more living rooms on the ground level, including bedrooms, bathrooms and a kitchen. There was also a sitting room, and the explorers knew Stella and Scarlett must be in this because they could hear scratchy music from a gramophone spilling out of the open doorway, as well as the low murmur of their conversation. The explorers fluttered up to perch on a nearby chandelier and had a hurried talk about what they should do.

'One of us could go back to full size,' Max suggested. 'And just run into the room with a snow globe?'

Jai shook his head. 'You probably wouldn't have the chance to say Scarlett's name before the hyenas attacked you or Stella blasted her ice magic at you. And even if you did manage to trap the Collector, we'd still have alerted Stella to our presence. I think using Ursula's voice is a better idea. If Ursula can persuade Scarlett to walk up to the room where the empty snow globes are of her own free will, then one of us can be waiting to turn ourselves back to human size and trap her at the last moment.'

Ursula was worried about the plan. Her skin burned and itched and she could almost feel her mermaid magic draining away from her. It would have been much better if she'd only had to freeze Scarlett where she was for a moment. Persuading her to go all the way up the stairs to a different room was something else altogether – but it seemed they didn't have any choice.

So they agreed that Ursula would venture into the study, staying close to the ceiling in the hope that neither Stella nor Scarlett would look up and spot her. That way, Ursula would know as soon as Scarlett was alone and vulnerable to her singing.

Ursula said goodbye to the others, who were going to stay hidden on the chandelier, and then she spread her fairy wings and swooped silently and swiftly through the open doorway. She found herself in a room full of globes – not magical snow globes, but old-fashioned revolving ones showing the world in all its glory. A large fireplace took up one side of the wall, but rather than a fire burning in the grate, it showcased the leaping lava surging up behind a wall of ice. No heat could radiate through, and this room was just as cold as all the others, but it was a spectacular sight. Along with the globes, there were several bookcases and a couple of tall wing-backed chairs, in which Stella and Scarlett sat. The two hyenas gnawed on bones in front of the fireplace.

Ursula flew up to the top shelf of one of the bookcases. There were several busts of previous Collectors there, including Eli Sauvage, Scarlett's father. Even in the face of his bust, there was a great deal of cruelty in his expression and Ursula shuddered a little at the sight. Still, it was easily big enough to hide her from view, so she tucked herself behind the bust and listened to what Stella and Scarlett were saying. To her dismay, she realised they were discussing which place they should snatch up next. Scarlett thought Pittypat Island was best, whereas Stella seemed to favour Banana Island.

'There are a lot of very rare monkeys there,' Stella

pointed out. 'They seem prime candidates for one of our jungle rooms.'

'Yes, but Pittypat Island has the elusive moon flowers,' Scarlett replied.

'That's true,' Stella acknowledged. 'Perhaps both islands ought to be moved to the top of the list?'

They talked around it a little longer before Stella finally said in a casual tone, 'You know, if you'd finally trust me properly and treat me as the partner you profess me to be, then we could take the submarines from the Ocean Squid Explorers' Club and retrieve both islands at the same time.'

A guarded look came over Scarlett's face. 'Or we could just use the miniature subs,' she said. 'And then there's no need to involve the club at all.'

Stella shrugged. 'It's your choice,' she said. 'The mini subs are all right, but they don't have anything like the speed or strength of the club's submarines. Besides which, if I'm going to be travelling by submarine, I'd quite like an actual bed to sleep in, to say nothing of a bathroom and all the other conveniences there are on board. They even have a skating rink and an ice-cream parlour from what I understand.'

To Ursula's irritation, one of the hyenas found a particularly noisy part of his bone to chew on just then so she had to strain her ears to hear what was being said.

Scarlett laughed. 'Well,' she said. 'You are an ice princess. I suppose I can understand you wanting to travel in style. And you *did* help with those explorers today ...' She leaned forwards in her chair slightly. 'I so want to trust you, Stella, and for us to be partners. But ... I have had my trust betrayed before, you see.'

Her hand went to the little red fish pendant at her throat and she toyed with it in an absent-minded sort of way.

'I don't know how else I can prove myself to you,' Stella replied.

'Let me think about it,' Scarlett said. 'We'll discuss it again in the morning. In the meantime, you know that I haven't hidden the Polar Bear explorers. I'm well aware that the old you would have been desperate to rescue them.'

Ursula's ears pricked up at the mention of the Polar Bear team. The hyenas were still chewing noisily and she could only just make out what was being said, so she leaned forwards a little way. She'd thought she would still be hidden behind the Collector's bust, but she had forgotten about her wings. As she moved, one of them peeked out above the statue. It was only a wingtip and perhaps it wouldn't have mattered if they'd been ordinary fairy wings, but these were galaxy fairies and the wings sparkled with starlight. The glow from the molten lava in the fireplace caught them at just the wrong angle, making them flash. This startled Ursula and she stumbled.

She spread her wings to prevent herself from toppling over the edge of the shelf and – just for a moment – she could see around the corner of the bust to the room below. To her horror, Stella was looking straight up at the bookshelves. Perhaps she'd noticed the flash of light too. Either way, Ursula was sure Stella's pale blue eyes had been fixed directly on her for a second before she managed to scoot back behind the bust. Her heart was racing at a hundred miles an hour and she felt sick. Stella had seen her. She was sure of it. Any moment now she'd say something to Scarlett . . .

'Put the Polar Bear explorers wherever you want,' Stella said in a bored-sounding tone. 'It makes no difference to me. I *would* like to have my polar bear back at some point, though. It hardly seems fair that I'm denied my pet when you get to keep both these slobbering brutes beside you at all times.'

Ursula hardly dared to breathe. Had Stella missed her after all?

'We'll talk about it tomorrow,' Scarlett said again.

'Fine.' There was the scrape of a chair as Stella stood

up. 'I'm going to the kitchen for a snack before dinner. As long as that's OK with you, of course?'

'You know you don't need my permission,' Scarlett replied.

Ursula pressed her back up close to the books behind her, but Stella didn't glance towards the shelves even once as she walked out of the door. Perhaps the hyenas recognised the word 'kitchen' or 'snack' because they trotted after Stella eagerly, both drooling slightly. Ursula waited a few moments to be sure that Stella had really gone, all the while hoping that Scarlett would stay where she was. She longed to remain in safety on the bookshelf, but the kitchen wasn't too far away and she was worried that Stella might hear her singing from there.

And so, taking her courage in both hands, Ursula fluttered down to hide behind Scarlett's armchair. She knew that another chance like this might not come along again and that there was no time to hesitate. In this moment she was part fairy and part mermaid, and she could only hope and pray that the combination of the two would be enough to persuade Scarlett up the stairs.

Ursula took one final deep breath to steady herself. Then she focused her mind on the magical song she'd been practising for weeks, first on the puppets, and then more recently on the swamp monsters. She'd proved to herself she could do it. Now she just needed the magic to work one final time. She opened her mouth and let the song pour out.

Tiny golden notes immediately shimmered in the air around her and, to her delight, Scarlett stood up at once. Ursula continued to use her voice to guide her towards the door, fluttering close behind her the whole time. Hope started to rise in her chest. Perhaps this really would work! Perhaps she could get Scarlett up the stairs and safely put away in one of the snow globes. They would finally have done what no one else had managed to achieve, and lock up the Collector where she couldn't do any more damage.

But as they reached the doorway, something went wrong. Scarlett tried to glance over her shoulder, and it was such a sudden gesture that it took Ursula by surprise. She had to increase her concentration to force Scarlett to keep looking forward. But the Collector must have been aware that there was something behind her, exerting influence upon her somehow, and she kept trying to turn around. The magic seemed to slip slightly in Ursula's grasp as she struggled to keep hold of it. By concentrating extra hard she managed to get Scarlett to walk out of the room and towards the staircase.

Glancing up, Ursula saw that her friends were still waiting for her on the chandelier, and they all looked very excited to see Ursula and Scarlett surrounded by the tiny golden notes. They thought that the plan was working, but Scarlett's willpower was unlike anything Ursula had ever experienced before – far stronger than both the swamp monsters and the practice puppets. It was taking every last ounce of her strength to keep her moving forwards.

Perhaps it would have been all right if Ursula wasn't already feeling a little ill due to her withdrawal from the ocean, but as it was she could feel beads of sweat starting to form at her hairline. Her hands shook slightly and it was impossible to concentrate on her fairy wings at the same time, and so her flying became a little erratic too.

Her friends realised she was struggling and they hastily flew ahead to the snow-globe room in order to be ready the moment Scarlett walked through the door. The staircase seemed to go on and on, and Ursula could feel Scarlett mentally struggling against her more fiercely with every step. They were close, though! They'd almost reached the top of the stairs now and

Ursula could see the doorway to the snow-globe room straight ahead. There'd been no sign of Stella or the hyenas either. If she could just persuade Scarlett to walk a few more paces . . .

She got her all the way to the landing before the Collector finally managed to look over her shoulder. She saw Ursula fluttering behind her and a furious look came into her eyes. Ursula managed to force her forward another step, but she could feel she was losing her grip on the magic. Scarlett knew for a fact that she was being controlled now and fought against her with everything she had. With the last of her strength, Ursula managed to shove her through the doorway. The Collector stumbled slightly and then Ursula couldn't hold on to the magic spell any longer. It finally broke apart, the little golden notes collapsing into glittering specks.

Ursula half fell and half fluttered to the floor, landing with a thump that knocked all the air out of her. She propped herself up on her elbows in time to see that her friends had all returned themselves to human size. Genie held an empty snow globe in her hands and began to say Scarlett's name, only it didn't work. Before she could finish, Scarlett leaped at her with a cry of anger, knocking the globe from her hands and smashing it on the floor.

CHAPTER TWENTY-FIVE

The three explorers all threw themselves at Scarlett at once, trying to pin her down. Ursula shrugged out of her fairy wings and transformed herself back to full size. She desperately wanted to help her friends, but as soon as she tried to stand, her head spun and she staggered back down to the floor. Bess had materialised in the room too – or at least as much of her as would fit. Her tentacles flailed about in panic but she was as powerless to help as Ursula. To make it worse, Scarlett was yelling out for assistance at the top of her lungs and they all knew that Stella and the hyenas would be there in a matter of moments.

Ursula felt a wave of despair crash over her. They'd been so close, but not quite close enough, and now their one chance to catch Scarlett by surprise was slipping through their fingers. If only Ursula had been able to find some seawater to transform into a mermaid somewhere along the way she would have been at her full strength. But where was someone likely to find seawater in the middle of the Terrible Valleys?

'STELLA!' Scarlett roared again as she threw a punch that sent Max crashing to the ground.

Genie had snatched up another empty snow globe, but so had Scarlett and she beat her to it. The base came off in one practised twist and then Scarlett gasped, 'The entirely human explorers!'

Jai, Genie and Max were immediately sucked up into the magic globe. Ursula was left sprawled on the floor and could only watch in dismay as Scarlett screwed the lid on tightly and then slammed the globe down on a nearby shelf with an angry thud. Ursula could see her three friends trapped inside and she groaned. The door opened just then and Stella appeared, along with the two hyenas.

'You took your time!' Scarlett snapped. 'Didn't you hear me shouting?'

Stella quickly took in the scene, her eyes lingering on Ursula where she lay sprawled on the floor. 'What happened?' she asked.

Scarlett gestured at Bess's tentacles, still writhing unhappily.

'The Ocean Squid lot are here,' Scarlett said. 'This girl tried to use her mermaid singing on me.' She glared down at Ursula. 'You know, you don't look so good. I suppose you've eaten some poisonous berry or been bitten by a rabid duck-billed platypus, or some such thing. That's what explorers get for always poking their noses in where they don't belong.'

'Shall I grab a snow globe for her?' Stella asked.

'No,' Scarlett replied. 'Of all the explorers, this one might actually be useful to us.'

She walked over and, to Ursula's surprise, stuck out her hand. 'I don't think we've been properly introduced,' she said. 'I'm Scarlett Sauvage, the first female Collector of the Phantom Atlas Society.'

'I know who you are,' Ursula said, making no move to take her hand.

Scarlett let it fall to her side. 'Stella you know too, of course,' she said. 'I'll offer you the same chance I gave her. Why don't you join us? The world would think we were villains, of course – a Collector, an ice princess and a mermaid. But I daresay your voice will come in useful, especially when it comes to persuading people that what we are doing here is valuable and good.'

'But I *don't* think it's valuable and good,' Ursula replied. 'Stella wouldn't either if you hadn't managed to freeze her heart. And mermaid singing doesn't work like that anyway. I can persuade a person to do something they don't want to do, and that magic will hold for a few minutes, but that's all. I can't make somebody change their mind about something or go against their beliefs.'

'Well, that is a pity,' Scarlett said, her eyes suddenly hard. 'Because it means you're no use to me at all.'

She walked over to the shelf of snow globes and selected another one – only this one, Ursula noticed, wasn't empty, but full of turquoise-blue water.

'Isn't this remarkable?' Scarlett said, holding it up to the light. 'Stella filled some of the globes with seawater on the way here so that we might safely contain endangered sea creatures.' She gazed into the bright blue for a moment, before going on. 'Do you know, when I was a child, mermaids were always my favourite? My father was ... well, he was a cruel and difficult man, and I did not shed a tear for him when he finally died. It was a relief to be free of his tyranny, quite frankly. He would go out on his missions and leave me with nothing but tins of soup stacked high in the kitchen, along with a tin opener. When he returned home he always went straight to his study, hardly seeming to care whether I had survived without him or not. But he knew I loved mermaids, you see, and every now and then he would come home in a good mood, and on those occasions he brought me back a mermaid gift. A shell from one of their cities or a mermaid picture to hang on my wall. I always wanted one of his snow globes containing a real mermaid, but it was forbidden. Father said they weren't toys with which to decorate a child's playroom, and I suppose he was right about that. Yet still, how I longed for those snow globes in the mermaid room. I take a special delight nowadays in surrounding myself with mermaids wherever I can. You will make an excellent addition to my own personal collection.'

Ursula felt her heart sink as she realised Scarlett was going to trap her separately from her friends, doomed to spend goodness knows how long in her own little sea bubble. She thought about trying to use her magical singing once again to freeze Stella and Scarlett just long enough to escape, but she knew it was no use. If she hadn't been able to handle Scarlett alone then she definitely wouldn't be able to take on both of them. Part of her thought about begging to be imprisoned with her friends, yet the other part thirsted for the cool blue waves of the ocean she could glimpse within the snow globe.

Her mind raced, trying to find an escape route, or some daring, courageous plan that would save the other explorers. But time had run out and Scarlett was already unscrewing the base of the snow globe. The ocean inside must have been held in place with some kind of enchantment, since none spilled out on to the floor.

The next second, Scarlett looked right at Ursula and spoke her name loudly and clearly. 'Ursula Jellyfin.'

There was a rush of magic and then the room around Ursula vanished and an ocean seemed to spring up around her instead. She felt a wave of despair at her imprisonment, but at the same time, when the water flowed over her, it was like finally being able to breathe again after too long half-suffocating. Her legs immediately turned into a mermaid's tail, ripping through the fabric of her explorer trousers, which drifted free to settle on the sand below. Her burning skin felt soothed and cooled and it was the most delicious feeling. In that moment she was glad that Scarlett had singled her out to go into a prison of her own. She would worry about escaping and finding her friends, and all the things that had gone wrong later. For now, she could only revel in letting her mermaid-self free once again and the silkiness of the sea against her tail.

Ursula could feel herself rejuvenating by the second.

It seemed that she didn't need to be in the water for long before she felt better again, and after a few moments, she looked around and took proper stock of her surroundings. Of course Ursula had never been trapped within one of the enchanted snow globes herself, but she had read the accounts of those who had, including Stella's own flag report. She was therefore expecting not to be able to see the glass walls of the snow globe at all, but instead just a thick fog crowding in around her. But these ocean-containing snow globes must have been different because Ursula could see the glass walls. She could even swim right up to them and press her nose against the smooth surface.

She was able to see all the way through to the room beyond, stretching out beneath her from her place on the shelf. Scarlett and Stella were still there but she couldn't hear a word of what they were talking about. When Ursula looked up she saw the glass dome of the globe curving above her too, just a short distance above her head. The floor beneath her was covered in a thin layer of sand and a couple of shells, as well as a little bush with some sort of sea fruit growing on it. She was inside a space about the size of a room. The realisation made a panicky feeling rise up inside Ursula's chest. She was like a fish in a tank and mermaids were meant for the vast, open water. It felt very wrong having walls hemming her in and she swam from one side of the globe to the other, pressing her hands against the cold glass, looking for a way out. But there was none to be found. She was trapped.

There was another snow globe placed beside her own on the shelf, and this contained her explorer friends. She could see them walking around inside their own prison, and Ducky was flapping his wings in an agitated fashion. Bess had morosely stuck the tip of a tentacle through the glass towards them but was powerless to do anything else. Ursula waved to try to get the others' attention but they didn't seem to be aware of her, and she guessed they couldn't see out of the snow globe like she could.

The next moment, Ursula's globe rose up into the air and when she looked over her shoulder she realised that Scarlett had picked her up and was leaving the room. She felt another wave of panic crash over her, even stronger than the first. Where was Scarlett taking her? It was one thing to be separated from her friends when they were right next to each other, but this was a thousand times worse. Even if the others somehow managed to escape, they would have no idea where Ursula had gone . . .

But then the chances of them being able to escape were slim. After all, no one else was coming for them, and people and places had remained locked inside these snow globes with time frozen around them for hundreds of years. It made Ursula feel sick to think that she might be stuck inside this globe for years on end, not aging in any way, only to finally get out and find that her friends and family had died – her mother, Old Joe, Minty, all of them long since gone, along with the world she'd known. The only person who'd ever managed to escape one of the snow globes was Stella, and that was because ice princess magic was the thing that had created them in the first place.

In desperation, she hammered her fists against the glass, but of course it did no good and only made her hands hurt. Scarlett had walked back down the staircase now and Ursula watched as the Collector carried her into a little sitting room. Ursula guessed at once that this was Scarlett's own private space. It was small but comfortable, with a single armchair and a desk. The walls were hung with paintings and there was a shelf behind the desk with a row of snow globes on it, each containing a lone mermaid who looked as wretched and miserable as Ursula felt.

Scarlett put Ursula's globe down on this shelf and

then peered in at her. She was so big in comparison that she seemed like a giant and the red fish pendant on her necklace was as large as a person. Ursula felt the urge to recoil but glared at the Collector instead and slammed her fist against the glass once more.

'Let me OUT!' she shouted.

She knew that Scarlett wouldn't be able to hear her and that she wouldn't pay any attention if she could, but it was impossible not to say the words anyway. A cruel smile twisted the corner of Scarlett's mouth as she gazed in at her, but then she turned on her heel and walked out of the room without a backward glance.

Ursula looked across at the mermaids in the globes next to hers and saw that they were just swimming around in a listless sort of fashion. It reminded her of the fish she'd seen in too-small fishbowls, and she shuddered at the thought that this might be her life for the foreseeable future. She couldn't accept it. She wouldn't. There had to be a way out.

And yet ... She spent the whole afternoon trying all the magical mermaid songs she knew in case one of them might break the snow globe, but none of them did any good. At one point the mermaid in the globe next to hers caught her eye and shook her head, indicating that it was hopeless. Ursula kept trying anyway, but there were plenty of other adult mermaids trapped here, and if their singing could get them out then they would probably all be free by now. She thought again of Mercadia and her mother, and wondered whether the mermaid city might already be imprisoned in a snow globe somewhere too. Ursula's friends were trapped, the Polar Bear team were imprisoned too – nobody was coming to rescue them. Things seemed very bleak indeed.

Time passed and it grew late. There were no windows in this room so it was impossible for Ursula to get a real sense of the hour of day, but she knew it must be night when the mermaids around her started to curl up on the sandy floors of their globes and prepare for sleep. Ursula was tired too, but the thought of copying them horrified her. It would be like giving up, like admitting that she was a prisoner here the same as they were and that she wasn't getting out. So she continued to swim around her globe, looking for weak points in the glass even though she knew there were none.

A couple more hours passed and the other mermaids were all asleep when a shadow fell across the floor and someone entered the room. Ursula assumed it must be Scarlett, but when she looked up she saw that it was Stella. Only something wasn't quite right. The ice princess was moving stealthily, as if she didn't want to be discovered here. Her eyes went to the shelves and when she saw Ursula, a smile lit up her face. Then something even more surprising happened – Stella *waved* at Ursula!

Ursula narrowed her eyes suspiciously. Was this some kind of trick? And yet ... for the first time, Stella looked like the girl Ursula remembered – clever and fun and smart and loyal, and most importantly of all, warm-hearted. Ursula wanted to believe it really was Stella but she didn't dare get her hopes up. She simply watched as Stella reached up to take Ursula's snow globe from the shelf and then hurried out of the room with it. They followed the curve of the volcano wall a little way before Stella walked into another room, closing the door behind her. Ursula got a glimpse of a small bedroom and guessed it must belong to the ice princess.

The next second, Stella gazed into the globe and waved at Ursula once again, still grinning. Then she raised her finger to her lips and, to Ursula's astonishment, unscrewed the base of the snow globe. As before, the enchantment kept the ocean water inside, but Ursula herself toppled out, instantly transformed to her usual size. She fell to the floor, dripping wet and still in her mermaid form.

'Hello at last!' Stella said, beaming down at her, her face alight with pleasure. 'I'm SO pleased to see you! And I'm really sorry about ... well, before. I've got so much to tell you, but first of all, just know that I'm still your friend and I'm on your side and my heart isn't frozen.' Her smile got even bigger and a sparkle came into her blue eyes. 'And together we're going to rescue your friends and mine.'

CHAPTER TWENTY-SIX

Stella passed Ursula a towel to dry off her tail so she could get her legs back. She had a pair of spare trousers waiting for her too. As Ursula got changed, Stella explained that Scarlett was currently asleep but there was still no time to waste.

'She's a terrible insomniac,' Stella explained. 'She finds it extremely difficult to sleep for more than a few hours at a stretch, so we can't dilly-dally.'

Stella hurriedly told Ursula how she'd managed to keep her heart from freezing by using a charm to protect it.

'You build a little chamber of ice around the warm heart, you see,' Stella said. 'And that keeps it protected no matter how much ice magic you do. I found the spell in my *Book of Frost*, but I'd never used it until now because I was afraid it might not work and I thought it safer to avoid ice magic altogether. When Scarlett kidnapped me though, I no longer had a choice.

Anyway, it seems to have worked. Even when I froze this entire volcano, I never stopped caring about my friends and family. I never stopped being myself.'

'But you pretended to in order to fool Scarlett?' Ursula guessed.

'Exactly. I knew she'd never believe the old me would join her voluntarily, but there was a chance she might fall for it if she thought I'd become a traditional ice princess. I've been trying to earn her trust since then.'

'But why didn't you just freeze her solid the moment you were able to?' Ursula asked. 'And find some way to escape?'

'I thought about it a few times,' Stella admitted. 'It's been so lonely and miserable here, and such hard work pretending. I was constantly worried I'd slip up and say or do something that would give away my true self. I wanted nothing more than to escape back to the safety of home. Only I don't have one any more – my house was one of the first places Scarlett stole when I made her some new snow globes. My father wasn't inside at the time, obviously, but many of our household staff were, as well as my pets. Scarlett is quite happy to put most of the snow globes on display, but some of them she's hidden away and I don't know where they are. My house is one of the hidden snow globes, along with the ones containing the explorers' clubs. I've been hoping to gain her trust in order to find out where they are, so I could take them with me when I escaped. There's no way I was going to abandon our housekeeper Mrs Sap or the groom Mr Pash, and I *definitely* wasn't going to leave my polar bear Gruff behind, or my tiny T-Rex Buster, or any of the other little fairy dinosaurs. So far though, Scarlett hasn't trusted me enough to tell me where they are.'

'So that's why you turned the Polar Bear team in to Scarlett?' Ursula replied.

Stella nodded. 'I knew she was just in the next room so she was going to see them anyway. Even if we managed to overpower her together, she'd then know where my true loyalties lay and she might never tell us where the snow globes have been hidden. We'd lose the clubs and my home forever. But it's different now that you're here because your mermaid magic gives you the power of persuasion. I know where our friends are being held so I thought we'd go and let them out first, and then you could use your singing voice to get Scarlett to tell us where the other globes are.'

Stella looked carefully at Ursula. 'What do you think? Can you do it? It seems like you almost managed to get her into a snow globe earlier, but I guess she's very strong-willed?'

Ursula nodded and explained that she'd been weakened by being away from the sea for a few days. 'But the snow globe has actually made me feel a lot better,' she said. 'It restored the part of me that needs to be in the ocean and I'm feeling a lot stronger now. I should be able to influence Scarlett for long enough to tell us where the globes are, I think.'

The two girls looked at each other and shared a smile. Ursula's head swam with relief. Not only was she out of the snow globe, but Stella was on their side as well, and they would soon be reunited with the others. Things no longer looked quite as bleak as they had before.

'I know you must have loads of questions and I've only told you a tiny part of what I'd like to,' Stella said. 'But we'll have to catch up on all that later. For now, shall we go and find our friends?'

Ursula nodded. 'Absolutely.'

She couldn't wait to see the expressions on her friends' faces when they realised that Stella was still herself and working with them after all.

'I coaxed the hyenas into the kitchen with some bones and shut them in,' Stella explained. 'So they shouldn't get in our way. We should still go quietly, though, just in case Scarlett wakes up. Her bedroom is down the hall.'

Ursula nodded and followed Stella from her room, both girls walking on tiptoe to create as little sound as possible. The ice volcano seemed eerie in the darkness, especially as it emphasised the red lava leaping and glowing beneath the floor of ice. They made their way up the staircase towards the snow-globe room where the two teams of explorers were trapped. Ursula felt her heart lift with every step. She would soon see her friends – they were so close to achieving what they'd set out to do and then, at last, they could finally go home and she would see the Ocean Squid Club again, and Old Joe, and Minty . . .

But then they reached the snow-globe room and Stella flicked on the light, only for both girls to jump in shock. Scarlett wasn't in bed as they had thought. She was right there, sitting in one of the armchairs, which she had positioned to look towards the door. There was a hard, angry expression on her face, mixed with bitter disappointment.

'So,' she said, 'the truth reveals itself at last. You would betray me after all, without a second's thought.'

Ursula's mind raced for some plausible explanation

as to why she and Stella might be together like this, but she couldn't think of anything and nor, it seemed, could Stella. Instead, the ice princess took a deep breath and said, 'Surely it's you who has betrayed me. You say you want to be friends and equals and partners, but you've kept me captive this entire time and endangered the people I love. You can't blame me for trying to get them back.'

'I'm not surprised,' Scarlett said in a flat tone. 'Not really. Perhaps some small part of me hoped you were on my side, but I always had a feeling that something wasn't quite right. Now I know for sure.' Her eyes flicked to Ursula. 'But it seems I made a mistake of my own. I assumed you would come for your father and friends first, rather than the mermaid girl. Still, no matter.'

Ursula thought she shouldn't hesitate this time but should start to use her magical singing straight away. She took a breath in but Scarlett said sharply, 'Stella! Freeze the mermaid's tongue.'

Stella looked appalled by the instruction, but of course she was still wearing the cuff and so there was nothing she could do except obey the direct command. Ursula managed to get out a single magical note but it wasn't enough to prevent Stella from throwing up her hand and sending a blast of ice magic straight at her. To Ursula's horror, she felt her tongue freeze into a useless cold lump inside her mouth and she was unable to utter anything more than a whimper. Ursula and Stella gazed at each other helplessly. Scarlett had managed to prevent both of them from using their magic, and without it they were powerless.

'I could never voluntarily join forces with you!' Stella burst out. 'You're too selfish!'

'Selfish?' Scarlett raised an eyebrow. 'What mental gymnastics did you employ to reach that conclusion? It was pleasant living in the Hanging Gardens of Amadon for a while, I'll admit, but I very much doubt anyone would choose to live in the middle of the Terrible Valleys, surrounded on all sides by lava and swamp monsters and vultures and carnivorous plants. Yet someone has to do it. Someone has to be the caretaker for all the precious places I've saved. No one else will shoulder the burden, so it falls to me.'

She let out a long sigh and said, 'I don't want to keep working with you under these terms, Stella. It seems we are doomed to forever misunderstand one another. I told you once before that I have no interest in keeping prisoners, and I meant it. If I can't persuade you to my way of thinking, then I shall have to find some other snow queen who is more amenable. Perhaps she'll be able to create a special globe to contain an ice princess and then you can join your friends in my collection. You won't be able to do any more damage there. It's not a fate I would have chosen for you, but it gives me some small element of satisfaction to think that you will be forced to spend decades – perhaps even hundreds of years – a powerless spectator from within the walls of the Phantom Atlas Society, watching as we rise from the ashes like a phoenix and finally achieve what we planned from the outset.'

'You're wrong,' Stella said. 'It's not what the society set out to do from the outset. Queen Portia was one of the founding members and I've met her, remember? She didn't want to steal the entire world – she only wanted to protect those parts most in need of it, like endangered species. She'd never approve of what you're doing, Scarlett. I know life hasn't been kind to you, but can't you at least try to give the world a second chance? People aren't perfect and the explorers' clubs aren't perfect. We know that. But that doesn't mean you should just throw it all away. Sometimes it's better to try to fix a broken thing.'

'That's where we differ,' Scarlett replied in a hard voice. 'Because it seems to me that if something is broken then you're far better off tearing it down, chucking it on the fire and starting over. Speaking of which, I'd better fetch a new water globe for your mermaid friend—'

She broke off abruptly as there was a crash and a bang from the hallway, followed by some ferocious howling and yapping.

'*Now* what?' Scarlett exclaimed, looking frustrated.

She strode to the door and summoned her hyenas, who came tumbling into the room. To Ursula's horror, each of them had one of the full-size jelly-legs aliens clamped in their jaws, their long limbs wriggling and squirming. Bertie was there too, her silver wings sparkling as she fluttered alongside one of the hyenas and thumped its nose with her fist.

'Leave!' she ordered. 'Bad dogs! Bad, bad dogs!'

It seemed that the fairy could pack more of a punch than her small size would suggest because the hyena instantly dropped the jelly-legs, who landed on the floor in a slobbery pile. To Ursula's relief, he didn't look harmed, only bemused. In another moment, Bertie had whacked the other hyena on the nose too, and the second jelly-legs landed on the floor with a thump beside the first.

Bertie looked up just then, saw Ursula and winced.

She lifted her hand in a wave and said, 'Sorry, Ursula. I got worried when you didn't come back and thought I'd mount a rescue, but I couldn't find you. When we went into the kitchen we got cornered by these horrible beasts.' She gestured at the hyenas.

Scarlett shooed them out of the way and leaned forward to inspect the jelly-legs. 'But how interesting!' she exclaimed. 'I've never seen their like before.' Her gaze flicked to Bertie's sparkling starlight wings and she said, 'A galaxy fairy, I assume. And so these must be creatures you picked up in outer space. How marvellous. You know, I'd actually be quite interested in working with the galaxy fairies. Why stop at protecting the world when you might protect the whole universe? But as you seem to be in league with the explorers, I'll have to ask Stella to freeze you in place for now. I can't have you trying to use your fairy magic on me.'

Bertie started to protest, but before she could finish, Stella blasted some magic at her and the little fairy was immediately frozen into a statue, covered in a coating of ice that made her sparkle all over. She tumbled to the floor and, worried that she might be shattered by the hyenas, Ursula hurriedly snatched her up, wincing at the coldness of the ice against her bare hands as she slipped the fairy into her pocket.

'Stay exactly where you are,' Scarlett ordered Stella. 'And keep an eye on the mermaid. If she tries to make a move against me, freeze her where she stands.'

Ursula watched as Scarlett bent down beside the jelly-legs, who seemed none the worse for their encounter with the hyenas and were waving their feet in the air at Scarlett hopefully. The Collector reached out to give them a tentative tickle and they immediately began giggling and hiccuping in delight, the usual little blue flowers rising up into the air.

'Extraordinary,' Scarlett murmured. 'Yes, space is definitely the next step for the Phantom Atlas Society. And these creatures will make a charming addition to my collection.'

Scarlett proceeded to ignore the two girls as she tickled the alien creatures. Ursula watched, and with her frozen tongue she was unable to warn her about what was likely to happen, even if she'd wanted to. Scarlett had no idea what the jelly-legs were capable of if she didn't stop tickling them. Ursula felt a flicker of hope that they might hiccup out an object or creature startling, or large, or dangerous enough to cause a diversion. Her eyes went to the shelf of snow globes and at once she saw the two with the explorer teams trapped inside. Scarlett had told Stella to freeze Ursula if she made a move against the Collector, but she hadn't said anything about freezing her if she went towards the snow globes . . .

'How peculiar!' Scarlett exclaimed.

Ursula looked back and saw with excitement that one of the jelly-legs had moved past flowers and had just hiccuped up a rather pretty flowering cactus. Scarlett turned to the other alien and tickled its foot, immediately causing it to hiccup out a small brown object.

'And what's this?' Scarlett asked. 'Some sort of nut?'

But the little brown thing was no nut. And it only stayed small for a couple of seconds before suddenly erupting into full size. Ursula recalled what Bertie had told them about the bear the jelly-legs had produced once before.

A big grizzly bear it was. It ate everything in the hold before it finally vanished . . .

Now it seemed that the alien had repeated the trick because they were all confronted with a huge beast of a grizzly bear. Scarlett cried out and leaped away from the creature as it rose up on its hind legs and gave a rumbling growl. The hyenas bared their teeth and Stella stared in shock. Ursula felt a thrill of fear at being so close to a bear, but she lost no time. She raced straight towards the shelf, snatched up the Ocean Squid snow globe and unscrewed the base from the glass lid. At once, her friends tumbled out, looking very confused to find themselves suddenly released and in a room with a large bear.

Ursula grabbed Genie's arm and hauled her to her feet, seeing that she had the sock with the dizard in her hand. She longed to tell her friends what was going on, but of course her tongue was still frozen solid so she could only gesture frantically as she plucked the dizard from the sock and hurled it over to Stella.

The fire magician had been telling the truth about it knowing what to do. The little dragon creature unfurled its wings and bit down hard on the bracelet surrounding Stella's wrist. At once, the fire inside it went out, the glass cracked and bright green musical notes filled the air as the merboy's voice escaped.

'No!' Scarlett yelled, appalled.

She dodged the bear and lunged towards Stella, but it was too late. Ursula held up the shell necklace that Mrs Parnacle had given her and the merboy's voice vanished straight into it. The cuff cracked even further and dropped harmlessly from Stella's wrist. At last, she was free.

CHAPTER TWENTY-SEVEN

Stella looked up and a wide smile spread over her face as Scarlett let out a shriek of rage. The Collector lunged towards her but the princess threw magic at her feet and a pair of ice boots immediately encased them, pinning Scarlett to the ground so abruptly that she toppled forward. Then Stella turned to Ursula and threw a spell to unfreeze her tongue.

It was a glorious relief to feel the burning ice melting away at last. Ursula pulled Bertie from her pocket and Stella quickly unfroze the fairy too. Bertie shook off the last of the ice from her wings and seemed perfectly unharmed.

At the same time the bear raised its giant paw, looking as if it might take a swipe at Jai, who was nearest to it, so Stella threw out her hand and froze it in place, along with the hyenas. Max snatched up the snow globe containing the Polar Bear team and unscrewed the base to release their friends, who came tumbling out alongside them. Stella immediately ran straight to Felix and threw her arms round him in a hug.

'I'm so happy to see you!' she said, squeezing him tight. 'I'll explain everything properly later but I never stopped caring about you all. I just had to turn you in to persuade Scarlett I was on her side.'

Felix returned her embrace in delight. 'You superbly clever thing,' he said. 'I never doubted you – not for a moment.'

Shay, Ethan and Beanie all crowded around Stella too, happy to be reunited, although Ethan seemed a little bit miffed as well.

'You might have sent us a secret signal or something,' he huffed. 'It was a bit of a dirty trick to make us think you were in league with the Collector.'

'Dirty trick!' Stella exclaimed. 'I like that! Isn't it exactly what you did to me back at Queen Jezebel's castle? You pretended to the magic mirror that you were happy to abandon me there because it was the only way to mount a rescue later. Not that I hadn't already rescued myself by the time you finally came back, but still, it was a sound enough plan if you'd just dawdled a little less.'

'We did not dawdle!' Ethan exclaimed indignantly. 'We came back as soon as it was possible to do so.'

Ursula left them to their arguing and turned to greet her own friends. Max, Jai and Genie put their arms round her in a group hug and Ursula felt a great wave of relief to be reunited with them once again so soon after believing they might be separated in their snow-globe prisons for years.

'I don't know how you managed it, but well done,' Jai said, beaming at Ursula.

'Nice work, Jellyfin,' Max added.

Genie squeezed Ursula the tightest of all, and Bess poked one of her massive tentacles into the room to curl around everyone affectionately.

'This is all very touching,' Scarlett sneered. 'But I wouldn't be celebrating just yet if I were you. Seeing as every volcano in the valley is going to erupt in less than half an hour.'

Stella turned to face her. 'What are you talking about?'

The others fell quiet and looked at the Collector too. With a sneaking sense of dread, Ursula noticed that something had happened to the little red fish pendant Scarlett wore – it was glowing a fiery-red colour.

The Collector fixed Stella with a look full of loathing. 'Don't you remember what I told you once before?' she asked. 'You asked me about your biological parents and how my father had managed to kill them and I told you that fire melts ice. Why do you think I chose the Valley of Volcanoes as our hideout? Being typical explorers with no knowledge of the place you're blundering into, I don't expect you have the slightest notion that these volcanoes are controlled by lava fish?'

None of the explorers said anything since none of them had ever heard of lava fish.

'Thought so,' Scarlett said with a curl of her lip. 'And so it follows that you also do not know that if you have a lava fish stone then you can control the fish?' She touched the glowing necklace at her throat. 'I've just told them to erupt the volcanoes,' she said, looking smug and horribly determined. 'Every single one in the valley. Including this one.'

'You're bluffing,' Ethan scoffed. 'If we all get washed away in a sea of lava, then you will perish too.'

'Indeed,' Scarlett replied, a gleam in her eye. 'The Phantom Atlas Society has been my life's work and I would rather go down with my ship than allow you to cart me off to some prison.'

'But Scarlett, what about all the places you've collected?' Stella asked, frowning in confusion. 'You've always said that preserving them is the most important thing in the world to you. Surely you wouldn't deliberately destroy any of them?'

'The snow globes won't be destroyed by the volcanoes,' Scarlett said. 'I've tested it. We will all die, of course, but the globes will be encased in lava. Perhaps they'll stay there for thousands of years or more, but I hope that by the time they're discovered the world will be a more enlightened place and that the people in it will be more deserving of all the riches I've managed to collect and preserve.'

'Use your voice,' Max said, nudging Ursula. 'Make her tell the fish to stop.'

'You can't stop them now,' Scarlett replied with a grim smile. 'Once they've started the process of erupting the volcanoes, it's too late.'

With a worried look at the others, Ursula started to sing anyway, reaching her powers of persuasion deep into Scarlett's head, but she could tell at once that the Collector was telling the truth. It felt different this time, like her magic was coming up against a brick wall. The problem wasn't that Scarlett was too strong-willed, it was that Ursula was asking her to do something impossible. She might as well have asked her to levitate into the air. Even a mermaid's power of persuasion couldn't compel somebody to perform an act they weren't physically capable of.

'She's telling the truth,' she said with a hopeless

look at the others. 'She can't prevent the volcanoes from erupting.'

'You see?' Scarlett said. 'I'll even tell you where those beloved explorers' clubs of yours are. It hardly makes any difference now. You'll find them in a safe behind that painting.' She pointed across the room at a canvas of some grazing wildebeest. 'You can have the combination code too if you like. It's seven-nine-one-two.'

Stella hurried over to the painting and took it down from the wall to find that there was indeed a safe set behind it. The combination code worked and the door swung open to reveal the missing snow globes – all of the explorers' clubs were there as well as Stella's house. Stella gathered them up, pleased to get her hands on them at last ... but it looked as if it might all be for nothing because the volcanoes had started to rumble.

The explorers were too low in the frozen volcano to be able to see much through the window, especially as it was dark outside, but they could hear the noise, and they could feel it too – shuddering up through the ground and into the soles of their boots. The frozen volcano shook in an extremely ominous way.

'Your ice can't compete with that lava,' Scarlett said with a triumphant look at Stella. 'Not when it gets to maximum heat. The lava will burst through at any moment.'

Ursula pulled her fairy wand from her pocket. 'We need to shrink as many snow globes as we can!' She glanced at the Polar Bear team and added, 'Then we can take them with us.'

'Take them where?' Scarlett sneered. 'Even if you left this second, you wouldn't be able to escape in time on a magic carpet.'

'We didn't arrive on magic carpets,' Ursula replied. 'We arrived in a fairy rocket.'

Scarlett looked worried by this for a moment, but she quickly recovered and said, 'Well, you'll never get away in time, regardless. Lava fish volcanoes erupt quickly and ferociously. You'll be burned to a crisp before you can take off.'

'What a cheerful thought.' Ethan scowled at her. 'But perhaps you're forgetting that there's an ice princess and a magician here too.'

'That's right,' Stella said. 'You say that fire melts ice but that isn't always true. Ice can put out fire.'

Scarlett's eyes narrowed. 'Not when it's an entire valley of volcanoes, it can't.'

'We'll see,' Stella replied with a look of determination. The lava below them roiled hotter than ever and, just at that moment, there was a great *cracking* sound and a jagged line appeared across the ice floor. There was no time to waste. Stella looked down and focused her ice magic at the floor, trying to hold off the explosion for as long as possible. Meanwhile, Ethan went to the top of the volcano to create one of his magical shields in the hope that it would offer protection from the eruptions taking place around them.

Ursula and her friends shrunk all the snow globes in the room, while the rest of the Polar Bear team ran through the volcano collecting up all the globes they could find and bringing them back. Three of the magic carpets helped too, while the fourth was despatched to the cave in the mountain to pick up Jewel. Together, the Ocean Squid team were able to shrink all the globes in record time. Bertie was loading them on to her rocket as quickly as she could, and Ursula and her friends shrunk themselves and the Polar Bear explorers down to help, as well as Jewel when she arrived, leaving only Stella full size.

They'd worked as quickly as they could but it seemed they were still running out of time. Melting ice was running down the wall of the volcano and cracks had appeared there too, as well as more in the floor.

'You'll never make it,' Scarlett said, although she looked uncertain for the first time.

'I can't hold the lava back much longer,' Stella gasped, looking at Ursula. 'Are you almost done?'

'Almost!' Ursula replied. 'There's just the lost islands still to load up.'

It seemed that Ethan was having trouble with his shield now too because they could see fiery drops of lava beginning to rain down through the centre of their volcano, melting great holes in the ice staircase. The magician tumbled into the room a moment later, a burning smell emanating from his clothes and hair.

'The shield can't take it any more,' he gasped. 'In a few minutes, this place will be flooded with lava! We have to go right now!'

Ursula threw the last of the snow globes into the hold and then Stella and Ethan both ran over so they could be shrunk to fairy size and enter the rocket too.

'Wait a second!' Stella said when it was her turn. 'We can't just leave Scarlett here.'

'What?' Ethan glared at her. 'Why not? She'd condemn all of us to die if she could, not to mention steal half the world. She's only getting what she deserves.'

'But she doesn't think she's stealing it. She believes she's saving it.'

Before anyone could stop her, Stella ran back to

Scarlett. The Collector's frozen boots were melting through the heat, but one of her feet was still stuck and she was desperately trying to tug it free as sweat poured down her furious face.

Stella reached out a hand and said quietly, 'You can come with us. If that's what you want.'

Scarlett looked up at her, panting. A great multitude of cracks were appearing all up the walls and across the ice ceiling.

'Has she gone nuts?' Ethan asked, glancing back at the others. 'We don't have time for this.'

'I agree with Stella,' Felix said quietly. 'It's the right thing to do.'

'It's going to get us all killed,' Ethan huffed.

Ursula didn't much like the idea of leaving Scarlett to burn to death inside the volcano either, but they *were* running out of time.

'Why would you take me?' Scarlett asked, looking baffled. 'What kind of trick is this?'

'It's not a trick,' Stella said calmly. 'I'm offering to save your life, if you'll let me.'

'You'll put me in a prison cell.' Scarlett spat out the words.

'You can stand trial and face the consequences of what you've done,' Stella said. 'Or you can stay here.

It's your choice.' To the others' surprise, Stella suddenly reached out to clasp the Collector's hand and leaned forward slightly. 'Please, Scarlett, come with us,' she said. 'Don't end your life here. I know you think we're enemies, but I don't disagree with you about everything. In fact, we both want the same thing – to protect the world and all its wonders. I just think we need to go about it differently. There has to be a route forward, a way that we can all work together. Please. Don't let this be where it all ends.'

The heat was almost unbearable now and the ice around them was melting rapidly. Lava began to bubble up through the cracks in the floor and drip through the walls.

'Stella!' Shay called. 'This is it! We really have to go!'

Stella looked down at Scarlett. 'I'm leaving,' she said. 'Are you coming with me?'

Scarlett paused for just a moment. The room was lit with a fiery-red light from all the lava, and with a look of despair she nodded. There was no need for Stella to melt the ice boots, because the last of them broke apart at that moment anyway, and then Stella and Scarlett were running towards the rocket.

Ursula and Max were ready with the fairy wands to shrink them and Jai and Max closed the door as soon as they tumbled inside. The explorer teams found themselves in a heap with the jelly-legs, the magic carpets and the sugar-tooth tiger in the hold. Bertie must have been watching from the cockpit because she immediately started the engines and the rocket lifted off.

'This is the tricky bit!' she yelled back to the others. 'As soon as we're out of the volcano I can take us to full speed, but we've got to navigate the lava first. Hold on to your hats!'

The rocket shot out of the room and into the centre of the volcano. Ursula immediately saw that they were a long way from being safe yet. Lava rained down all around them, glowing bright red through the windows. Each drop was the size of a house to the little fairy rocket, and they felt the impact as a couple of them landed on the wings. At once, there was a horrible burning, smoking smell.

Luckily, Bertie was an expert pilot and, with much weaving and dodging, she managed to fly them up through the centre of the volcano and then all the way out through the top. The explorers gave a cheer, but then they saw the valley spread below them and their triumph turned to despair. It was awash with lava glowing brightly in the darkness, with every

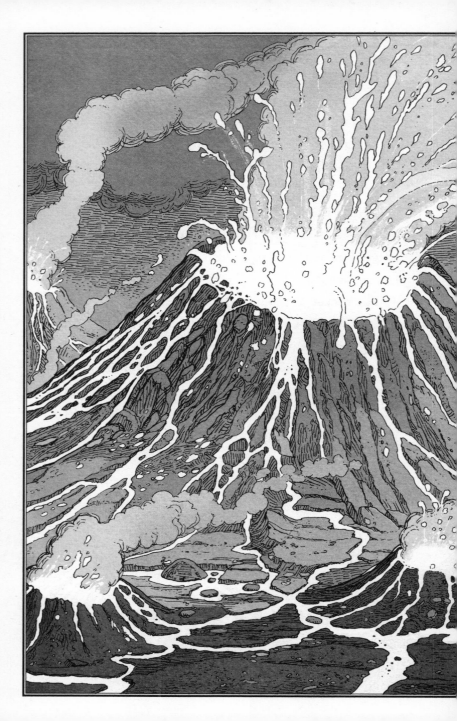

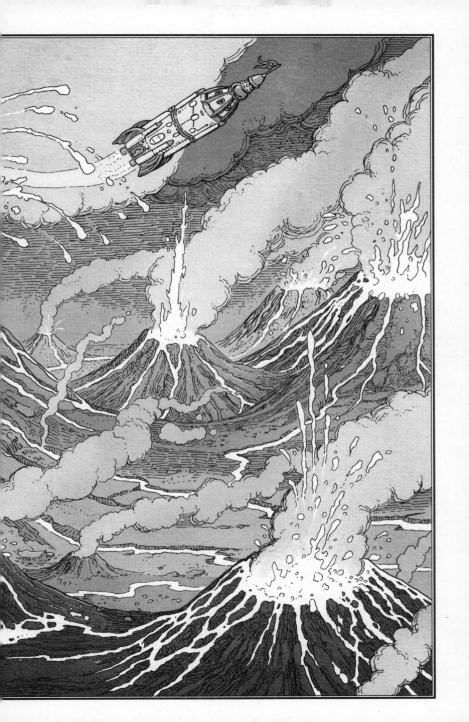

single volcano smoking and erupting at the same time, shooting streams of fire high into the night sky.

We're not going to make it, Ursula thought in a panic. The fairy rocket was too small and the walls were too thin, and there was too much lava raining down around them. But then Stella threw herself over to the nearest window and pressed her hand against the glass, sending bursts of ice magic out into the air.

With a final shudder, the last of the ice around the volcano below finally cracked and fell apart, and a great torrent of lava raced up to meet them. They all knew Bertie would be switching the rocket to full speed but it looked as if she wouldn't quite have the moments required to get them clear ...

Until Stella blasted a great rush of ice magic down through the floor, freezing the lava mid-arc. It stopped just short of the rocket, giving Bertie the seconds she needed to turn the engine power to maximum. The rocket raced straight up into the air, going higher and higher and higher. The Valley of Volcanoes was quickly lost from view and they were surrounded on all sides by fluffy white clouds, followed by a glittering night sky and then, finally, the star-filled darkness of outer space.

CHAPTER TWENTY-EIGHT

For a moment everyone stood at the windows and gazed in wonder at the extraordinary, beautiful sight that was their planet spread out below them. Ursula thought the colours looked more vivid than they'd ever done before – the world was a glorious blue, green and white marble. She felt a surge of affection and protectiveness towards their world then, and a sudden burst of hope rose up in her that perhaps the Phantom Atlas Society and the explorers' clubs could work together after all, in pursuit of the same shared goals and interests . . .

But then Scarlett lunged towards the cockpit, perhaps with some vague idea of trying to take control of the rocket. Stella quickly shot some ice ropes at her and the Collector crashed to the floor with her arms and legs bound.

'For goodness' sake!' Stella exclaimed. 'Why can't you just work with us for one second?'

Scarlett looked up from where she lay sprawled on

the floor. 'I'm grateful to you for taking me with you,' she said. 'You didn't have to do that and I won't forget it. But I won't live out my life in some prison either. I won't.'

'You won't have any choice,' Ethan replied. 'Not after all the crimes you've committed.'

They set a course for Stardust City, arriving there the next morning. Bertie had radioed ahead to let the galaxy fairies know to expect them and the explorers were given a hero's welcome when they exited the rocket. But the celebrations would have to wait. There were hundreds of stolen places to return, including the explorers' clubs themselves. Many people and locations in the enchanted globes had been held prisoner for too long already, and the fairies were eager to do their part to set them free.

Ursula was relieved to find that Mercadia was not amongst the snow globes and so her mother must be safely back at home. She couldn't wait to see her again soon and felt a burst of pride that she and her friends had succeeded in stopping the Collector once and for all. A little later, a lump rose in her throat at the sight of all the gleaming rockets standing ready to return the stolen places back to where they came from.

There was a great air of excitement in the hangar

as the explorers and fairies scampered this way and that, distributing the globes to the various rockets and consulting the *Phantom Atlas* to check and double-check where each place ought to go. It was almost over – the end was in sight and soon they'd be reunited with all their lost friends, as well as the places they'd never realised were missing in the first place.

Perhaps that was why, in all the excitement, no one thought too much about Scarlett. After all, she was held securely as far as they were concerned. Stella said the ice ropes wouldn't melt for days and days, so they had time to deal with the globes first before turning their attention to the Collector.

Except when the explorers finally came back to Bertie's rocket, Scarlett was nowhere to be found. The ice ropes hadn't melted; they had been cut and lay curled on the floor of the storage hold.

'The ends are scorched,' Stella said, peering at them. 'She used fire magic to cut them.'

'But how?' Jai asked. 'She didn't have a staff with her, did she?'

Stella shook her head. 'No, but perhaps she had some other weapon that we didn't know about. Or maybe she used the lava fish pendant somehow?'

Either way, Scarlett was gone. At first they assumed

she must be in the city somewhere and Bertie assured them she wouldn't have got far.

'Every fairy here knows who she is,' she said. 'We'll find her all right.'

But Scarlett Sauvage had vanished. They searched every inch of Stardust City and there was no sign of her whatsoever.

'This is ridiculous!' Ethan exclaimed. 'She can't have just vanished into thin air!'

'Perhaps she snuck on to one of the fairy rockets before it took off?' Beanie suggested.

The explorers fell silent at this suggestion, feeling glum. Dozens of fairy rockets had left the city in the last few hours. Many of them had already delivered their snow globes and were on the way back. When they radioed the pilots, the fairies searched their rockets at once but everyone came back with the same answer: Scarlett wasn't there.

'We're just going to have to accept that she escaped,' Stella said. 'We've got more important things to worry about right now.'

Ursula was concerned about the Collector's absence but she agreed with Stella. They had succeeded in their rescue mission and now, at last, it was time to go back where they belonged too. She had no idea whether the

Ocean Squid Explorers' Club would agree to let her become a member or not, or indeed whether she would be allowed to live there now that they knew of her mermaid heritage, but she wasn't going to find out the answers to those questions by hiding in Stardust City. They would make a brief stop at the mermaid academy to return Kieran's voice, and then Ursula was going to visit Mercadia for some long overdue quality time with her mother. After that, it would be time to return to the club and discover her fate.

FIVE MONTHS LATER

Ursula stood on the boardwalk at the Ocean Squid Explorers' Club and gazed out over the sparkling blue sea. It was a beautiful day with not a cloud in the sky, and the air smelled of ocean salt and coconuts. After a short while, her dolphin friend Minty stuck his grey snout out of the water, clicking out a greeting. Ursula knelt down and ran her hand over his smooth head.

'I can't come swimming right now,' she told him. 'I promise I'll come later, though. Once everyone is in bed.'

Now that her secret was out, Ursula no longer needed to keep her mermaid swims secret but she still enjoyed the cool, dark peace of the ocean at night, and besides, she was too busy during the day. Not only did she have her engineering duties to attend to, but she was planning a new expedition with Jai, Max, Genie and a few other Ocean Squid explorers as well.

They planned to take two submarines and attempt to be the first explorers to reach the deepest part of the ocean. It would be a long journey, full of peril and danger – and Ursula couldn't wait to get started. A team had been sent to retrieve the *Blowfish* from the edge of the Nebula Sea and Ursula very much hoped it would be assigned to their expedition. It would be like old times to be on board once again.

Suddenly, there was the sound of footsteps on the boards behind her and Ursula turned round expecting to see Old Joe coming to tell her that tea and toast were being served in the engineers' room. But it wasn't Old Joe – in fact, it wasn't someone from the Ocean Squid Club at all. It was Stella Starflake Pearl, dressed in the pale blue robes of the Polar Bear Explorers' Club, her white hair tied back in a neat plait. Ursula broke into a grin when she saw her and ran the last few steps to hug the other girl tightly.

'I heard you weren't getting here until next week!' Ursula exclaimed. 'I thought I'd miss you.'

'I came earlier so that I could say goodbye,' Stella said with a grin. 'They told me your expedition is going to be a long one and you might be at sea for a while. Congratulations, by the way.' She indicated the black cloak Ursula wore, the official uniform of the Ocean Squid Explorers' Club. 'I'm so glad they finally saw sense and let you become a member.'

'Me too.' Ursula beamed. 'And I'm so pleased that you're back with your club as well.'

It hadn't been easy. In spite of everything the explorers had achieved, the presidents of both the Polar Bear and Ocean Squid clubs were still sceptical about the girls' memberships. Fortunately, a large chunk of both clubs felt differently. There had been strikes and protests and, eventually, the presidents had changed their minds. Genie had been allowed to become an Ocean Squid member too and Max had been reinstated. It looked as if the clubs were finally ready to start changing their minds about a lot of things.

Stella and Ursula sat on the edge of the boardwalk, taking it in turns to throw a Frisbee for Minty, while Stella told Ursula how all the clubs had now agreed to officially recognise a new expedition role – that of conservationist. This was part of the reason why Stella was at the Ocean Squid Club now. It seemed that being snatched away by the Collector was the wake-up call the clubs had all needed and they were finally going to start sharing their knowledge and work together.

'I think it's a really exciting time to be part of the explorers' clubs,' Stella said. 'Some big changes are coming. Who knows? Maybe there'll even be a female president one day?'

Ursula's heart lifted at the thought. Perhaps it was possible.

'And what about Scarlett?' she asked. 'Has anyone seen or heard from her?'

'Not a thing,' Stella replied. 'Although the galaxy fairies say that one of their wands is missing, so it looks like she might have taken it with her when she escaped.'

'Do you think she'll ever come back?' Ursula asked with a flicker of worry. 'That she might try to rebuild the Phantom Atlas Society and cause trouble again?'

'Who knows?' Stella replied. 'The snow globes have all been destroyed so she'd have to come up with another means of stealing places away. But she's extremely clever and determined so if she wants it badly enough then maybe she will find a way. And I guess we'll just have to deal with that problem when it happens. I hope not, though. I like to think that she's out there somewhere, perhaps working at a turtle sanctuary or something like that. I hope she's accepted that there's no way to save the whole world and has settled for saving one little piece of it instead.'

The two girls lingered on the boardwalk for a while longer, talking and laughing together as the sun slowly sank beneath the horizon. Finally it was time to go in for dinner.

'I'd wish you luck on your expedition,' Stella said as they went past the submarines. 'But I don't think you need it. Perhaps we might join each other for a joint expedition one day?'

Ursula smiled. 'I hope so,' she said. 'In fact, I can't think of anything I'd love more.'

POLAR BEAR EXPLORERS' CLUB RULES

1. Polar Bear explorers will keep their moustaches trimmed, waxed and generally well-groomed at all times. Any explorer found with a slovenly moustache will be asked to withdraw from the club's public rooms immediately.
2. Explorers with disorderly moustaches or unkempt beards will also be refused entry to the members-only bar, the private dining room and the billiards room without exception.
3. All igloos on club property must contain a flask of hot chocolate and an adequate supply of marshmallows at all times.
4. Only polar-bear-shaped marshmallows are to be served on club property. Additionally, the following breakfast items will be prepared in polar-bear-shape only: pancakes, waffles, crumpets, sticky pastries, fruit jellies and doughnuts. Please do not request alternative

shapes or animals from the kitchen – including penguins, walruses, woolly mammoths or yetis – as this offends the chef.

5. Members are kindly reminded that when the chef is offended, insulted or peeved, there will be nothing on offer in the dining room whatsoever except for buttered toast. This toast will be bread–shaped.

6. Explorers must not hunt or harm unicorns under any circumstances.

7. All Polar Bear Explorers' Club sleighs must be properly decorated with seven brass bells, and must contain the following items: five fleecy blankets, three hot–water bottles in knitted jumpers, two flasks of emergency hot chocolate and a warmed basket of buttered crumpets (polar–bear–shaped).

8. Please do not take penguins into the club's saltwater baths; they *will* hog the jacuzzi.

9. All penguins are the property of the club and are not to be removed by explorers. The club reserves the right to search any suspiciously shaped bags. Any bag that moves by itself will automatically be deemed suspicious.

10. All snowmen built on club property must have appropriately groomed moustaches. Please note that a carrot is not a suitable object to use as a

moustache. Nor is an aubergine. If in doubt, the club president is always available for consultation regarding snowmen's moustaches.

11. It is considered bad form to threaten other club members with icicles, snowballs or oddly dressed snowmen.

12. Whistling ducks are not permitted on club property. Any member found with a whistling duck in his possession will be asked to leave.

UPON INITIATION, ALL POLAR BEAR EXPLORERS SHALL RECEIVE AN EXPLORER'S BAG CONTAINING THE FOLLOWING ITEMS:

- One tin of Captain Filibuster's Expedition–Strength Moustache Wax.
- One bottle of Captain Filibuster's Scented Beard Oil.
- One folding pocket moustache comb.
- One ivory–handled shaving brush, two pairs of grooming scissors and four individually wrapped cakes of luxurious foaming shaving soap.
- Two compact pocket mirrors.

Ocean Squid Explorers' Club Rules

1. Sea monsters, kraken and giant squid trophies are the private property of the club, and cannot be removed to adorn private homes. Explorers will be charged for any decorative tentacles that are found to be missing from their rooms.

2. Explorers are not to fraternise – or join forces – with pirates or smugglers during the course of any official expedition.

3. Poisonous puffer fish, barbed wire jellyfish, saltwater stingrays and electric eels are not appropriate fillings for pies and/or sandwiches. Any such requests sent to the kitchen will be politely rejected.

4. Explorers are kindly asked to refrain from offering to show the club's chef how to prepare sea snakes, sharks, crustaceans or deep-sea monsters for

human consumption. This includes the creatures listed in rule number three. Please respect the expert knowledge of the chef.

5. The Ocean Squid Explorers' Club does not consider the sea cucumber to be a trophy worthy of reward or recognition. This includes the lesser-found biting cucumber, as well as the singing cucumber and the argumentative cucumber.

6. Any Ocean Squid explorer who gifts the club with a tentacle from the screeching red devil squid will be rewarded with a year's supply of Captain Ishmael's Premium Dark Rum.

7. Please do not leave docked submarines in a submerged state – it wreaks havoc with the club's valet service.

8. Explorers are kindly asked not to leave deceased sea monsters in the hallways or any of the club's communal rooms. Unattended sea monsters are liable to be removed to the kitchens without notice.

9. The South Seas Navigation Company will not accept liability for any damage caused to their submarines. This includes damage caused by giant squid attacks, whale ambushes and jellyfish plots.

10. Explorers are not to use the map room to compare

the length of squid tentacles or other trophies. Kindly use the marked areas within the trophy rooms to settle any private wagers or bets.

11. Please note: any explorer who threatens another explorer with a harpoon cannon will be suspended from the club immediately.

UPON INITIATION, ALL OCEAN SQUID EXPLORERS SHALL RECEIVE AN EXPLORER'S BAG CONTAINING THE FOLLOWING ITEMS:

- One tin of Captain Ishmael's Kraken Bait.
- One kraken net.
- One engraved hip flask filled with Captain Ishmael's Expedition-Strength Salted Rum.
- Two sharpened fishing spears and three bags of hunting barbs.
- Five tins of Captain Ishmael's Harpoon Cannon Polish.

Desert Jackal Explorers' Club Rules

1. Magical flying carpets are to be kept tightly rolled when on club premises. Any damage caused by out-of-control flying carpets will be considered the sole responsibility of the explorer in question.
2. Enchanted genie lamps must stay in their owner's possession at all times.
3. Please note: genies are strictly prohibited at the bar and at the bridge tables.
4. Tents are for serious expedition use only, and are not to be used to host parties, gatherings, chinwags, or chit-chats.
5. Camels must not be permitted – or encouraged – to spit at other club members.
6. Jumping cactuses are not allowed inside the club unless under exceptional circumstances.
7. Please do not remove flags, maps or wallabies from the club.

8. Club members are not permitted to settle disagreements via camel racing between the hours of midnight and sunrise.

9. The club kangaroos, coyotes, sand cats and rattlesnakes are to be respected at all times.

10. Members who wish to keep all their fingers are advised not to torment the giant desert hairy scorpions, irritate the bearded vultures or vex the spotted desert recluse spiders.

11. Explorers are kindly asked to refrain from washing their feet in the drinking water tureens at the club's entrance, which are provided strictly for our members' refreshment.

12. Sand forts may be constructed on club grounds, providing explorers empty all sand from their sandals, pockets, bags, binocular cases and helmets before entering the club.

13. Explorers are asked not to take camel decoration to extremes. Desert Jackal Explorers' Club camels may wear a maximum of one jewelled necklace, one tasselled headdress and/or bandana, seven plain gold anklets, up to four knee bells and one floral snout decoration.

UPON INITIATION, ALL DESERT JACKAL
EXPLORERS SHALL RECEIVE AN EXPLORER'S BAG
CONTAINING THE FOLLOWING ITEMS:

- One foldable leather safari hat or one pith helmet.
- One canister of tropical-strength giant desert hairy scorpion repellent.
- One shovel (please note this object's usefulness in the event of being buried alive in a sandstorm).
- One camel-grooming kit, consisting of: organic camel shampoo, camel eyelash curlers, head brush, toenail trimmers and hoof-polishers (kindly provided by the National Camel Grooming Association).
- Two spare genie lamps and one spare genie bottle.

Jungle Cat Explorers' Club Rules

1. Members of the Jungle Cat Explorers' Club shall refrain from picnicking in a slovenly manner. All expedition picnics are to be conducted with grace, poise and elegance.
2. All expedition picnicware must be made from solid silver, and kept perfectly polished at all times.
3. Champagne-carrier hampers must be constructed from high-grade wickerwork, premium leather or teak wood. Please note that champagne carriers considered 'tacky' will not be accepted onto the luggage elephant under ANY circumstances.
4. Expedition picnics will not take place unless there are scones present. Ideally, there should also be magic lanterns, pixie cakes and an assortment of fairy jellies.
5. Oriental whip snakes, alligator snapping turtles, horned baboon tarantulas and flying panthers

must be kept securely under lock and key whilst on club premises.

6. Do not torment or tease the jungle fairies. They *will* bite and may also catapult their tormentors with tiny, but extremely potent, stink–berries. Please be warned that stink–berries smell worse than anything you can imagine, including unwashed feet, mouldy cheese, elephant poo and hippopotamus burps.

7. Jungle fairies must be allowed to join expedition picnics if they bring an offering of any of the following: elephant cakes, striped giraffe scones, or fizzy tiger punch from the Forbidden Jungle Tiger Temple.

8. Jungle fairy boats have right of way on the Tikki Zikki River under *all* circumstances, including when there are piranhas present.

9. Spears are to be pointed away from other club members at all times.

10. When travelling by elephant, explorers are kindly asked to supply their own bananas.

11. If and when confronted by an enraged hippopotamus, a Jungle Cat explorer must remain calm and act with haste to avoid any damage befalling the expedition boat (please note that the

Jungle Navigation Company expects all boats to be returned to them in pristine condition).

12. Members are courteously reminded that – due to the size and smell of the beasts in question – the club's elephant house is not an appropriate venue in which to host soirees, banquets, galas or shindigs. Carousing of any kind in the elephant house is strictly prohibited.

UPON INITIATION, ALL JUNGLE CAT EXPLORERS SHALL RECEIVE AN EXPLORER'S BAG CONTAINING THE FOLLOWING ITEMS:

- An elegant mother–of–pearl knife and fork, inscribed with the explorer's initials.
- One silverware polishing kit.
- One engraved Jungle Cat Explorers' Club napkin ring and five luxury linen napkins – ironed, starched and embossed with the club's insignia.
- One magic lantern with fire pixie.
- One tin of Captain Greystoke's Expedition–Flavour Smoked Caviar.
- One corkscrew, two Scotch egg knives and three wicker grape baskets.

ACKNOWLEDGEMENTS

Many thanks to the following wonderful people:

My agent, Thérèse Coen, and the Hardman and Swainson Literary Agency.

The lovely team at Faber – especially Natasha Brown, Leah Thaxton and Susila Baybars.

Tomislav Tomić for the amazing illustrations.

My family.

All of the children's booksellers and teachers who take the time to champion books and nurture a love of reading in young people.

And, finally, to all of the children who have read and enjoyed Polar Bears and Ocean Squid. When you dress up as the characters, or write letters to me, or create things in the classroom, or share your amazing ideas at events, you remind me of what a special thing it is to be a children's writer. I hope you enjoy this book too.

COLLECT THE
EXPLORERS' CLUBS SERIES!